Lilly's Wedding Quilt

A Patch of Heaven Novel

Kelly Long

Thomas Nelson
Since 1798

NASHVILLE   DALLAS   MEXICO CITY   RIO DE JANEIRO

For John Evans, a Champion of the Cross
And for his beloved family: Kimberly, Chris,
Deanna, Sarah Jan, and Andrew

May we all someday be found "washed up on heaven's shore."

Published in Nashville, Tennessee, by Thomas Nelson. Thomas Nelson is a registered trademark of Thomas Nelson, Inc.

Thomas Nelson, Inc. titles may be purchased in bulk for educational, business, fundraising, or sales promotional use. For information, e-mail SpecialMarkets@ThomasNelson.com.

Unless otherwise noted, Scripture quotations are taken from the NEW AMERICAN STANDARD BIBLE®. © The Lockman Foundation 1960, 1962, 1963, 1968, 1971, 1972, 1973, 1975, 1977, 1995. Used by permission.

Publisher's Note: This novel is a work of fiction. Any references to real events, businesses, organizations, and locales are intended only to give the fiction a sense of reality and authenticity. Any resemblance to actual persons, living or dead, is entirely coincidental.

Library of Congress Cataloging-in-Publication Data

Long, Kelly.
    Lilly's wedding quilt / Kelly Long.
        p. cm. — (A patch of heaven novel ; 2)
    ISBN 978-1-59554-871-9 (pbk.)
    1. Amish—Fiction. 2. Amish Country (Pa.)—Fiction. I. Title.
PS3612.O497L56 2011
813'.6—dc22   2010051161

Printed in the United States of America

11 12 13 14 RRD 5 4 3 2 1

GLOSSARY OF PENNSYLVANIA DUTCH WORDS AND PHRASES

ach—an exclamation like *oh* or *my*

aentis—aunts

appenditlitch—delicious

boppli—baby/infant

bruder—brother

buwe—boy

daed—dad/father

danki—thank you

derr Herr—God

dumm—dumb/stupid

eck—bridal table

Englisch—non-Amish people and their ways

fraa—wife

gōtt—God

grossmudder—grandmother

guder mariye—good morning

gut—good

hallich gebottsdaag—Happy Birthday

hiya!—hi

hoech-nawszich—high-nosed or high-browed

hund—dog

jah—yes

kapp—prayer cap

kinner—children

kumme—come

maedel—girl

mamm—mother

munn—moon

naerfich—nervous

narrish—crazy

nee—no

rumspringa—running-around time

schnee—snow

schtecklimann—groom's go-between

schweschder—sister

sei so gut—please

wunderbaar—wonderful

Author's Note

*I*n researching this novel I discovered the fact that Amish communities differ from one to another from both simple to larger-life activities. For example, there are dialectal differences in the spelling of such words as "dawdi" house, which may also be spelled "doddy" or daudi," depending on the region in question. In addition, praying aloud at the dinner table may also, at times, be a voiced prayer when there is a particular praise offered.

The Amish man who was my main source of information, the truly forthright and dry-humored Dan Miller, told me that it would be difficult to find two Amish communities exactly alike. While all may share basic beliefs in the Lord, family, and work ethics, diversity still exists.

It is a lesson to me as an *Englischer* that though the Amish may appear to live "the simple life," their differences provide a rich culture for both fact and fiction, and it is my honor to represent some small threads of their ways of life.

—Kelly Long

Prologue

*I*n the moment between heartbeats he heard the ominous report of a gun, then lurched forward from a burst of blinding pain. He groaned aloud and stared down at the dark sleeve of his left arm in the moonlit winter night. He tightened his muscular thighs against the horse. *Stay on. Stay on.* The voice seemed both his own and that of a fading echo. He wavered, then concentrated on the saddle horn, the reins, and the lead of the other horse behind him. Primal and metallic, the smell of his own blood mingled in his senses with the distancing shouts of the shooter, and he managed a grim smile. He was now, among supposedly other intriguing things, a horse thief . . .

CHAPTER 1

*L*illy Lapp was late. Of course, in the whole scheme of things, no one was bound to notice a missing school-teacher from the ceremony. Not that her job wasn't deeply valued, but she knew that the eyes of all the Old Order Amish Community pressed into the King family's largest barn would be torn between watching two things—the wedding of the season and the face of the man who was not the groom.

She adjusted herself on the hard buggy seat and gave a brisk slap of the reins in an attempt to encourage her horse, Ruler, who plowed along with disinterest through the bleak cold of the late November day. She wished she'd remembered her gloves, but the visit by the *Englisch* police officer had thrown her normally practical frame of mind and she'd left home in an uncollected hurry. A wounded horse thief hiding in the area, indeed.

Fortunately, her mother had still been asleep when the officer had arrived. Lilly was sure that her widowed *mamm* would not have given him permission to search the barn and the outbuildings. But Lilly felt that it was her duty to cooperate with the authorities, no matter how strange their notions may be. She just could not believe that any of her own community would ever steal a horse from an *Englisch* farm, not when there were so many horses available as part of everyday life. Besides, it was wrong. Though, of course, there was always the possibility that someone could have done this. The Amish were certainly not perfect. Still . . . she could not imagine it.

She felt that Ruler might be picking up speed when the first crystalline drop of icy rain hit her cheek through the open front of the buggy. Soon it was pouring, a thick deluge that struck with all the intensity of a thousand miniature knives. Ruler began to toss at the reins, and Lilly swallowed, nervous at his behavior. She knew she had to get him into shelter of some kind, but the wedding home was still a good two miles away.

She blinked as the rain slanted, pelting into the buggy and soaking her dark cape. Ruler had given in to the onslaught and stopped stock-still along the side of the road. There was no help for it; she'd have to get out and lead him to shelter. From what she could gather, they were somewhere near Deacon Zook's property. The shifting wind moved the fog and revealed the reassuring bulk of an outlying barn. She slipped from the buggy, quaking from the cold, as she went to the horse's head and unhitched him, grabbing the reins. She reasoned that the storm would soon pass and the buggy would be all right along the roadside. She pulled, and Ruler lifted his head to roll a baleful eye at her before finally beginning to move forward.

It seemed miles to the barn, though it was only several hundred feet. Trudging in the freezing rain in her best shoes and long dark dress—which were meant for socializing and not warmth—made the walk almost unbearable. Finally, she pressed her hands against the closed door of the barn, taking deep, panting breaths and searching for the latch with numb fingers.

To her amazement, the door slid open from the inside, and a tall, dark-haired Amish man stared down at her with a grim look.

She blinked her eyes, licking surreptitiously at a splat of rain that dripped past her mouth, then spoke the first thing that came to her mind.

"Jacob Wyse. What are you doing here? Today's the—" she broke off as his handsome face tightened beneath the brim of his black hat.

"The wedding?" he snapped. "Right. But wedding or not, I'd like to know why you're fool enough to have a horse out in weather like this. You surely must have seen the rain coming."

He brushed past her to grab Ruler's reins, and she sagged backward out of the way as the horse followed Jacob like an obedient lamb, leaving her to cling to the barn door with limp hands and suppressed words of ire on her lips at his assumption that she was some sort of weather vane.

"Come in here out of the cold," Jacob ordered from the dim interior of the barn. She tried to make haste to obey, though her legs seemed too numb to move. He finally came back and hauled her into the shelter without ceremony, sliding the door closed with a strong arm. He sat her down on a bale of hay and returned to Ruler where he ran caressing hands over the animal's back with a dry rag and made soft, soothing sounds in his throat.

Lilly tried to slow her breathing as she listened to the sudden quiet of the barn, insulated by bales of hay and stacks of feed bags. Although she was soaked to the skin, she couldn't seem to think to do anything about it and surveyed the interior instead. She recognized Jacob's bay gelding, Thunder, in a stall, munching at some hay, while another horse's head appeared over a half door near the far wall. Then she glanced up at Jacob as he finished wiping Ruler down and led him with ease to an empty stall. He filled the hayrack, turned back to her, and sighed.

"Why are you here?" he finally asked, looking at her like she was an unwanted bug at a picnic. Indeed, considering her bedraggled appearance, she probably looked more hag than girl. But there was nothing she could do about it at the moment, so she slipped off her soggy bonnet.

"I asked you the same thing. Though, in my case, it's rather obvious that the storm brought me here. Shelter for my horse, you know."

He shook his head, and she tried to ignore the pull of interest that she felt being so close to him. Jacob Wyse was, in face and form, the most attractive man in the community. She'd thought so ever since they'd been in school together and she'd watched him tend to a stray and starving dog that some other boys were trying to drive away. Jacob had stared the boys down one by one, then went to lift the animal into his strong arms, never knowing he was also stealing Lilly's impressionable young heart at the same time. But now at twenty-four, Jacob's tall muscular form, rich hazel eyes, and dark chestnut hair with lighter streaks from the sun were all the more appealing. Still, he'd never spoken more than a few words of any consequence to her in all the time she'd known him.

In the community where everyone knew everything about everyone else, it had been well understood for years that Jacob Wyse only had eyes for the beautiful Sarah King, and every other girl was just part of the mountainous landscape. But today, Sarah King was getting married . . . to another man.

Lilly snapped her attention back to him when she realized he'd been speaking.

"Wh—what?" She shivered, trying to subdue the urge to let her teeth chatter.

"I said, for the third time, that you're soaked. Go back into one of the stalls and take off as much as your decency will allow. I'll find you a stable blanket."

"I will . . . not." She meant to sound outraged, but her voice came out in a thready squeak.

"Look, I'm not having the beloved schoolteacher of Pine Creek come down with pneumonia on my time. Move!"

She sat still, her practical nature telling her that what he was suggesting made sense, but the woman in her felt insulted at his tone and the casualness with which he commanded she undress. She knew that Jacob Wyse didn't especially care for the idea of schooling and schoolteachers, at least he didn't when he was younger. His opinions must not have changed much.

"A gentleman . . . would offer me . . . his coat." There was no holding back her teeth chattering now. She watched as a grim smile spread over his handsome face.

"A gentleman might," he agreed.

She reminded herself that he looked good but his temperament had always been wild and brooding. She realized the unpredictable weather might be easier to deal with than him and wondered if the rain had lifted any so that she might just leave.

"It's still pouring; you can hear it."

"How did you know what I was thinking?" Lilly asked.

He smiled a real smile then, just briefly, and she felt her heart catch in her chest.

"What's in a woman's mind is easy enough to figure out—it usually involves what they think they want and what they wish they had."

She tried to ignore the blush that warmed her cheeks; his arrogant words made her fume.

"You should open a shop . . ." she suggested. "Doctor Wyse's thoughts on women and the summation of their brains."

"Stop the *hoech-nawszich* schoolteacher talk and undress, or I may take it into my professional head to help you out."

She tried to stand, outraged at his words, but her skirt had frozen to the hay. She could only flounder in an undignified manner.

He bent to lift her, then staggered as if her weight was too much for him. She huffed in embarrassment until she realized that he'd reeled backward in a sudden wash of pallor. "What's wrong?" Lilly asked.

He shook his head. "Nothing."

A bead of sweat dripped down his cheek.

"Jacob, are you ill?"

He seemed to rally at her question and stood upright, wiping his cheek. "*Nee*," he said in a hoarse voice. "But neither am I . . . a gentleman."

She stared at him as he opened his heavy black coat and slid it off. She gasped when she saw the blood that stained his white shirt, beginning near his left shoulder and expanding downward to his elbow. "Jacob! What happened?" A dawning awareness struck her. She glanced to the horse in the far stall and then back to the man who nearly sagged before her. "You're the one they're looking for? The horse thief?"

"Smart girl," he acknowledged, his eyes narrowing with pain.

Jacob allowed himself to sink down onto a bale of hay. He slid off his hat and closed his eyes. For some reason, it felt all right to reveal his wound to the serious, wide, blue eyes of the schoolteacher. She might talk high, but he knew from overhearing conversations that she loved the *kinner* she taught. And anyone who had a heart for children had compassion, and he needed some right now.

He heard her tussle with her skirts and then opened his eyes to watch her come forward and kneel between the sprawl of his legs. She was nothing if not practical, he thought as she matter-of-factly reached to examine his wound with slender fingers. She leaned close to lift the edge of the handkerchief he'd used to help staunch the blood flow.

"Before the cancer took *Daed* he taught me a lot about veterinary science, so I learned something about wounds," she murmured.

Of course you did. He had to think to keep from muttering the comment aloud.

"You were shot from behind, obviously. From what I can see of the exit wound, it looks clean. No arteries were hit or you would have bled to death by now."

"Thanks for the thought."

"What happened exactly?"

He looked away from her, staring up at the broad barn beams above them. "I was fool enough to give in to—let's say a reckless urge—and stop by Tom Granger's farm because I heard a horse in pain and distress. I got sick of all the unfairness in life, and when that idiot farmer left the barn with a bloodstained whip in his hand, I went in and put the mare on a lead and led her away. Granger saw me, shot me, and I've been hiding out here since last night. I'm lucky no police have come knocking."

He glanced at her eyes, warm with respect, and he wanted to duck away from her open emotion. Another woman might have played the game of feigning shock at his actions. Clearly, the schoolteacher didn't understand the affectation of womanly wiles and, more than that, she seemed to hold some kind of misguided admiration for him. And he didn't think that rescuing a horse from Granger was worth admiring, even though everyone around knew Tom Granger was a surly *Englischer* who mistreated his wife, son, and stock, and who cursed loudly as Amish women and children walked past his farm.

Jacob roused from his musings when Lilly replaced the handkerchief and folded the torn edges of his shirtsleeve back over the makeshift bandage, fussing with the fabric.

"You are fortunate that you've escaped the notice of the police. They've searched the area but probably overlooked this outlying barn."

"Well, that's one thing in my favor, I suppose. But I've got to face them sooner or later, and I—"

He realized that she peeked at his mouth while he spoke, and he recognized the brief, veiled glance. Girls had studied his lips with speculative interest since he'd turned sixteen, and impetuous instinct now drew his eyes to her lips.

He was bone weary, wounded, and besides the physical pain, his heart hurt more than the time an anxious stallion had broken his ribs.

But he was also alive and sick of feeding on ideas about what might have been. *Now* mattered. That was all. What was right in front of him. He ignored the prick of conscience that might have checked his words and tilted his head to one side.

"I know what you want," he said evenly and without conceit.

She startled, a ready denial in the depths of her eyes.

He shook his head. "Don't. I want it too."

"I have no idea what you're talking about."

Then the schoolteacher knows more about books than she does about herself, he thought, leaning forward.

He cupped his callused hand around her fragile chin before she could draw away.

"I'm talking about escape," he whispered. "Just for a moment. No responsibilities. No wedding. No heartache. Nothing—but now."

He lowered his lashes until all he could see was the petal pink of her mouth against the paleness of her skin and then he dipped his head. He kissed her until he felt her resistance melt into tentative response, and then he closed his eyes. He wanted to banish the image of Sarah that burned in his brain and slanted his chin to deepen the kiss. He heard his own frantic intake of breath when she laid a hand on his chest, and he surrendered helplessly to the fantasy of another man's wife—a vision that he longed to deny.

CHAPTER 2

*L*illy envisioned a thousand granules of sugar quickening through a funnel to some dark, waiting center. She was sliding with them, covered in sweetness, until the rational part of her mind intruded. *Substitute.* Substitute teacher. Sarah's substitute. She wrenched backward and Jacob made a strangled sound in his throat that jarred her senses, leaving her longing to soothe him. But she sank back to rest on her legs. Her mouth stung and her chin burned from the dark shadow of his jaw. She prayed that the Lord might forgive her for allowing such a thing. And then added her request that He also might bring someone, someday, to love her with as much passion as she felt through Jacob's kiss.

She watched him come to himself, like a dreamer waking with reluctance. His heavy lashes lifted from his flushed cheeks and he sighed.

"I'm sorry."

"No, you're not," she replied, surprised at the steadiness of her voice. "You wanted an escape; you got it."

His green-gold eyes narrowed. "I think you got a bit of it too, Miss Schoolteacher."

"You're right, of course. I've never had the kiss of a man, only a father's."

A tenseness appeared around his handsome mouth at her admission, and he looked away.

"You need medical attention."

He nodded, still concentrating on some unknown spot at the back of the barn. "*Jah*, but the only doctor around is the good Grant Williams, veterinarian at-large. And he, as you know, has other plans this morning."

Lilly didn't need to listen hard to hear the bitterness in his tone.

Dr. Williams was an *Englischer* who'd been baptized into the community only a few months past, but he was as accepted as one to the bonnet born. And, he was the man who had won Sarah King's heart.

Lilly tapped her lips with her index finger as a half-formed idea began to take shape.

"What?" He swung his penetrating gaze back to her.

"If we go anywhere in town to have you treated by the *Englisch*, they'll tell the police. Lockport is too small for the town not to know about the horse. So, you only have one person to treat you—the groom."

"Have you lost your mind?"

She raised an eyebrow at him. Not for nothing was she a teacher, easily engaging stubborn students. "Have you lost yours? And have you stopped to think of how it will look if you don't show up for the wedding?"

He glared at her. "What does it matter?"

"It matters because you're not going to run away. You're going to live here, work here, and so will the Williamses. And you also know how this place is—everyone is just waiting to see how you will react to the wedding. To not show up suggests weakness; something I'm sure is not part of your character."

He snorted. "Really? You just got a literal taste of my weakness, Lilly Lapp. And seeing Sarah today—well, it's something I could live without, no matter what people think."

She shrugged. "It's your life."

The words hung with cunning in the chill of the air until he shifted on the bale of hay with a sigh.

"*Ach*, all right. But tell me, teacher, how do I separate the beloved groom from his beautiful bride so that he can do some stitching without her or anyone else's notice?"

"At the *eck*, or as they're going to be seated, I'll create some kind of diversion."

"A diversion? You, the schoolteacher, who's supposed to be beyond reproach in behavior? What will the school board say? What will your *mamm* say?" He asked the right questions, but his tone provoked, as if he doubted she'd be capable of doing anything out of the ordinary.

She loved a challenge and smiled at him. "Likely, everyone will have something to say, but so what? I'm twenty-three, my own person, and I—" She swallowed; she'd almost said she cared about him even though she only really knew him from childhood and at a distance in the community. "I can do as I please—relatively." She ignored the niggle of doubt that warned her that her widowed *mamm* would not be pleased by any diversionary wedding tactics and plowed on. "So, we'll go back to your house and put up Granger's horse. I'll borrow a dress of your *mamm's*, and we'll go to the wedding."

She waited to see if he'd dismiss her out of hand because she was a woman, and as her mother often pointed out, probably too decisive a woman at that.

But his own eyes narrowed in consideration and he finally

grinned at her. "Lilly Lapp. Who'd have thought? But I don't really want to get you involved in all of this."

"*Derr Herr* involved me," she pointed out. "The minute you opened that stable door. Sometimes things happen for a reason, Jacob."

"I suppose there's truth in that. All right, help me up then, Miss Independence."

He leaned against her for just a moment as he got to his feet, and she tried not to notice the heat of his body through his cotton shirt. She helped him with his coat and hat, added her collapsed bonnet to the mess of her hair, and then they turned to the horses.

"The rain has slowed down," he said, cocking an ear to the barn roof. "We'll hitch Ruler to the buggy and tie the little mare behind with a lead. I'll come back later for Thunder. Deacon Zook'll figure I left him for shelter in the weather."

And somehow, despite his injury and her hampering skirts, they made it back across the field with Jacob talking low and easy to the horses as if in some long-forgotten language. Lilly, only half-listening, concentrated on staying upright on shivering legs. She breathed a sigh of relief as she clambered into the buggy with the help of an undignified push from behind.

"Move over," Jacob instructed. "I'll drive."

"But your arm—Ruler's stubborn."

"Is he now? I think he's a lamb."

"That's not how he seems to me," she complained.

Jacob glanced at her. "Is it just Ruler or are you uncomfortable around horses in general?"

"In general, I suppose. Actually, Alice Plank's little brother, Jonah, usually comes over in the morning to help me get Ruler hitched up and ready. It was something Father arranged when he knew he was growing very ill. I really don't care much for horses."

"What about horse thieves?"

She sniffed. "Slightly more tolerable."

"In that case"—he laughed—"I'll say *danki*, Lilly, for tolerating this horse thief—for helping me."

She nodded and he set the buggy into easy motion down the wet road.

CHAPTER 3

*I*f he found it odd that he'd chosen to steal a horse, survived a gunshot wound, and then decided to escort a soaked schoolteacher back to his home after he'd forced a kiss from her novice mouth, it could be no stranger than his automatic actions over the past few months. He'd become more and more restless as Sarah's wedding date approached. There was no sense denying it—when he'd realized he'd lost Sarah, that in truth he'd never had her, it had devastated him. And there seemed no reason to pretend otherwise. So he'd mentally agonized through the summer and fall, trying to pray, trying to work, and generally feeling more and more despondent as winter set in.

He gave a sidelong glance at Lilly Lapp as she hugged her arms across her chest and shivered, her lips visibly blue—lips he'd deliberately warmed with his own. It had never occurred to him that it might be her first kiss. Now he had to push away a wave of chagrin when he thought about his behavior. Lilly Lapp was someone who'd never even registered in his passing vision let alone his thoughts. Of course, he'd gone to school with her and seen her occasionally about the Lapp farm, often in the shadow of her father. Old Dr. Lapp had been the local veterinarian since Jacob was a child, and he'd learned much about horses and their care from the cheerful Amish man. But Dr. Lapp had passed away, leaving behind a grieving wife, and Lilly, his only child. More than that, Jacob's mind whispered, the death of Dr. Lapp had made room for Dr. Grant Williams to appear and nothing had been the same since. There was no use dwelling on it. The Lord knew he'd spent long enough doing that these past months.

"Come over here," he said, indicating the small distance between them in the buggy.

"*Nee*. I'm fine."

He sighed. "If we're going to be coconspirators, I can't let you freeze to death before we can accomplish our plan. I promise I mean you no impropriety." He choked on a sudden laugh at his formality after the brazen kiss in the barn.

She threw him a wry look that suggested she knew what he was thinking but scooted a bit closer under his outstretched arm anyway. He enclosed her cloaked shoulder in his big hand, sliding her firmly up against his side. He felt her quaking even through the thick wool of his coat and frowned.

"We're almost there," he soothed kindly, raising his chin toward the large Wyse horse farm and barns visible over the next rise in the road. "I just don't want to make the mare go too fast."

"It looks like her right side took the brunt of the lashings."

"*Jah*," he agreed, his jaw squaring when he thought of Granger. "Those will soon heal well enough. The two on her rump are the deepest. I'm most worried about those—and her spirit."

"Are you going to take her back?"

He looked down at her. "Are you asking if I'm going to come clean with Granger? Yes, teacher, right after today's big doings, but I need to get through the wedding first." He watched her lips part on a sigh, revealing perfect white teeth, and went on.

"Perhaps I could let money talk to Granger. He might overlook the theft if I offer a more-than-fair price for the mare."

She looked back at him, understanding dawning in her eyes. "You've thought that all along, haven't you? Even when you took her? Then why didn't you just buy her outright? Why go to all this trouble? And what did you think would happen when you did steal her—especially if Granger caught sight of you? That he would merrily wave you off?"

He shrugged. "It's not like I asked to be shot." He gave her a wry smile. "I was wrong—that's it. I have no excuse. I was mad and I gave in to the sin of anger. I wanted to do violence to Granger. I wanted to . . . to break something. The hold he held on the mare, maybe."

"Just like a fairy tale," she remarked.

"A what?"

"Rescuing the damsel in distress—only this one happens to be a horse."

He felt baffled. What did a fairy tale have to do with anything?

"Too bad it wasn't Sarah you rescued, eh?"

He could feel the heat rising in his cheeks. "Are you comparing Sarah to a horse?" he tried to quip, hoping to change the direction of the conversation.

"No."

He pursed his lips. "Well, let's just say that you've got quite the imagination, but I guess you need it to work with children. Here we are."

He swung the buggy down the narrow lane and avoided the palpable sensation of her stare.

I'll take the mare into the barn and tend to her a bit. Go on in. My *mamm* and *daed's* room is the first door off the sitting area.

Help yourself to whatever you can find to wear, although *Mamm's* clothes may be a bit short on you."

She looked away from his measuring gaze and tried hard to forget about the sensation of his fervent kiss. Taking his offered hand, she stepped from the buggy, hastened past him, and took the steps up to the porch. She glanced back to watch him lead the mare to a nearby barn, then slipped through the unlocked door.

Lilly had only been to the Wyse home for Meeting, and then it was always so crowded that she'd never really had a chance to look around the beautiful downstairs with its detailed woodworking, comfortable-looking chairs, and pristine kitchen with wild winter roses growing from a watering can on the bright windowsill.

It was such a contrast to her own home where heavy, dark furniture blocked the windows of most rooms and the stinging scent of pine oil often permeated the air. Her *mamm* had so changed since the death of her *daed* that she now seemed to hide from the sunlight. The Wyses' home, on the other hand, gleamed with light and smelled like a combination of fresh baking and starched linen, presenting quite an inviting atmosphere.

Despite Jacob's invitation to be bold, she slipped off her shoes and tiptoed into the bedroom, turning up a kerosene lamp on a lovely cherry bedside table. She removed her ruined bonnet and soaked prayer *kapp* and then pulled as many hairpins as she could find from the tangled mass of her dark hair. Then she caught sight of the walls and her lips parted in surprise and wonder.

She pivoted on wet, stockinged feet to stare with amazement at the paintings that decorated the light wood. She drew a deep breath at myriad striking watercolors portraying Amish life in bright detail. *Kinner* and men with long beards, planting and harvest, all seasons of life and earth seemed to be represented by the artist's brush. She marveled at the irresistible beauty of the images. She knew that some Old Order Amish communities eschewed art as being impractical, but the local bishop encouraged the use of the Lord's given talents. And these paintings certainly seemed purposeful in capturing the life and vitality of her people.

A quick knock on the door sounded. She responded in an absent tone, her mind enraptured. "Come in."

There was a distinct moment of silence, a sudden drifting awareness, and then the dawning knowledge that Jacob had entered the room, and that her hair hung loose and damp below her waist. It was only the privilege of a husband to view his wife's hair unbound, and her lack of haste had put her in this awkward situation. She started to bundle the dark mass up with frantic fingers but to no avail. She discarded the passing, childish thought to run and jump into the bright, quilted bed and hide under the covers.

"Jacob—I—the paintings. They're amazing. Who does them?"

"Seth. It's kind of a thing he only shares with the family. That's why the paintings are in here. I've got one in my room."

Lilly thought of Jacob's younger brother. Twenty-three-year-old Seth Wyse, with his golden hair and bright blue eyes, seemed the absolute antithesis of the dark Jacob. Although the brothers were similar in attracting the girls, Seth had an infectious grin, a cheerful disposition, and the deepest baritone at singings. He was a charmer to be sure. Yet his paintings revealed a side of him that she never imagined existed. The depth and maturity of the art drew both heart and spirit.

She held her hair back over her shoulders and wished Jacob would go out, seeking for something to say to break the moment.

"You must be very proud of Seth."

"He's my little *bruder*, but he's my best friend. I'd ask you not to say anything of his painting though. It really is a private thing."

"Of course, but it's also a gift from *Derr Herr*." She tried not to shiver. "Do you think he might come to school one day to give the *kinner* a drawing lesson?" She smiled at the thought while a frown appeared on Jacob's face.

"Seth's finished his schooling."

"*Ach*, I know but—"

"You'd best hurry. And, if you don't mind, I could use a bit of help bandaging this arm again before I change my shirt."

Politely snubbed, Lilly thought. She began to tap one slender foot in the same rhythm she used when dealing with stubborn students.

"Am I in trouble?" he asked, his mood quicksilver and his deep voice laced with humor. "I always seemed to rub teachers the wrong way when I was in school; things must not have changed much."

She stopped tapping when her arms began to ache from holding her hair back. "You know perfectly well that I'm standing here, with my hair down, and you should show enough respect to—"

He laughed aloud and she frowned at the provoking sound.

"After aiding a horse thief, checking out a gunshot wound, and time alone in a deserted barn, you're worried about your hair being down?"

"Yes," she snapped, ignoring the faint guilt that added a heated kiss to his list.

"Your priorities are strange, teacher, but if you still want to go, you need to hurry. The ceremony will be over and they'll be at the food soon. I will go out while you change, of course."

"Of course," she said. As his eyes sparkled at her, she felt foolish for losing her temper. He gave her a parting grin, and she went to the bureau to find dry underclothes and socks and then hastened to change into a dark green blouse, black dress, and apron. She bundled her hair back up into a dry *kapp*, then glanced ruefully down at her borrowed attire. The clothes were too short on her, revealing both black-stockinged ankles and long white arms.

Nevertheless, she really had no choice; she couldn't return home for her own things. She'd have to explain the situation to her mother, who would have risen from her bed by now but would be ensconced on a couch downstairs. And she'd gone to all the trouble of securing a substitute teacher from Elk County for her class. This wedding, like most winter weddings, was being held on a less busy weekday instead of the weekend. More than that, she did not want to miss this social opportunity, even if it had become one of the most upside-down days of her young life.

She prayed as she extinguished the lamp and left the room, wanting to greet Jacob with encouragement and an apology for her snap of temper. When she went into the sitting area, she stopped when she saw him standing next to the kitchen sink, his shirt off and his back toward her. She did have an interest in the study of anatomy, but it was one thing to read it in a book and quite another to see it clearly delineated in broad musculature and well-shaped bones. And, she reasoned, she'd been so used to caring for her *daed* in the latter stages of his illness that she'd nearly forgotten what health looked like in the human frame. Thus reassured, she approached him and he turned his head over his shoulder.

"I cleaned the exit wound as best as I can, but I can't reach all the way round."

She nodded, sidling next to him to wash her hands with soap. She ignored the scent of his body—something like pine and summer mixed together—and dampened a fresh cloth to clean the back of his arm. He flinched when she dabbed at the small entry wound.

"Sorry."

He shook his head. "Just go on."

She proceeded while he gripped the sink edge with white-tipped fingers. She felt *naerfich*, nervous, at his proximity, then told herself that the feeling was ridiculous in light of their kiss. But if she moved forward in any direction, she'd come in contact with his lean hip, the fall of his suspender, or the warmth of his tanned arm, and it made her skittish.

She ignored the faint groan that came from his lips as she bandaged the wound in haste. Then she avoided looking at him entirely as she helped him into the clean blue shirt he'd gotten.

"Look, I'm not going to kiss you again, all right?"

"I didn't say you were."

He worked at tucking the shirt into his dark waistband with one hand and frowned at her. "*Nee*, but you're as *naerfich* as a cat."

"Cats are actually remarkably sedate." She slid across the room and bent to feel the everyday reality of the damp leather of her soaking shoes. Clearly he did make her nervous, and she decided she didn't like the rattling of her normal composure. It would be best to help him and be done with it.

"Here's a cloak and bonnet of *Mamm's*. I'll be outside waiting."

She caught the fall of wool that he tossed to her and watched him leave, now properly covered in shirt and another coat, and exhaled a breath she'd been holding for a very long time.

CHAPTER 4

*A*s they neared the King farm, a seemingly endless row of horses and buggies came into view. The whole adult community must have been invited; most weddings were smaller. Jacob began to doubt his actions in allowing the schoolteacher to be part of any of the mess he'd gotten himself into. Yet, at the thought of insisting she enter the well-lit King home alone, a soft voice, gentle but persistent, came to him from inside his heart. He'd experienced enough of his faith to recognize that it was *Derr Herr* who'd brought the girl to the barn this morning, and, for some reason, he understood that she was supposed to be involved. Still, as he angled the buggy into a spot, he felt he should give her one more chance to choose—but he already could guess her response. *She has a strong will*, he thought with a private smile.

"Sure we shouldn't rather have a Doc in town take a look at this arm?" he asked her. "We know the bullet passed clean through; the bleeding's pretty much stopped. It's not too late for you to just slip out of the buggy and forget the whole thing."

"Everyone will have seen us by now—together," Lilly said,

glancing at the wide, uncurtained windows of the King house where figures passed in gay motion, illuminated by many kerosene lamps.

Together. He blinked at that. He hadn't considered how it might appear if they showed up late—and together—for the wedding celebration. He, who'd spent years dodging, or merely ignoring, advances from the ladies of the community, was arriving late to a wedding with a rumpled and ill-clothed schoolteacher. He bent his head and ran through the social implications of such an arrival. Of course, it could be as simple an explanation as him finding her along the road, stuck in the icy rain, and he just happened by. He nearly groaned aloud. More lies. And all his fault. But before he could think further, she'd slipped down from the buggy and stood on the ground looking up at him expectantly.

There was something brave about the way she stood in his mother's socks and the too-short cloak and dress she wore. Her blue eyes were steady and trusting. But she had far more to lose in this situation than he did. Why, she could be forced to give up her teaching position if there was any question about where they had been. And he knew well enough the wagging tongues that some women in the community enjoyed using against others. He needed to just forget this whole thing and go see Granger, alone.

He looked up to see Lilly on the porch, looking back at him. He hastened to get down from the buggy and to reach her side. Before he could get there, the door was flung open by a young woman—Kate Zook. Jacob stifled a sigh. The newly-turned nineteen-year-old Zook girl was as spiteful as her mother, and he and Seth had spent many a social engagement trying to avoid the overt advances of the wily female. The girl was currently looking Lilly up and down with raised, questioning blond brows.

"Why, Jacob Wyse . . . and Lilly Lapp." The girl's voice carried insinuation. Jacob squared his jaw as those nearest the door stopped still to glance in their direction.

He took Lilly's arm. "Kate. Good to see you. The cold is a bit much today. Would you mind letting us in?"

The girl widened the door, and Jacob kept a hand on Lilly's arm as they pushed into the crowded room. The space seemed overly full of speculative and all-too-interested eyes. Jacob nodded to the men closest to him, then removed his hat, hanging it on a nail. A stirring in the crowd brought forth a petite older woman with a careworn face and anxious hazel eyes, who reached out small hands to touch his sleeve.

"Jacob, we've been so worried," the woman said in a low voice.

He smiled down at her. "It's all right, *Mamm*. It's just been a busy morning." He glanced at Lilly and Mrs. Wyse extended her hand to greet the schoolteacher.

"Lilly, it's *gut* to see you." His mother's smile was warm; then she turned to her son. "Last night, Jacob—Seth and your *daed* went looking when you didn't come home."

Jacob loved his mother, though at the moment he wished she'd contain her concern; she certainly wasn't making the situation look any better for Lilly.

He smiled again with reassurance, ignoring the group who'd now gathered about the door. "I'll explain later, *Mamm*. Let's take some time to celebrate. I, er, we must congratulate the bride and groom."

"*Jah*." His mother nodded, patting his arm. "You both, take off your outdoor things and come and have something warm to eat."

He hesitated to take off his coat, unsure if his arm had started to bleed again and shot a quick glance at Lilly. She appeared confident as she prepared to remove the borrowed cloak, but he knew how odd she'd appear once it was off.

"Uh, *Mamm* . . . Lilly, I mean, Miss Lapp, would surely like to keep her cloak on, as I would my coat, at least until we warm up a bit."

He almost breathed a sigh of relief as Lilly's fingers paused.

Then Kate Zook spoke loudly. "Not home last night, then late to the wedding, with the schoolteacher not wearing her own clothes—they do appear rather short. Were you two in some kind of trouble?"

Jacob saw his mother's eyes flash green fire at the girl, and Lilly opened her mouth to speak. He cut her off.

"Kate, *danki* for your concern, but we must see the bride and groom before we enjoy any of the delicious food. If you'll excuse us."

He grabbed his mother's arm and Lilly's hand, figuring it was best to keep them close by in case anyone raised more questions. He plowed through the crowded front room into the next sitting room. Lavish food tables lined the area, with the *eck*, or bridal table, in one corner of the room. He squared his shoulders as he approached the bride and groom and their attendants with the two women in tow. He was perfectly aware of the attention he was attracting, not just with his mother and Lilly, but also because of the interest people had in what his reaction to the bridal couple would be.

His determined eyes took in the beauty of the bride, Sarah King—*nee*, Sarah Williams now—and her dear, familiar face; a face he'd known and loved since childhood. He couldn't help it; when he saw her he forgot that she was the bride of the day—another man's wife. He only thought of the years that he'd harbored a love for her that harrowed his heart and mind and robbed his will of reason. It was beyond him, beyond his ability to solve or escape. Then, unbidden, and against his will, he found himself praying a prayer for another love, a love that would sweep all before it like a driving spring rain. He almost smiled as he finished the thought. He must be addled in the head, from his wound and the wedding, because he knew without a doubt that he wanted absolutely nothing to do with another woman. His whole focus of living for the moment would bear no place for a second-best love.

He refocused and forced himself to acknowledge that Sarah looked happy, even radiant. He'd rehearsed this moment a million times, wondering how he'd get through it. But never had he imagined approaching the table with a concealed gunshot wound and two women in tow.

Sarah and Grant beamed at them as they came forward. *Lovely diversion*, he thought, plastering a smile on his face. He stood about as much chance of getting his arm looked at now as an *Englischer* did at hiding out at an Amish baptism.

He was within a foot of the *eck* when sudden, loud voices from the front door echoed across the rooms and he turned with everyone else to see what the disturbance could be. He heard Lilly's sharp, indrawn breath as a young police officer, with gun drawn, entered the main bridal party room. The bishop, Ezekiel Loftus, an elderly and outspoken man, followed closely behind.

"I tell you to stop, young man! You've no right to be here at such a time as this. It's a wedding and our people's own doings."

The police officer stood amidst the crowd of stunned guests. The Amish, as a rule, did not believe in violence against fellow human beings and the handgun was an insult to Sarah and her day. Jacob wanted to rap the young man in the head.

"It's *my* doings if there's a horse thief here," the officer returned. "And I say there is. I've been watching from the woods for the past hour and I noticed you had a late guest or two. One was a big Amish man, no beard, dark hat and coat."

The bishop nodded. "And what Amish man doesn't have a dark hat and coat?"

"You know what I mean." The officer's gaze swung through the crowd and lighted on Jacob, still dressed in his outerwear. "You! Take off your coat."

All eyes turned to Jacob and he let go of his mother and Lilly. "As you like." He reached for the closures on the heavy wool and would have slipped it from his shoulders when Lilly's voice rang out, clear and resonant.

"You're mistaken, Officer. It's true that Jacob Wyse was late, but he was with me." From the corner of his eye, Jacob saw her small jaw tighten as she stepped forward.

The policeman nodded. "Uh-huh, and so would a hundred others of you say to protect one of your own. But the horse was stolen last night, Miss . . . late."

Lilly's voice dropped and her lashes lowered. "He was with me then as well."

A collective gasp followed her words. Jacob couldn't believe what she was saying. The girl had just thrown away her reputation, her very livelihood—for him—in front of everyone.

"What are you talking about, Miss Lapp?" The bishop demanded, turning toward her, the police officer forgotten, as the guests began to murmur. The bishop was also the chairman of the school board and in charge of Lilly's position.

Jacob moved between Lilly and the old man, and something in his spirit forced his voice to carry with level force. From far away he heard the compelling words he pronounced as if they were spoken by someone else. "*Jah*, sir. It's as Miss Lapp says, but not as you all may think." He let his eyes flash to the encircling crowd and reached out to take her hand in his own. "Lilly and I were together, but we were talking—about our future. *Sei so gut* congratulate us on our engagement."

CHAPTER 5

*T*hey say you never hear it coming," Grant Williams remarked as Jacob forced himself to be still while the vet sutured.

"What? The bullet?"

Grant laughed. "Or the engagement."

Jacob wanted to hit something. He found himself actually liking the man who'd taken Sarah's heart. They were in a back room at the King house and the sounds of the crowd were subdued by the thick wooden walls.

Lilly Lapp had gone along with his *narrish* announcement, then apparently explained the situation of his wound to Grant under cover of a congratulatory embrace. He'd soon found himself hustled off by the groom and no one seemed to notice as they surrounded Lilly. The last he saw of her, she was composed and smiling, fending off more questions than trout nibbles during a storm.

"I'm putting a small drain in. You can see me in a week to have it out. The stitches need another two weeks after that. Which—"

Grant grinned at him. "Should put you somewhere around your wedding date, right?"

"Yeah. Thanks."

Grant cleaned up the small mess from a table and put a few things back in his bag. "Guess it's lucky that around here folks expect me to be able to treat people sometimes as well as animals. I've learned to stock up on a few supplies."

Jacob sighed. "Look, Grant, you can turn me in, all right?"

"What?"

"You know it's a gunshot wound and that I stole the horse. I don't want to intrude on your day any more than I've done. You could probably get in trouble for helping me."

"You think I'd turn my wife's best childhood friend in to the police? On our wedding day?" He snapped his bag closed. *"Nee, danki."*

"All right, then—thank you. And congratulations."

"Danki. Now make sure you get those antibiotics down every day and no lifting saddles or anything else heavy. I don't want those stitches torn out. I'd offer you some pain medicine but you wouldn't take it. Right?"

Jacob shook his head and Grant grinned. "Stubborn Amish man. All right. See me in a week and I'll see you—back out there with your lovely betrothed." Grant smiled and closed the door behind him, leaving Jacob to rest his head against the wall. His mind whirled as he wondered in surreal confusion what he'd been doing with his life—especially over the past twenty-four hours.

I thought that you weren't a gentleman."

"I thought that you couldn't really create a diversion."

They were in the long queue of buggies heading home from the wedding in the winter twilight. Lilly scrunched her eyes closed for a moment against the headache of recalling the afternoon. She sought for something else to say.

"Well, at least the police are no longer interested in you."

Jacob nodded, and she swallowed, thinking about the moment when the young officer's apparent superior had entered the room. He'd seemed appalled at his junior officer and had sent the young man out. The older officer then apologized profusely to the bishop and the room at large, assuring them that they would look elsewhere for the horse thief.

"And how is your arm?"

He shrugged. "Sore. Thank you for telling Grant."

She nodded, then spoke in a brisk tone that didn't match how she felt. "So, shall we go tomorrow and tell the bishop that the engagement is broken?"

"What?" He turned to face her in the dim interior of the buggy.

She stared ahead, resolute. "The engagement. I didn't expect you to speak back there. You should have just let them believe my excuse."

"What kind of a man do you think I am to hide behind a woman's skirts? And you, throwing away your teaching position—how are you going to support your mother?"

Lilly clenched her lips tight against his words. She knew why she had spoken in defense of him, no matter how strange a reason it seemed, even to her. She searched her heart and felt the conviction of *Derr Herr* to tell him the truth.

She pressed her hands together and found her voice. "I would imagine that you haven't ever given me more than a passing thought in this life, but I've always admired you—since we were in school together and you saved that dog."

"What dog?"

"It's not just that. I don't want you to think I was angling for an engagement. I wasn't." She took a deep breath. "When you kissed me in the barn, I know you thought of Sarah. I pulled away because I do not wish to be a substitute for her."

"Then how could you even consider an engagement, a marriage, when you know that I—"

"That you still love her, and I'd be second-best?"

"*Jah*," he whispered miserably.

"At the reception, *Derr Herr* gave me an idea before I ever stepped forward to speak in your defense. Maybe you'd call it an affirmation. Anyway, I had this vision of quilts."

"Quilts?"

"Yes, quilts are made from scraps and secondhand things—but never from the original whole piece of cloth."

"I don't understand."

"I like quilting. I don't have time for it much anymore, but I used to love taking secondhand fabric scraps and making something beautiful from them. If *Derr Herr* gives us the ability to do that with pieces of cloth, how much more of a gift does He give us to patch scraps of lives together to bring Him glory?"

"But no girl is willing to settle for scraps or to be thought of as secondhand."

Lilly laughed. "I could simply tell you that some leftovers are better than the fresh dish itself."

"You're serious, aren't you?"

"I guess I am."

He stared at her in the dim light. "You're strong, Lilly Lapp. Courageous. And I think you know how to meet life with all of its unpredictability. I admire those qualities, but I'm not going to lie to you—I guess I can't anyway if you knew what I was thinking in the barn. I don't have much of a heart left to give, in fact, it's mostly scraps itself—a secondhand heart." He grimaced. "I think it's one thing to have an ideal like your quilt notion, and a whole other challenge to actually live it out."

"It's a challenge to live anyway sometimes," she said low. "At least for me."

The sound of horses' hooves echoed in the stillness as she finished speaking. She stole a glance at him, now in profile, as he eased his hat back on his head, revealing more of his handsome face. "Yeah, me too." He took a deep breath. "You're like your father. When he'd treat a horse, he'd kind of mutter to himself for a moment, decide what to do, and then he did it. No doubting, no worry—he just moved ahead."

Lilly smiled in the darkness. "He used to quote that Scripture verse, 'Where there is no vision, the people are unrestrained.' So, I guess he'd get a vision of the way things are supposed to be and hang on to that."

"I haven't had much vision lately, but I know this much about horses—certain jobs go better with two at the pull rather than one. And you and I are strong, Lilly Lapp."

"Is that a real proposal, Jacob Wyse?" she asked, her voice laced with humor.

"It's a lean proposal; I'll admit that. But it's honest."

She thought for a moment, her heart beating with a mixture of excitement and trepidation. "So we go through with the engagement?"

"With the wedding. Bishop Loftus cornered me at the root beer table and pressed for a date." He grinned at her, a flash of white in the growing dark. "So I gave him one."

"You did?" An Amish engagement was supposed to be a secret thing, with courtship carried out just as secretly until the engagement announcement was made at Meeting, at least two weeks prior to the wedding. But what did she expect, announcing herself to being with Jacob alone?

"I did." He chuckled. "No one's likely to forget our engagement for a long time to come."

"True enough," she said, wondering at the stepped-up beating of her heart. "What date did you give?"

"December twenty-third. They'll announce it at the next Meeting."

She looked at his big hands, wishing he'd squeeze her cold fingers with reassurance.

"Our school Christmas program is on the twenty-first." Her head swam at the idea of things to be done in the coming short weeks.

"The bishop wants you to finish the spring term and to go on teaching until—" He broke off.

"Until what?"

"Nothing."

"What?"

He sighed. "Until the *kinner* start to come."

"Oh . . ." she whispered.

Jacob cleared his throat. "Let's have this out in the open then, Lilly. I have no desire to force you into a marriage, a marriage in truth anyway, until we've had a chance to get to know one another—for quite a while."

"For quite a while," she agreed, wishing she could slide down the buggy seat and disappear into a spot on the floor.

"*Gut . . . gut.* So, here we are. Let's go in and tell your *mamm.*"

Lilly gave a wild glance out the buggy window and realized they'd turned into her own lane. This was what she'd been dreading the most—facing her mother. And she didn't expect that he'd accompany her. She hadn't thought that far.

"I assumed I'd just go in by myself," she said.

"*Nee,* you don't have to do it alone."

You don't have to do it alone. His words echoed in her mind with layers of meaning. *Ach,* if only it were true, and he became someone she could share her everyday fears and burdens with, like she had done with her father. Of course, there was *Derr Herr* and His Word, but sometimes even He felt distant.

She realized that Jacob had gotten out of the buggy and stood waiting, hand extended to help her down. She gave his palm a light touch as she jumped down and then squared her shoulders to face the white house. Only a single lamp burned in a downstairs window, its flame little welcome against the night.

"I don't know how my *mamm* will be, and I—"

"Lilly, I understand about your mother. I mean, well, not everything. Don't try to apologize for her or anything she says. Sometimes people are just hurt, and they need time to heal."

"All right." Lilly nodded, thinking he had absolutely no idea what he was in for.

CHAPTER 6

So you're the miserable thief? Amish, ha! Think you're all high-minded and separate from the world with your clothes and your talk. You ain't no better than a common criminal and jail's where you belong. I'll be calling the police now."

Jacob had expected the malevolence from Granger and knew he deserved it. What the *Englischer* was saying was true, at least about him as an individual, but not about his people. He sighed silently and resisted the urge to rest his weight against the door-jamb as he let the man splutter out.

"Mr. Granger, please call the authorities. As you say, I'm a common horse thief. I made a mistake, and I deserve the consequences."

"You bet you do."

"But, I could have handled things differently maybe . . . maybe instead of stealing the mare I might have offered to buy her outright from you. You obviously aren't happy with her for some reason."

"Buy her from me?" The man sneered. "At a bargain no doubt, and a waste at that. She can't handle a bit and deserves what she got."

Jacob had to remind himself that he should not want to grab the man by the throat, especially when he mentioned the abuse of the animal as something deserved. But he collected himself and calmly offered the man triple the highest value of what the mare was worth.

"You're crazy." Granger eyed him with suspicion but also with a growing interest in his demeanor, which could only be called greed.

"In cash. Right now. I take the mare home. You give me a bill of sale and we keep the—purchase between us."

The man stroked his chin. "Add another thousand. I've heard it said that you Amish are tighter with money than any people around. So, I guess making you pay is really making you pay— more than time in jail might." Granger chuckled at his own joke.

"Fine."

Jacob paid the ridiculous price without hesitation and waited for the receipt, all the while praising *Derr Herr* that he'd been allowed the lightest of consequences. Of course, Granger could always come looking for him, bringing the police, but Jacob had the feeling that all the Amish would look alike to the angry man, so he didn't worry too much since he held the bill of sale.

He left Granger's feeling sullied and exhausted, and he knew he needed rest badly. But the thoughts of the day kept him upright in the saddle. He was engaged to Lilly Lapp.

She said what?"

Alice Plank, Lilly's best friend and fellow teacher, choked on the question with a look of horror on her pretty, round face. The two were seated at the Planks' kitchen table in the light of early dawn, drinking tea. Alice's father and brother were doing chores outside the small farmhouse that was situated next door to the Lapps'.

"She said, 'No.' Short and sharp—just like that."

"Well, what did he say?"

Lilly sighed, reflecting on the night before. Jacob had not been very happy, to say the least. She wrapped her hands around the mug.

"Well, are you going to tell me the story or not?"

"Long or short version?"

"Long, of course, don't leave any details out." She leaned forward, eager to hear it all.

"All right then. I let Jacob inside—the hallway was dark of course. *Mamm* had set no light on the table. As usual, it smelled like pine disinfectant and mothballs. I so wanted to apologize for the smells, but I decided he might as well experience everything. I remember swallowing my apprehension as I made my way into the sitting room where the single lamp burned. He caught my hand in the dark and squeezed my fingers."

"How sweet," Alice said.

"I know. And I was so grateful. It made me feel strong enough to face *Mamm*. But I supposed that one meeting with her and he'd be running to the bishop to retract the engagement."

"No kidding," Alice said, then quickly put her hand on Lilly's arm. "I mean no respect toward your—"

"Alice. It's okay. It's nice to have someone who understands what it's like."

Alice smiled. "So? Don't stop now."

"Before we even got to the sitting room, *Mamm* called, 'Is that you, Lilly? I've been worried sick. It's way past the time I told you to be home—whatever happened?'"

"I was so embarrassed. I felt like a *boppli*. But Jacob spoke up. 'Forgive me, Mrs. Lapp. It's my fault Lilly's been gone so long.'

"'Who do you have with you?' *Mamm* cried out. I felt bad for her. I could see her *kapp* was actually quivering. She shrank back on the couch like he was going to attack her."

"Your poor *mamm*," Alice said. "It must be awful to be so afraid."

"Well, it didn't last for long. I took him into the small circle of light near her. I told her, 'It's all right, *Mamm*. It's Jacob Wyse. He brought me home.'

"We walked into the room and I tried to see her as Jacob might. She looked so tiny with all those quilts round her. About all you could see were the lines on her face and dark shadows under her eyes as she peered up at us. That might have been okay. But then she started in on him.

"'Jacob Wyse? Bringing you home? And on Sarah King's wedding day.' She looked at him like he was an insect getting into her bread dough. 'I'm surprised you could bear to attend the service.'"

Alice sucked in a breath of shock. "What did you say?"

"I tried to plead with her to be silent. Then it got worse."

Lilly closed her eyes as Jacob's calm voice echoed in her head. "He said, 'Yes, Mrs. Lapp, we both attended the celebration today, but we were delayed some by the weather and by our own talk.'

"*Mamm* wiped her nose with a hankie and stared at him. 'What's that now?'

"Jacob tried to be polite. He told her that we were delayed by our own talk—of our future together. '*Sei so gut*,' he said kindly. 'Forgive me for not following tradition and sending a *schtecklimann* to ask your permission first, but I was . . . caught up in the moment. I've announced our engagement to both the bishop and the community.'"

"Wow," Alice said. "He sounds as though he was very formal and polite."

"Yes, he was. I was impressed. But I hadn't thought about the *schtecklimann* until he mentioned it."

Lilly poured more tea into her mug and took a sip, thinking about the *schtecklimann*—a potential groom's go-between.

Normally Jacob would have asked one of the deacons to go in secret to ask her mother's permission for her hand in marriage. Of course, it should have been her father who received the request.

"Then *Mamm* bolted upright. 'What? Lilly? What's he saying? That you're engaged?' I don't really blame her. It was a shocking announcement."

"What did you say?" Alice asked.

"Actually, I didn't say anything. Jacob spoke up right away. 'Yes, Mrs. Lapp,' he said. 'Lilly and I are engaged.'"

"For a brief moment I thought *Mamm* might have apoplexy as she choked and coughed into her hankie. 'Say it isn't true,' she said, giving me that glare."

"I know the one," Alice said.

"I tried to speak in a soft voice, hoping that might help her hear the shocking news. 'It's true. Jacob and I are engaged, *Mamm*. I'm sorry for the short notice and the surprise. I hope you'll be happy with the wedding though.'

"'The wedding! When is the wedding—in a year's time, surely?'

"'*Nee*,' Jacob said. 'The wedding date has been given to the bishop as the twenty-third of December—this year.'

"'*Nee*.'"

Alice gasped.

"'What, *Mamm*?' I asked her.

"'I said no.'

"'Does the date displease you, Mrs. Lapp?' Jacob asked.

"'No, young man, the engagement displeases me, and setting a wedding date for a few weeks out is entirely unacceptable.'"

"Oh boy," Alice muttered.

Lilly nodded. "Of all the possible reactions from *Mamm*, this is one I didn't anticipate. I didn't know what to say. I started to open my mouth to say something, anything to fill the awkward silence. But Jacob cleared his throat and stood up to her again. His voice came out low, husky. It sent shivers down my spine."

"Mmmmm." Alice sounded as though she had just eaten fresh strawberry ice cream. She gave Lilly an understanding smile.

The image of Jacob's bare back danced behind Lilly's eyelids like a mirage just out of reach. She would keep that thought to herself.

"He said, 'I understand you're upset, Mrs. Lapp, but you can rest assured that I have Lilly's best interests at heart.'

"*Mamm* actually snorted. 'Don't try to horse talk me, young man. You forget that I lived for more than twenty years with an animal whisperer; it'll get you nowhere. Now tell me, is she pregnant?'"

Alice burst out laughing, then clapped a hand over her mouth. "*Ach*, I'm sorry, Lilly. But I can't believe she'd say that."

Lilly stared down into her cooling tea and resisted the urge to rub her temples. "Well, she did."

"And—Jacob?"

"He wanted to wring her neck, I think, but he took it. Then he just said straight out that he was marrying me, with or without her approval."

"And then she said yes?"

"Nooo, then she was mad enough to spit."

"It sounds like they're a matched pair," Alice observed.

Lilly laughed. "Maybe so. But she finally settled down when he told her that he was moving in with us instead of me going to live at the Wyses'."

Alice stared at her. "Lilly, really? He must genuinely care for you."

"I wish I could believe that, but I think he's just doing what's right—to see to my mother's health and provision. He said he spoke to the bishop about it at the wedding. I don't even know when he found the time."

Alice added a spoonful of sugar to her cup, then stirred thoughtfully.

"What is it, Alice?"

"*Ach*, I don't know. I mean, I know how you've felt about Jacob all these years and that this wedding probably seems like some kind of dream. But, are you sure it's what you really want? I mean—with Sarah and all."

"I've got to believe that it's the Lord who's guiding this." She swallowed the edge of anxiety that laced her words, then looked determinedly at her friend. "I know it's the right thing for me to do."

"Lilly, tell me how it could be right! It was so fast. A whim. A mistake."

Lilly shrugged her shoulders and stared into the mug with the dregs swimming at the bottom. "I can't explain it, Alice." She looked up. "It's a little like the way you felt about David before he moved away."

Alice set her mouth into a grim line. "Intuition is risky, Lilly."

"I don't think it's all intuition. I think it's *Derr Herr's* whisper."

Alice looked at her with resolve. "Then I will stand by you. Always."

"Besides." Lilly laughed. "If I didn't marry Jacob, I don't think another man would survive my mother's tongue."

Alice laughed with her. She picked up the mugs and put them into the sink. "Did she finally give her blessing?"

"*Jah*. But she told Jacob he'd have to earn her approval."

"*Ach*, Lilly. This is going to be some marriage."

"I'm beginning to see that." She glanced at her brooch watch and groaned. "I'd best move before *Mamm* wakes up. I'll see you later. Oh, and thank you for being willing to be my wedding attendant."

Alice stood with her and gave her a big hug. "I wouldn't miss it, Lilly. Not for anything."

CHAPTER 7

*L*illy hurried home from the Planks', wondering if the daylight would dispel the sense of unreality from the day before. But there was no sense denying it, she was engaged to Jacob Wyse. She almost laughed out loud at the absurdity of the thought. She felt both excited and anxious, and no matter how confident she'd tried to sound to Alice, she wasn't sure what it would be like to actually be his wife—not when he readily admitted his feelings for another. She shook her head at the sudden well of tears that filled her eyes. It didn't matter that he loved Sarah; she was used to being lonely. She could withstand it in marriage as she could as a daughter, sometimes as a teacher. Besides, she knew that at the very least he would be courteous and that was good enough for her. And, she reasoned, brushing away her tears, the Lord could accomplish much with time. Then she swallowed hard as she considered her mother.

Weekday mornings always heralded the worst in her *mamm*, and the day after her announced engagement would be no exception as far as Lilly was concerned. She went into the kitchen and had just hung up her cape when her mother's voice came plaintive and shrill from up the stairs.

"*Jah, Mamm*. I'm coming." She hastened up the stairs to her mother's doorway. The room was darkened, as usual, by the heavy press of bulky furniture placed against the drapes covering the width of the windows. When *Daed* had died, her mother had moved from the bright master bedroom on the first floor to the much smaller guest room on the second floor.

Lilly stood poised in the doorway, not really wanting to enter because of the oppressive feeling that her mother would continue to have more to say about the engagement and Jacob Wyse. "What would you like for breakfast, *Mamm*? I've got more than enough time to do bacon and eggs."

"Fried cinnamon toast. My stomach might not hold much else. I had barely a moment's rest last night after you shocked me so."

"I'm sorry, *Mamm*," Lilly said with sincerity. "But you know how much *Daed* liked Jacob. I'm thinking he would be proud."

"He may well have been; your father loved anyone who loved animals. But that doesn't excuse the fact that this hurried engagement doesn't sit well with me. Not one bit."

"*Jah, Mamm*. I realized that last night."

"Well then, go on and get my breakfast and give me a moment's peace."

Lilly blew out a breath, then went down to the kitchen and turned up two kerosene lamps, remembering the brightness of the Wyse home. She got the woodstove going and set about beating an egg with ground cinnamon and milk and sighed aloud as she stirred. It was at this time of the day that she missed her father the most. *Mamm* had always been last to rise, and Lilly and her *daed* had a playful and merry time cooking breakfast together until *Mamm* came down to join them. Lilly knew that it wasn't what other Amish mothers did, but she didn't care. Not when she had her father's steady smile and kind eyes to reassure her that every-thing was all right, even if it was different. *Mamm* had been normal in her own way—waking late, but working long into the night on quilts or fine needlework for other women. She'd had a tendency to be sad and angry at times, but nothing like the despair she seemed to sink into when *Daed* was gone.

Lilly dragged her thoughts back to the present, dropped a pat of butter into the frying pan, and set about cooking the piece of bread she'd soaked in the cinnamon mixture. It was soon fin-ished, and she pulled out the usual tray, then added a small jug of maple syrup to the plated food and a brimming cup of tea. She gulped down her own tea, then snatched up the tray and went back upstairs. She settled the tray on her mother's lap and stepped back, waiting.

"It looks soggy, but I suppose it's the best you can do. I want you home directly after school today. Mrs. Stolis is bringing over some fabric from the dry-goods store for me to choose from, and you'd better be here to take proper measurements. I was going to have a blouse made, but now I fear I will need a new dress for the wedding instead."

Lilly's head began to throb at the thought of what she herself would wear to her wedding. Her mind couldn't remain there long because of the more pressing issue of what they owed on the vari-ous debts her mother continued to incur. It seemed as though her *mamm* had taken to spending money on things she didn't really need as a way to try and comfort herself. Lilly knew even Mrs. Loftus, the bishop's wife, had tried to speak to her about it. But the talk hadn't deterred her mother; she didn't seem to find comfort in the things Lilly might have expected.

"*Mamm*, I could easily go to the Stolises' with your measure-ments. There's no need for her to come by on a weekday with all of her work at the store. And I thought we'd talked about the fact that my wages can only stretch so far—you had three new blouses the month before last."

Her mother frowned as her teacup rattled against its saucer. "We've talked of this before, Lilly. I told you that I am trying to cut back on the spending that brings me pleasure. I guess at least, with Jacob Wyse's money, we will stand some chance of you not bringing this up again."

Lilly slid from the doorway and pressed her thin fingers to her temple as she escaped down the staircase. Here was another thing she hadn't considered—the Wyse family wealth. Would Jacob's family think she sought to marry him for money? Of course, the bishop made sure that all the widows of the community were tended to with food and help with work about the house and farm, but what was needed did not always extend to what was wanted. And her mother did seem to find temporary solace in material things.

Lilly wished that she could improve her relationship with her mother, but when she tried to talk to her, it either produced a furious tirade, hours of wrenching tears, or a silent withdrawal into the darkness of room, bed, and soul. Lilly felt she could not bear any in great amount for much longer. Yet, she had to; she'd promised her father. It had been one of the last things he'd asked of her before succumbing to cancer—that she would care for her mother. Although she had no idea what havoc his death would bring to her heart and spirit, she could not break her word to the man who'd loved and nurtured her throughout her young life.

Today her teaching waited for her. It wasn't until after she left the house to go to the barn that she recalled that she was without transportation. She'd insisted last night that Jacob take Ruler and the buggy since she felt it would be difficult for him to walk the distance to get Thunder. He'd promised to return the horse the next morn.

She frowned as she opened the barn and found what she

expected—no buggy and no horse. She was puzzling out what to do next when she heard the sound of sleigh bells echoing down the lane.

She turned, her heart beating with expectancy, as she watched Ruler appear from around the house. But instead of Jacob, it was Seth Wyse who hopped out of the buggy, his hat off and a wide smile on his handsome face as he came toward her with an outstretched arm.

He bent and pulled her into a quick embrace, then set her back on her feet. "Lilly Lapp, my dear and soon to be *schweschder*-in-law. Let me offer my most sincere congratulations." He gave her a contagious grin until she had to smile back, then he swept her up into the buggy.

"I added some sleigh bells to Ruler's tack this morning. Hope you don't mind. He's got a tendency to lag a bit and the cadence of the bells might improve his trot."

"It's—fine." Lilly felt overwhelmed by his greeting and wanted to ask about Jacob.

Seth laughed aloud. "My *bruder's* still in his bed. I let him sleep. Even Jacob's got to have a bit of a rest after a gunshot wound and an hour with Tom Granger."

"So, he talked to Mr. Granger?"

"Bought the mare, free and clear. You don't have to worry that your future husband will land himself in jail."

Lilly felt a rush of relief but was still unsure of how to converse with Seth Wyse. If Jacob was dark and brusque, then his brother was all cheerfulness and light. She felt flustered by his obvious and enticing charm. Yet she remembered his paintings and the serious depth they conveyed. Perhaps Seth's demeanor was as much a cover as she suspected Jacob's could be. Of course, in reality, Seth had spoken to her many more times in the past than his brother had, and she decided to just relax and enjoy his goodwill.

She felt Seth glance at her and decided that he, too, must share his brother's talent of perception because he casually touched her arm as she hugged her book satchel to her chest.

"Lilly, seriously, I don't know everything about you and Jacob, but I'm glad to welcome you to the family."

She turned to smile at him. "Thank you, Seth. I appreciate your welcome, and I hope I can make a difference in Jacob's life."

"Oh, you'll make a difference, Blue Eyes, don't worry about that."

Lilly couldn't help the blush that she felt stain her cheeks. She wasn't used to compliments, especially teasing ones. She couldn't help the feeling of pleasure that rushed through her at his words.

"Now, that's a rare thing in the ladies of my acquaintance," Seth remarked as he turned Ruler easily.

"What?"

"A true blush. You're a beauty, Lilly Lapp."

Lilly opened her mouth to speak but shut it again when no words surfaced.

Seth's thoughtful glance brushed over her, his own blue eyes like the color of the sea. "Sometimes, a rose grows in winter, and we miss it for all the snow."

She blinked as her heart began to race a bit at his strange comment. It was the artist in him, she realized, that made poetry of words, and she couldn't help but feel intrigued. But this was Jacob's *bruder*.

He laughed, breaking the awkward moment. "Never mind. Here we are."

She was surprised that they were already at the school.

He came around to help her down and then tied Ruler to the wooden hitching post.

"*Ach*, how will you get home?" Lilly asked in alarm.

"Easy." He grinned. "A good mile jog across two sodden fields never hurt any man." He tipped his hat to her. "Have a good day, sweet *schweschder*."

CHAPTER 8

$\mathcal{S}$o, tell me why you did it."

Jacob entered the warm, morning-lit barn where Seth was tending to the mare's wounds. It had always been like this between them—an unspoken ability to understand each other and to not have to ask too many questions. But he didn't feel in the mood to give answers he wasn't sure of himself.

"You should have got me up." Jacob rubbed absently at his shoulder which had ached all night, leaving him drained and irritable.

"I guess I should have."

"What does that mean?"

"Nothing."

"What happened? Was she upset?"

"You mean your betrothed? *Nee*. We just—talked. She was fine."

"Well, *gut* then."

He blew hot air through his cheeks and lifted a bucket of feed with one hand. He felt like he had the beginnings of a cold, and recollecting Mrs. Lapp's reaction to the engagement made his head throb.

"Don't hurt that shoulder any worse."

"Don't worry about me, little *bruder*."

Seth snorted. "Right. Now, tell me—why the engagement?"

Jacob put the bucket down and rubbed a hand on Thunder's neck. "I don't know," he admitted. "Maybe I wanted a way out of this mess in my head with Sarah, or I wanted to do what's right for Lilly."

"*Jah*, and getting married to an innocent woman while you're still in love with another sounds like a *gut* plan."

Jacob cast him a dark look. "It wasn't like I planned it ahead of time. And I didn't make Lilly say what she did about being with me."

"You didn't deny it either."

"Look—what I said, well, I know it sounds *narrish*, but it just came out of my mouth, like I was supposed to say it."

Seth turned from the mare to start rubbing wax on a saddle. "She has beautiful eyes, you know."

"Who?"

"Lilly. Eyes like winter jewels."

"Since when have you noticed?"

"I always notice girls' eyes. Besides, I went to school with her too, remember?"

"*Jah*."

Jacob ducked his head away from his brother's prodding. He thought with shame about the kiss he'd taken from Lilly yesterday in his own desperation to escape thoughts of Sarah.

How could he have been so selfish to think only of escaping his pain without considering the ramifications of using her? And the engagement—what if that was only a means of putting something right in front of him to focus on, to cling to, a distraction from his painful reality? Was it wrong for him to continue?

Yet, she seemed to be willing, with all her foolishness about quilt scraps and second choices—and a dog from school days.

56788901234567890

What *hund?*

"We'd best get outside. The buyer's coming early."

Jacob rolled his eyes. He was in no mood for the type of buyer his brother typically arranged.

"What?" Seth asked, sliding open the barn door.

"Nothing."

They went to lean against the fence as a BMW swung down the lane.

"Here we go," Seth said under his breath, a bit of pleasure edging his voice. "The game begins."

"*Jah.* But it's a game that grows old."

"You're growing old, big *bruder*. You know as well as I do that *Englisch* lady buyers who come here from Boston—or wherever—have an expectation of what us backward, innocent Amish boys are, and it's not always pleasant. So, what's wrong with treating the customer like a princess, changing her views, and getting us extra money for a horse to boot?"

Jacob sighed as the car ground to a halt. "I don't know."

Seth cocked his hat. "Think of it as advertising. The Wyse Brothers cater to a customer's every whim as well as providing the best horseflesh on the East Coast. Now, smile."

Jacob rubbed at his dark hair, then plastered a smile on his face. He felt like he'd rather be lying down nursing his shoulder instead of moving forward to greet the head-to-toe fur-clad, blond-haired woman who exited the car once the uniformed driver had opened the door.

"Mrs. Castleberrry." Seth had his hat off and was shaking her hand. "I'm Seth Wyse. We're so glad you made it despite the unpredictability of the weather this time of year."

The woman smiled, a dazzling flash of white teeth and an appraising glance from makeup-lined eyes. "Perhaps the pleasure is mine," she said, glancing past Seth to where Jacob stood.

Jacob yanked his hat off and extended his hand. "Ma'am."

"Oh, please call me Victoria, and I'll call you—"

"Jacob," he muttered. Seth took a false step backward and dug him in the ribs as he hurried to respond. "Uh, we've got the horse we discussed on the phone. If you'd like to come inside the barn, it's a bit warmer. Your driver is welcome too."

She gave an airy wave. "James can wait in the car. He reads. Frankly, I was surprised that you were able to use the telephone; I had heard that you Amish do not."

"Usually we don't, but for business we are allowed, Victoria." Seth had caught her arm against his lean side. "Please let me help you over this uneven ground."

"Thank you." She glanced over her shoulder at Jacob. "I should like to have the opportunity to see the area a bit while I'm here. Perhaps you might give me a private tour? It would also give me a chance to see the horse perform at an extended trot."

Jacob ignored his *bruder's* smiling profile and drew a deep breath. "I'd be glad to, Mrs.—uh, Victoria. My pleasure."

"Marvelous." She gave a triumphant toss of her fur-hatted head as Seth began to tell her about the farm in dulcet tones.

The beginning of Lilly's school days were occasionally a time of peace for her, and today looked promising. She opened the back door of the one-room schoolhouse—which had no lock—and concentrated on starting the woodstove, letting the familiar routine soothe away the tumultuous thoughts in her head. She unpacked her satchel of books and graded papers, laying them on her desk, then wrote the schedule for the day on the blackboard. Foremost in her mind, besides the incredible idea of her wedding, were preparations for the Christmas program.

The program was a joyful annual tradition in many Amish

communities. Almost everyone would come and crowd the schoolhouse to watch *naerfich* pupils perform. Only English was spoken in the program, and many of her younger students still struggled during practice to remember to speak English and not to slip into their Pennsylvania Dutch dialect. And, since even the bishop would attend to see how well the students' English was coming along, this gave both students and teacher reason to fret. This year was no exception in terms of anxiety, despite her forethought and planning to make the program unique. But there was never any telling how the students would perform. So, practice was key, and every school day afternoon from late November to the day of the program itself was spent rehearsing.

Lilly looked up from her desk as the stomping of boots on the back porch alerted her to her first students' arrival. John and Mary Zook, two of the eldest students in the eighth grade, and twin siblings as well, came well-bundled into the room. They wished her *"gut* morning," then went on squabbling in a friendly fashion over the lunch their *mamm* had packed to be shared. The little trio of Mast children arrived, ranging from first grade through the fifth. Then Lucy Stolis, in the seventh grade, came in shivering, bearing an apple for Lilly. She accepted it with pleasure, considering her own lack of breakfast. By the time she rang the handbell on the back porch, all fourteen of her students had arrived and found their seats.

News spread faster than spilled water in the little community, and Lilly could tell by the students' suppressed whispers and stray giggles that they knew of her engagement to Jacob Wyse.

"Is there something I should know?" she asked innocently, surveying the excitement on their faces.

"We think you know already, Miss Lapp," John Zook said, and the others laughed in delight.

To Lilly's surprise, Mary Zook slid a large handmade card of construction paper from beneath her desktop. "We wanted to say congratulations, Miss Lapp." She offered the card shyly.

Lilly took it with genuine pleasure, admiring the hearts and flowers and the signatures of all the students. Here was abundant goodwill that cheered her heart and helped set aside her worries of the future for the moment.

"Thank you, thank you all. I'll cherish it." She let her smile envelop the class, then she made a sudden decision. "And I have a surprise for all of you—I'd like each of you to come to the wedding. I know that students usually stay in school during wedding ceremonies, but as young ladies and gentlemen, I want you to be there."

The delight on their faces affirmed to her what an honor she was giving them; even the older boys looked pleased. She just hoped that Jacob wouldn't mind. She then pushed thoughts of the wedding away and focused on the moment at hand.

"All right, now let's look at our plans for the day."

There was a collective groan when they'd reviewed the schedule she'd written on the blackboard, and Matthew Mast raised his small hand.

"Yes?" Lilly asked with good humor.

"Miss Lapp, if we offer to give up Christmas holidays, can we not have the program?"

Several students nodded eagerly in agreement and Lilly had to suppress a laugh. "No, Matthew. You all know it won't be so bad."

"Badder than the dentist," Matthew suggested.

"*Worse.*" Lilly smiled. "*Worse*, Matthew. And, no, it won't be.

"Now I'd like each of you to take the quilt square you've been working on. You should be just about finished. I plan to baste them together this evening. Then, as you may know, some of your mothers have kindly volunteered to put our class quilt together for us."

Again, there was a chorus of faint groans, this time from the boys of the class, and Lilly had to stifle a smile. Making a class quilt to display at the Christmas program was something that was done in many schools, but the boys were naturally opposed to the idea. In the past, she'd seen more than one boy bring in a square that had obviously been completed by a mother or a *schweschder*, so she'd solved that problem by having them work on the squares only in class. Mothers had donated scraps from their quilting bags, and Lilly had given the option to either glue or hand sew to create a picture on the squares of cotton she'd passed out.

This year's class quilt theme was "Trees." Lilly had encouraged her students to think about all aspects of a tree, from seedling beginnings, to the multitude of colors during the fall and the stark beauty of winter. Now, as she walked among the desks, surveying their work, she was surprised and amazed at the variations of colors and patterns that made up the individual trees. The younger students' work was especially sweet with oddly shaped tree trunks in brown calico and masses of purple and red leaves.

She passed Lucy's desk, especially impressed by the dozens of tiny hand stitches the girl had used.

"That's lovely, Lucy."

The child's face glowed with the praise and she lifted her head to meet Lilly's eyes. "Will you have time for a wedding quilting, Miss Lapp?" she whispered.

Lilly paused, trying to think of what to say. She would dearly love a wedding quilting, but there was one secret part of her that questioned whether or not she actually deserved such a joyful celebration. After all, she'd done everything so impulsively with Jacob, upside down and out of order. Wedding quiltings were things of planning and coordination; legacies of a rich past and dear hopes for the future. It was enough, she decided with an inward sigh, if God would bless their life together. A wedding quilting was not necessary for marital happiness. She laid her hand on Lucy's shoulder.

"I promise to let you know if I do."

The girl flushed with pleasure and then returned to her stitching as Lilly passed on to the next desk. The idea of a wedding quilt led to other half-formed, tangled thoughts of what it might be like to lie in Jacob's embrace against a backdrop of imagined patterns. She wondered how often he'd be thinking of Sarah, then snapped her thoughts back ruthlessly to the moment at hand.

CHAPTER 9

*J*acob had to suppress a groan as the throbbing in his head increased with Victoria's chatter. Despite the even pace of the good-minded driving sorrel named Jim, Victoria sought to grab Jacob's arm with each dip in the road. He felt like shrugging her off like a bug.

But, remembering Seth's hissed admonition to "behave," he nodded and murmured at the appropriate times and hoped that the woman's desire for a lengthy tour would end soon. However, it seemed that she was enchanted with everything Amish, and when the school bell rang clear as crystal across a shallow field, Victoria squealed with delight.

"Oh, is that a real Amish school? I want to see it. I think I'll find it picturesque."

He cleared his throat. "Well, Victoria, the teacher likes her privacy and I'm sure that perhaps another time . . ." Jacob was surprised that he felt a little nervous about seeing his intended.

The woman pouted her red lips and sighed. "I don't know; the more I experience things the more I think that perhaps another horse to go with Jim here might be nice, but if you're sure about the teacher . . . I guess we could just go back."

Jacob could hear Seth now if he didn't give in to the infuriating woman's wishes, so he turned the horse without a word and started down the narrow lane to the school. As he squinted against the winter sunshine, he could see the playing figures in the distance. It had snowed a bit the night before and he realized that Lilly would be out for recess as well, keeping *gut* watch over her charges. The thought did not improve his headache nor his throbbing shoulder any as he considered the recklessness of the day before.

The children swarmed to the roadside when they saw the buggy stop and Victoria again grasped his arm. "Oh, help me down, Jacob. They're so darling in their outfits."

He helped her from the buggy then went to hold the head of the horse so that the children could pet it. He did not wish to pay attention to the carrying giggles and whispers of the *kinner* in Pennsylvania Dutch as they remarked upon his upcoming wedding to the school-teacher and questioned the presence of the *Englisch* woman.

"Oh, Jacob, tell me what they're saying. It's so delightful to hear a true backwoods dialect."

"Perhaps you should speak in *Englisch*, children, as you know you should be doing."

Jacob glanced up to see Lilly's slender form come across the *schnee*-dusted school yard. The children shushed themselves with haste.

"Mr. Wyse? Was there something you needed?" Lilly's tone was pleasant, almost distant, but then he met her eyes and saw the hesitant sparkle in the blue depths.

"*Nee*. I mean, no, Miss Lapp, thank you. I was just showing Mrs. Castleberry—"

"Victoria," the woman gushed, patting bonnets and hats, despite the odd looks from the students.

Jacob exhaled. "Victoria, the area. She's interested in purchasing Jim here."

"Ah," Lilly said and extended a hand to the woman. "It's a pleasure to meet you. Children, can you say good morning to the lady?" There was a dutiful chorus of greetings.

"Would you both like to come inside? We're practicing for our Christmas program."

"Oh, wonderful! I know Jacob will love that too; he's been absolutely the most perfect host," Victoria confided, sliding her arm through his once he'd tied Jim to the hitching post.

He avoided Lilly's gaze and the eyes of the *kinner*.

"Of course. I'm told Mr. Wyse, er, Jacob is always a perfect host," Lilly said.

Jacob felt amusement bubble along his spine. Lilly Lapp was full of surprises, like being in possession of a quick wit. He tipped his hat. "Why, thank you, Miss Lapp. I know, coming from you, that is high praise."

He ignored Victoria's speculative look from him to Lilly as they followed the troop of children onto the back porch of the one-room school.

They all stomped their feet and Victoria giggled, giving her own high-heeled boots a tap or two, then wobbling so that Jacob was forced once more to offer his arm. The class followed Lilly inside to hang up their outer things on nails inside the doorways, while Jacob kept his coat on as did Victoria. Once inside the warm room, the students found their desks with a subdued quiet, due no doubt to the *Englisch* visitor. Although Jacob knew that teachers usually drew students inside the school at the arrival of an overly interested tourist, he imagined Lilly allowed the guest because he accompanied her. He swallowed at the thought and wondered if she was the jealous type of girl, although what engaged woman wouldn't be jealous? He sighed to himself and let the thought drift away.

Lilly pulled two wooden folding chairs from behind her desk and started dragging them to the back of the room.

"Here, I'll do that." Jacob took the chairs from her and set them up, ignoring the draw of pain in his upper arm. He waited until Victoria had arranged her furs before taking a seat himself. The wooden chair creaked under his long form but held firm as he removed his hat and ran a hand through his hair.

Lilly moved about the room, passing out a stack of papers to the students and then coming back to offer the sheets to the visitors. Victoria accepted with a smile but Jacob shook his head.

"I'm fine."

"You won't be able to follow along," Lilly pointed out. She shrugged her shoulders when he frowned.

"Very well. Children, let's begin." She moved gracefully between the desks, returning to the front of the class.

Victoria leaned over to him and talked behind the program in a whisper. "She's quite a lovely girl. I've never seen such blue eyes against such fair skin."

Jacob grunted in response. He let his gaze trail over his betrothed's face in an objective manner. He was surprised to find that she was beautiful in a distant sort of way. He crushed the sudden image of Sarah that flared in his mind and shifted on his chair with an audible sigh.

Lilly looked in his direction. "Now, Mr. Wyse, if you're going to be in my class, you need to be quiet. No sighing over activities." Her tone was teasing, and a few of the girls giggled.

His first impulse was to return her light banter but as he felt some of the students' eyes upon him, he had a flashback to younger days when he'd always gotten in trouble in school for one thing or another.

His *daed* had always been against more than the bare minimum of schooling anyway, believing instead that his sons might learn better from experience than books. He'd kept both boys at home whenever possible to help with the horses or to go on day trips. His feelings had transmitted to Jacob who'd always acted up in school whenever he had the opportunity, and he'd made plenty of opportunities. Still, the law was the law, and Jacob had completed the eighth grade by the skin of his teeth and had gone on to do apprenticeship work under his father until he'd turned fifteen. By the time he was eighteen, he'd become an integral part of the horse breeding farm. And, at twenty-one, he'd set up his own breeding business with Seth as a partner.

Now he found himself annoyed with Lilly as a teacher for inadvertently reminding him of his difficult time in school. He smiled darkly. "Truth be told, Miss Lapp, I'm not very good at being quiet and following the rules."

Lilly looked up from her handout and flashed an engaging grin. "Somehow I sensed that about you."

"Did you now?" His tone was level.

"Yes, but I'm willing to accommodate all kinds of learners, Mr. Wyse. Even the most difficult ones," she said sweetly.

He was aware that Victoria rustled next to him and that he and the teacher had caught the interest of the class, but her use of the word "difficult" rubbed at an old wound, and he stared at her in blatant challenge.

"Oh, I don't think you've seen *difficult* yet, Miss Lapp. In fact, regarding difficult men, you might find that you actually have something to learn."

He watched her flush at his insinuation. The class looked back to her, awaiting her response. She tapped her slender finger against her lips and he saw the confusion in her eyes, but then she rallied.

"A good teacher is always willing to learn, Mr. Wyse."

"Yes, but is she willing to be taught?"

He watched her temper snap, as he instinctively knew it would.

Her blue eyes flashed like a lightning strike against the gray of the mountains, and he felt a moment of curious sensation like static electricity grabbing at his hair. She strode to her desk, her face set.

"I'm just taking a moment, Jacob Wyse, to write a note home to your mother, explaining that you've been excused from class today due to—impudence." She wrote fast, then marched back to him, licking the envelope as she went. She thrust the note at him, and he almost laughed, his humor restored. He took the envelope and tucked it into his coat pocket, then rose to his full height, his long legs brushing her skirts when she didn't back off.

He lowered his voice. "Miss Lapp, a pleasure as always. Although I will have to admit that sassing the teacher has never been so—interesting."

She flushed and he grinned as he replaced his hat and offered his arm to a bewildered Victoria.

Lilly nodded to the other woman. "Mrs. Castleberry, please come again anytime." She turned her back on them and walked to the head of the class. Jacob sauntered to the door, winking at the students and then tipping his hat at the teacher. Maybe a day at school wasn't as bad as he remembered it after all.

It took nearly an hour for Lilly to regain her internal composure. In truth, she had very nearly given in to the tears that welled behind her eyes but held on to the knowledge that her crying would only upset the students. So she listened to initial recitations of the various poems and readings she'd handed out without really hearing them until she found herself correcting John Zook on a certain pronunciation. As his face took on an embarrassed hue, she recalled with sudden vividness a similar expression on a young Jacob Wyse's face. He'd been a year ahead of her in school and she now remembered with surprising detail all of the times the teacher had snapped at him or called him out for his work or attempts to recite. He'd usually come back with some smart-mouthed answer that got him sent to sit alone outside while the teacher acted relieved that he'd gone.

Lilly sat up straight at her desk as she realized that she'd treated him the same way in her classroom, and she felt ashamed. She should have remembered how he must feel in a classroom setting. She smiled gently at John Zook.

"You're doing a great job with your recitations, John, really you are. It's perfectly fine to need help with one word here or there."

She'd said the right thing because the boy flushed with pleasure and took his seat. She only wished that she might have another opportunity to say kinder words to Jacob in the classroom, no matter what his attitude was about school. She decided then and there that she'd apologize to him as soon as she could and went back to listening with a proper ear to her students.

CHAPTER 10

y sunset, Seth still wasn't talking to him, and neither was his mother for that matter. Word had spread throughout the community that he'd brought an *Englisch* woman to school and then had tried to get the best of Miss Lapp, his intended, in some kind of argument. But then he'd been sent home with a note to his *mamm* instead. He still had to suppress a laugh when he thought about it. Truth to tell, it was the first time he'd had any fun in months. And even though his conscience pricked him that it had been at Lilly's expense, he still didn't really want to change a thing. Lilly had gotten him laughing again and that was priceless. Except, of course, there was the fact that Victoria Castleberry hadn't been all that pleased to not be in on the joke and had left without buying so much as a bridle. And, he knew that his mother was embarrassed and thought he'd truly lost his wits.

He knocked on Seth's door after supper.

"If it's you, go away," his brother called.

"Come on, Seth—it's been hours. Let me in. I said I was sorry."

"Not to her you haven't."

Jacob frowned at the wooden door. "*Ach*, all right. Let me in and we'll talk about it.'

"Come in then."

Jacob entered to find Seth painting in the slant of the sun's late-falling rays. His suspenders hung around his waist, and a loose, paint-stained shirt was half-buttoned up his chest. He turned with a palette and brush and raised an eyebrow.

"I'm listening."

"I'll apologize to her, of course."

"What possessed you in the first place? Not to mention losing the sale of Jim and that woman probably telling all of Boston that the Wyse Brothers are fractious Amish men. Why would you want to hurt Lilly?"

Jacob sank down on the foot of Seth's bed and rubbed at the back of his neck. "I just wanted to let off some steam. She did make me mad but I didn't want to hurt her. And I found out she's just— well, she's fun when she's thinking."

Seth turned back to his painting. "Uh-huh."

"Now what does that mean?"

"It means that you don't know the first thing about yourself, big *bruder* . . . or women, for that matter."

"What are you talking about?"

Seth set the painting materials down and wiped his hands on a rag. "Where's the note?"

"What?"

"The note she wrote you to give to *Mamm*. Where is it?"

Jacob reached into his pants pocket. "Here."

Seth took the envelope. "It's not even opened."

"Really?"

"Just carrying it around with you as a souvenir?"

"No, I just . . . never took it out."

Seth sighed, turned up a lamp, and opened the note. He scanned the words on the page then shook his head. "You don't want to know."

"What?" Jacob rose to his feet and stared at his brother.

"'Dear Jacob, Truly, for whatever I've done to make you angry at me, please forgive me. Lilly Lapp.'"

Jacob sucked in a breath, then hung his head. "I didn't think she'd write something like that."

Seth folded the note and slid it into his brother's shirt pocket, then he clapped him on the shoulder.

"Well, now you know."

Jacob lifted his gaze. "You know how I hate classrooms. But I've been a fool to hurt her so. It's my own problem—not hers."

Seth gave him a brief smile. "Well, you'd better get over your problem fast since you're marrying a teacher."

"I'm going over to the Lapps' now to apologize."

"Now?"

"*Jah.* Right now. I don't have to court in secret anymore since the engagement is known, remember?"

Seth turned back to his painting but shot him a wry grin over one shoulder. "*Gut* luck then, *bruder*—on your first courting attempt."

Jacob paused on his way out the door. "Seth—*danki.*"

*L*illy washed the few dishes from supper and sighed at the large remainder of the ham and bean casserole she'd made. Her mother had barely touched the supper, requesting tea and toast instead. Lilly wondered if she should encourage her *mamm* to see someone other than the local midwife for her ailments but knew she'd probably refuse as she'd done in the past. And tonight she'd gone to bed even earlier than usual, leaving Lilly with the whole of a Friday night to face alone.

She had just settled down with some papers to grade at the kitchen table when a quiet knock at the back door startled her. She rose and went to peer out the upper window of the door, seeing Jacob with his hat in his hands.

Her heart began to pound, and she knew that this was her opportunity to apologize to him for her behavior. She opened the door wide and a blast of chilly air bit across her shoulders.

"Jacob, *sei so gut*, come in."

"*Jah*, Lilly, *danki*. Uh, would you mind if Kate Zook comes too?" He stepped aside to reveal the pretty girl, her cheeks flushed from the cold, and her lips berry red.

Lilly nodded in confusion and felt a stab of jealousy. "*Nee*, please . . ." She widened the door.

They entered and she glanced at the back staircase. "My *mamm's* gone to bed early."

"We'll be quiet," he whispered. " Kate was out walking and—"

"I just lost track of the time," the girl confided. She let her dark eyes drift up to Jacob's face with a languid smile that did little to make Lilly want to welcome her. "Jacob saw me alone in the dark. He was kind enough to bring me—well, here first."

First, before what? Lilly wanted to snap, forgetting her desire to apologize to her intended.

"May I take your coats?"

Somehow, she managed to seat them both at the kitchen table, trying to ignore the way Kate sidled next to Jacob on the bench.

"I'm still cold," she shivered.

If he puts his arm around her, I'll rap him. Lilly had to swallow her absurd thought. If anything, Jacob looked stern and not interested in Kate's overtures.

"I could make hot chocolate," Lilly offered with reluctance.

It sounded rather tame to her ears, especially for someone who had been as socially sought after as Jacob Wyse, but he readily agreed while Kate pouted. Lilly concentrated on pulling out a saucepan from beneath the cupboard with the minimum of noise.

"I would have thought that your *mamm* would still be up," Jacob said, obviously trying to make conversation. Lilly's temper melted a bit; he sounded desperate.

"My *mamm* usually goes to bed very early."

"It must be lonely," he observed.

She felt a lurch in her heart as if they were the only two in the room. "Always," she said, then turned to add cocoa powder and milk to the pan.

As she stirred, she thought about his courting comment, concentrating on ignoring Kate's ill-contained murmured hints to leave.

Typically, a courting couple met alone, in secret, at the girl's house once everyone else had gone to sleep, but after the engagement announcement, they could meet anytime with anyone present. She thought how different things would be if her father were still alive, but then, perhaps she'd never have come to be engaged to Jacob. It occurred to her that her heavenly Father was the one who'd have to approve her marriage now.

She brought three blue mugs to the table and ladled in the steaming chocolate drink. She sat opposite them and stared down at her cup, unsure of what someone was supposed to do as part of a courting couple—or trio.

"Why are you uncomfortable around horses?" Jacob asked.

"What?" She looked at him in confusion as Kate yawned.

"You told me that you were uncomfortable around horses—I wondered why."

"I really don't think now is a good time . . ."

"Oh, come on," Kate snapped. "Even I know that story. I'm just surprised that you two—being engaged and all—wouldn't have talked about it."

Jacob gave her a quelling glance. "What story?"

Lilly played with the rim of her cup. "It's silly, really," she said after a moment.

"Yes, it is silly to tell old tales," Kate said.

"I want to hear it anyway." Jacob sipped his hot chocolate, his look encouraging Lilly to speak.

She took a deep breath and avoided Kate's bored expression. "I guess you don't remember it, but when I was seven years old the community prayed for my healing because of a horse."

"May I have more chocolate?" Kate interrupted. "It will help me to concentrate. I'm so easily distracted around a handsome man."

Lilly kept her voice even. "You needn't concentrate, Kate. Besides, you really must learn not to be swayed by every handsome man who picks you up—alone—at night."

"I would've been eight," Jacob interrupted, seemingly oblivious to the byplay of the two women. "What happened?"

Lilly sighed in faint exasperation. "My *mamm* allowed me the rare privilege of accompanying my *daed* on a veterinary call. It was a colicky horse over at the Millers'. The horse was down by the time we got there and thrashing its hooves in pain. I foolishly thought it would help my father if I tied up the horse's legs while he turned to retrieve something from his bag. I got a blow to the head that left me unconscious for more than a week. I guess no one knew if I'd recover, but *Derr Herr* was merciful."

"You could have been killed."

"The Lord moves in mysterious ways," Kate said.

"I was close enough that the horse didn't have as much power as he could have."

"I didn't know." His eyes softened. "Of course you're afraid. It's a wonder you're even willing to drive."

"Ruler can be slow and stubborn under harness, but he's quite docile when Jonah gets him ready. *Daed* sold his draft horse to buy him for me when he knew he had cancer."

Kate sighed loudly and plunked her elbow on the table and propped her head on her hand. She couldn't have looked more bored.

Lilly swiveled in her seat, turning slightly away from Kate, and fixed her eyes on Jacob.

Jacob set his mug down. "I remember *Daed* selling your *daed* that horse. He was one of the most mellow horses we ever had."

"We got him from you? Why didn't you say so?"

Jacob shrugged. "I thought you knew."

"Big deal," Kate said. "I can't see why a horse purchase is of such importance. One horse is as good as another—as long as it can pull a buggy."

Jacob didn't even look her way, keeping his focus on Lilly. "If you like, I can help you feel more comfortable around horses. Will you let me sometime?" Jacob reached across the table to grip Lilly's hand.

Her breath caught at his touch and she found herself nodding, lost in the intense pull of his eyes in the lantern light. "I—don't know if I'd like it, but I'd be willing to try."

He smiled at her and she returned the look, feeling a flood of friendship wash through her at his words. And friendship was a good thing to have in a marriage . . .

Kate broke the moment, drumming her fingers briefly before she abruptly rose from the table. "Jacob, my *mamm* will be worried. If you're not ready to go just yet, I guess I'll just walk. Thank you for the chocolate, Lilly."

Somehow, the girl managed to sound vulnerable, even to Lilly's practical ears, and she withdrew her hand from Jacob's.

"You'd better go," she murmured, not meeting his eyes.

She saw them to the door and out onto the porch when Jacob

turned back from the top step. He bent close and whispered in her ear. "I'm sorry, teacher. About today."

She smiled at him. "I'm sorry too."

He grinned and even the sound of Kate's tinkling laugh on the cold night air could not diminish the surge in Lilly's spirits.

CHAPTER 11

*W*hy the green shirt?" Seth asked as Jacob headed down the hall past their bedrooms.

"It's Meeting."

"*Jah*, but you haven't worn that shirt since—"

"Since I thought that I could win Sarah?" Jacob laughed over his shoulder as they went down the stairs.

"Did I miss some major lightning bolt in the middle of the night—besides your impending engagement?"

"Nope. Just feel like wearing my best shirt."

"And so you should," Mary Wyse interjected from where she stood at the cookstove. "It brings out the color in your eyes."

"Vanity, *Mamm*, vanity," Seth teased, encircling his mother's waist with a hug.

Jacob bent to kiss his mother, then took a plate to the table. "I suppose mothers are allowed a bit of partiality."

Samuel Wyse lowered *The Budget* from in front of his face and eyed Jacob. "Feeling well this morning, son?"

"Right as rain."

"And how is Miss Lilly?"

"She's *gut, Daed.*"

"She's had a lot to deal with since Doc Lapp passed. I imagine you'll lift a lot of weight from her shoulders once you marry."

Jacob nodded. "I'll try."

"We'll miss you here about," his father said from behind the paper, and his *mamm* made a soft sound of agreement.

"I'll be here for work every day and will come anytime you'd like to have us. I want to get Lilly used to the horses."

"*Gut,* maybe I'll teach my beautiful future *schweschder*-in-law to ride," Seth announced, sliding up to the table with his plate of bacon and eggs.

Jacob took a sip of coffee. "Too late, little *bruder;* I've already offered."

"*Ach,* my loss."

"I know quite a pretty girl who might be willing to have lessons from you, if you've got the time."

"Who?" Seth sat up straighter, eyes wide with interest.

"Kate Zook."

Seth sighed. "I find myself too busy for lessons after all."

"Boys!" Mary Wyse admonished from the stove.

Jacob shot a look at his brother and they smiled together in silence.

Lilly sighed under her breath as her mother continued her tearful explanation as to why she could not attend Meeting—yet again. Sometimes Lilly felt she could withstand her mother's sharp tongue more than her crying, but in all honesty, all *Mamm's* recent behaviors were becoming more difficult. Lilly had been praying lately to respond with more love to her *mamm's* needs, and so she tried again.

"Please, *Mamm*. There's plenty of time left to get ready. You could wear one of your new blouses. And besides, I miss your company. And, well, today the deacon will officially announce the engagement."

"Yes, but it's not your place to be there when it's announced. Every other girl stays home the day of the announcement."

"I know, *Mamm*, but Jacob already spoke of it before everyone. *Sei so gut*, won't you consider coming?"

"I don't feel well, Lilly, yet you're always trying to pressure me. Sometimes it feels like you don't really care about me at all."

Lilly blinked back her own tears at the accusation and sat down on a small chair near the bed. "*Mamm*, I love you. I always have. I don't mean to sound as though I don't care. I can remember when I was a little girl and we made applesauce together, and you'd sing the hymns from Meeting. You taught me so well."

Her mother sniffed. "I remember those times too, Lilly. You had such beautiful hair . . ." She reached over and touched Lilly's *kapp* with gentle fingers. "You still do. I loved to braid it before Meeting."

Lilly smiled. "And I always wanted to pull away from you and the comb!"

"You did. I'd chase you all over with your hair flying out behind you like a beautiful banner."

"And you never grew angry, *Mamm*—no matter how late we were. I loved that moment when you'd catch me up in your arms and laugh."

Her mother slipped her hand down to cover Lilly's. "Do you remember Sunday afternoons? We'd go down to the watermelon patch in the summer to play and thump the melons with our fingers, trying to find the ripest one?"

"*Ach, jah, Mamm*. And then we'd haul the melon back to the house in my little red wheelbarrow and ice it down for supper. There was nothing like that frosty sweet redness!"

"You loved to spit the seeds out—always having distance contests with your father." Her mother sighed suddenly and slid her hand away. "It seems like, since he died, I just forget things—even the words to our beloved hymns."

Lilly touched her arm. "*Ach, Mamm.* Let me help you remember."

Miriam Lapp shook her head. "I can't, Lilly. I just can't. It's just too hard to face all those people. You go on now. Forget about me." She turned her face resolutely to the wall.

Lilly rose from the chair, knowing when she'd lost the moment. "I'm sorry, *Mamm.* I won't trouble you again to go. I know you don't feel well."

She went down the stairs, mentally exhausted, and the day had yet to truly begin. At least, she told herself as she put on her cape, she could gain the comfort of Meeting, and that was something to be grateful about.

*H*ere she comes," Seth murmured, giving Jacob a poke in his lean ribs.

Jacob sighed as Kate Zook made her purposeful way to where the brothers were standing, waiting for Meeting to assemble.

"She may well be seeking you since I'm engaged."

"I don't think anything's going to derail that girl's train." Seth grinned. "It's an express headed straight toward you."

"But why?" Jacob pleaded.

"It's your shirt."

"Seth . . . Jacob." Kate smiled, baiting them with her attractive eyes. "It's so good to see you . . . again."

"Kate." Seth smiled. "Always a pleasure."

She nodded in an absent fashion but stared at Jacob until he wished he had kept his coat on.

Seth clapped him on the shoulder. "Gotta get to my seat."

When Jacob would have followed, Seth waved him still. "*Nee*, stay and visit with Kate a bit. I'll save you a place. No problem."

Jacob ground his teeth but smiled down at the coy face of the girl in front of him. "So, how are you feeling after your chill last night?"

"Oh, I'm fine, thanks to you—and Lilly Lapp, of course. And the buggy ride home. It was so warm . . ." She shifted her weight onto her other foot and briefly laid her hand on his arm. "I've been thinking, after seeing you and Miss Lapp together that . . . well, maybe this whole engagement thing is just a ruse. Will you tell me the truth?" She swept her lashes downward. "I can keep a secret."

Jacob controlled the angry words that came to his lips. He told himself that she was young and naive, impetuous, and not unlike how he himself had been at her age.

"No ruse, Miss Zook. Just a marriage, plain and simple. Now, if you'll excuse me."

She laughed deliberately, a high-pitched sound that caught the attention of several women nearby. Jacob straightened and frowned.

"*Ach*, Jacob Wyse, you are as entertaining as can be."

"Right, *danki*."

"I'm not like Lilly." She lowered her voice to a husky drawl. "I love horses and am not afraid of them at all. And it's finally perfect weather for a sleigh ride." She batted thick eyelashes while he plotted ambushing Seth in his sleep for leaving him in this situation. His gaze swept the barn for an excuse, any excuse. When he caught sight of Lilly's calm profile as she sat on the end of one of the hard Meeting benches next to Alice Plank, he tipped his hat to Kate.

"Miss Zook, a good day. Excuse me, I see Lilly . . ." He crossed over two empty benches with his long legs and escaped to the other side of the barn, leaving Kate's angry and speculative frown behind.

"Lilly, Alice." He pulled off his hat. "How are you both today?"

"Very well," Alice said.

Lilly looked up at him. "I'm fine. How is Kate Zook?"

Alice coughed.

Jacob looked at Lilly cautiously but was pleased to see the calmness in her blue eyes. "A bother to me," he confided.

Lilly raised an eyebrow, asking a question he couldn't discern.

"Maybe today's official announcement will scare her off," Alice offered.

"If it doesn't, maybe I'll tell her Seth likes her."

Lilly's unasked question changed to a smile, while Alice covered her mouth to hide hers.

Meeting was about to begin so he backed away, when Lilly handed him a green envelope. "I know it's not usually customary, but I just thought—well, read it and please let me know."

He took the note and nodded. "Surely."

He made his way to where Seth sat, taking his time to sit down, making sure to elbow his brother twice as he got situated.

"Ow," Seth hissed, rubbing his side. "All right. I'm sorry about Kate."

"No you're not."

"You're right. I'm not," Seth said, adding his mischievous grin.

Jacob shook his head and slid him the envelope under the cover of his coat.

"Now what did you do?"

Jacob shrugged. "Maybe nothing."

"Sure . . ."

"Just read it. I have to let Lilly know something."

The first hymn began and a sharp blast of wind whistled through the Stolises' barn. The green envelope danced from Seth's hold to twirl in the air and then land. Seth rose to make a grab for the paper, then stumbled backward onto the bench, but not before he'd caught the disapproving eye of many in the community.

"What are you doing?" Jacob growled, under the cover of singing.

"Don't worry. I'm sure she never even noticed."

Lilly saw her green envelope blown from Seth's hand and wanted to cover her face with her cape in embarrassment. How could he? How could Jacob show his brother the invitation? It was meant to be something private. It wasn't really personal, but private nonetheless. It seemed the two were having a joke at her expense. She tried to brush aside the thought that Jacob may even have told Seth the details of their engagement and the truth behind it. She told herself it didn't matter. But embarrassment soon gave way to simmering anger as the Meeting continued.

She would not speak to him—that was it—engagement or no engagement. To think that she'd begun to trust him. He apparently thought nothing of the feelings of friendship and camaraderie he'd created in her with his kind words of interest about her insecurity around horses. Perhaps he had learned to be kind and polite around other girls as a matter of necessity while he'd been waiting for Sarah. She put aside the internal voice that suggested Sarah was no longer someone he could wait for, urging her to see what truly happened, to give him a chance to explain.

She nearly jumped when Alice reached over and squeezed her hand. Lilly looked at her friend, who leaned close.

"Are you all right?"

Lilly nodded, managing a weak smile. She turned her face

to the front. But her attention was still highly focused on Jacob's insensitivity.

*W*hen Meeting ended hours later, she wanted to bolt from the bench like a pig out of the chute, but one of the deacons stood up with a piece of paper in his hand and a smile on his face. She'd nearly forgotten the engagement announcement, and now she'd have to endure pleasantries while she fumed inside. She should have listened to her *mamm* and stayed home.

The deacon always enjoyed his role and smiled and teased the crowd a bit before he would read the names of the couples to be married within the next month. Finally, he cleared his throat, and the crowd rustled expectantly. This time was usually a surprise for all but the couples and their immediate families.

"Mary Stolfus and Christian Esh, Naomi Glick and Benjamin Lantz all wish to announce their intention to—ah, just a moment, I seem to have forgotten one couple. So sorry."

Lilly wanted to crawl under the bench at the joke as Alice squeezed her arm.

"Lilly Lapp and Jacob Wyse also wish to announce their intent to be joined as man and wife before this community."

Everyone laughed and Lilly avoided looking in Jacob's direction. As people rose and turned to speak to her, she murmured politely. She excused herself from Alice with a promise to see her later in the week, then worked her way toward the barn doors. When she was finally free, she hurried up the lane to where the buggies stood in a line. She'd untied Ruler, climbed onto the buggy, and grasped the reins, when a large hand closed over her gloved fingers.

Chapter 12

"ove over. I'm driving you home."

She stared as Jacob jumped in beside her, and she opened her mouth to protest.

"Not one word until we're clear of here, then you can let go all you need. You don't want to make a scene."

She swallowed hard, realizing he was right.

People turned to stare with interest at the engaged couple who drove away without even bothering to stop for lunch in the main house.

She sniffed and tried to ignore the clean male scent of him that drifted to her as he turned the buggy onto the highway.

"All right. Go ahead," he said when they'd driven a short distance.

She held her tongue with perverse reason, not wanting to give him the satisfaction now of even so much as a word.

Out of the corner of her eye, she saw him shake his head.

"Women!"

"That's it, Jacob Wyse. You just—you just jump out right now and let me alone. Why I ever thought to give you that invitation is beyond me, but I was wrong. Absolutely wrong!"

He eased his hat back, exposing his dark hair, and exhaled. "It was—an invitation?"

"Of course it was an invitation! Didn't you have the decency to read it before passing it along to joke about with your brother?" She felt her eyes well with tears and clutched her hands together in her lap.

"I wasn't joking with Seth."

"Then what were you doing?"

She looked at him and noted the strange expression on his face, the sudden flush on his sculpted cheeks.

He paused a long time, his jaw working as though he was deciding what to say and how to say it. He finally took a deep breath and spoke. "I gave it to Seth to read for me."

"You what?"

He glanced at her, his eyes dark with a pain she couldn't understand.

"I can't read very well." He drew another deep breath and turned to face forward, his stony expression silencing her.

"I've never told anyone but my brother."

She struggled to find her voice as his admission washed over her. She knew by instinct that if she reacted with pity or concern he'd pull away, and she realized with sudden clarity that she didn't want that, not one bit.

"Well, then it seems we both have something we can teach each other in this relationship." Her tone was level, practical. "I let you teach me to ride, and you let me teach you to read."

He shook his head. "Riding's easy, but there's something in me with the reading. I can't do it."

"You can try."

"Do you think I haven't?" he spat out.

"I'm sure you have, but . . ." Feminine instinct came to her in a tingling rush of inspiration and she lowered her voice. "Maybe you've never had the right—tutor."

He responded to her soft suggestion; she knew it by the way his throat worked and how he glanced at her with a flash of speculative interest.

"Tutor?"

"Mmm-hmm. We can do it in complete privacy, after school, for a little while. Then maybe—in the evenings when we're married. And no elementary primers for you. I'll make up lessons that will hold your attention."

Her heart pounded as she listened to herself. Honestly, she sounded like she was inviting him to a series of very interesting dates, but her teaching instincts were too well engaged to give up now. She'd teach him to read all right, and he'd remember it as a pleasant experience or she wasn't the teacher she knew herself to be.

He smiled at her then. "I'd be willing to try, I guess."

She resisted the urge to clap her hands like a little girl and gave a simple nod instead. "*Gut*, after the Christmas program." She bit her lower lip.

"What's wrong?"

"Nothing. It's just—that invitation I gave you. It was to the Christmas program. I know everybody always comes but I just wanted to—invite you especially. I mean, it's part of wanting to share my work with you."

"I'll be there, front and center."

"*Danki.*"

They turned into her lane. "*Ach*, Jacob, how will you get back?"

"The walk will do me good. I'll put Ruler up and you go on in to your *mamm*."

She hesitated, wanting to ask him in for lunch but not knowing what frame of mind her mother might be in. Still, he should probably get used to it.

"Lilly, go on. I understand about your *mamm*."

She nodded and slipped from the buggy to make her way inside the house, closing the door behind her without looking back.

Jacob thumped his chest as he walked fast against the biting wind. He felt exhilarated inside, like the feeling he got when a new foal found its legs. He'd told the schoolteacher that he couldn't read and she hadn't batted so much as one professional eye. In fact, she'd made tutoring with her sound like a sensuous experience. Although, he could very well be putting more into her words than she'd meant. For all he could tell, Lilly did things with a calm logic, operating without the instincts he knew he had to rely on. Unless she got riled. He smiled as he thought of how blue her eyes were when she yelled. Blue like sea crystals.

"Jacob? Do you need a ride?"

He turned, so lost in his thoughts that he hadn't even heard the buggy coming up behind him, and he now faced Sarah and Grant Williams. Sarah looked concerned and Grant's smile was welcoming, but it was like someone had thrown a bucket of water over Jacob in the thick of the cold. He shook his head.

"*Nee, danki.* I'm fine. Just enjoying a bit of a walk."

"You're going to freeze," Sarah said, her hazel eyes, so like his own, flashing green.

He resisted the familiar urge to study the beauty of her face. He started to hug his arms across his chest, but the pain in his arm stopped him. He felt he must look silly with one arm giving a feeble attempt at warmth, and stomping his feet.

"*Jah.*" He forced a smile. "I will if I keep standing here. Go on with the two of you now. I'm *gut.*"

"All right." Grant lifted the reins. "Be seeing you—in about two days. Remember?"

"Sure." Jacob recollected that the drain in his wound had to come out.

"Goodbye, Jacob." Sarah turned a frowning face back to him and waved while he let the buggy get a good pace ahead.

He lifted his hand to wave back, then began walking again, but now he couldn't recall what he'd been so happy about in the first place.

CHAPTER 13

*T*he few weeks until the Christmas program passed in a flurry of activity inside the little school. Lilly had each student painstakingly make out an invitation to friends and family as she tried to ignore the excitement of Jacob's response to her own private invitation. She wasn't quite sure why his words were like a secret of delight that she treasured. They'd seen each other several times before the program, of course, deciding on a simple wedding with few guests. As was customary, Jacob delivered the invitations in person, while Lilly concentrated on her mother and all of the preparations for the day. But she couldn't fully focus on the wedding until the school program was past, so instead, she concentrated on last-minute rehearsals and the children's favorite—decorating the classroom.

The class quilt had been completed by several of the mothers and was strung in a delightful display across two windows on a piece of clothesline. The winter sunlight penetrated the thin quilt and made the vibrant colors and images stand out in vivid hues. Lilly had hand-stitched each student's first name on his or her particular square and knew that the parents, or at least the mothers of the community, would be pleased by the fine work of the students.

"How's this, Miss Lapp?" Reuben Mast held up a paper chain of red and green construction paper, while his paste-dabbed nose and cuffs gave evidence of his hard work.

Lilly smiled. "It's beautiful. Your *mamm* will love it."

"*Jah*. But—"

"Yes," Lilly interjected. "Use *yes*."

Reuben sighed. "Yes, but my *daed's*—my dad's—not likely to 'ppreciate all this decorating. 'Women's work' he would call it. That's what he said about the quilt square when I told him."

Some of the students laughed.

"I see, well, I'd like you all to know that decorating and making a community quilt are not just 'women's work.' It's art. And many of our greatest artists, even Amish artists, are men."

"No way," Reuben burst out.

"*Jah*. I mean, yes. They are."

"Like who?"

The whole class was listening now, and Reuben puffed out his fifth-grade chest with pride at having caught the ears of everyone in the room. Lilly enjoyed the moments when the younger students could be heard, so she chose to extend the discussion.

"Well, you've all seen the fine leatherwork that Amish men do during the winter to sell at spring festivals—the saddles, satchels, belts, and such. All of that could be called 'sewing' by some, but it's really art."

"That ain't art." John Zook interjected his voice, strident with adolescence.

"*Isn't*, John, and yes it is art. Don't you find that leatherwork is interesting to look at? The design details are inspiring and make you think that what you see is more than just a piece of cowhide."

The youth considered. "Ye-es, I guess so. But why care about art that men make anyway? Isn't *Derr Herr* the best artist at nature and stuff, like the bishop says at Meeting sometimes?"

Lilly felt the thrill she always did when a student pushed back, stretching and thinking on his or her own. "You're right, John, of course. But He has blessed us as well that we can create beauty with purpose, like the intricate belt that still holds up a man's pants."

Lucy Stolis raised her hand. "Well, what about women's art, Miss Lapp?"

"What about it? Don't women do quilting and gardening and sewing which results in beauty with a function?"

Lucy frowned. "I guess, but it seems more like the women's art is work."

John grinned at her. "Like it should be."

"John," Lilly admonished. "No, Lucy, a woman's work is different from a man's, but you know that both must work very hard to make a happy home, right?"

"Yes, ma'am."

"Good! Then let's get this room decorated artistically for the purpose of giving our guests tomorrow a *wunderbaar* program."

*J*acob had the vague idea that it might be nice if the kitchen floor would open up its fine grooved planks and swallow him whole. He'd come in from the stables for lunch, only to discover Mrs. Zook and Kate sitting down to a cup of tea with his *mamm*. He'd tried to back out, but his mother seemed oblivious to his silent plea. He had a sudden notion who Seth took after.

"Ladies." He hung up his coat and hat on pegs behind the door and made his way to the coffeepot.

"Jacob," his *mamm* urged. "Come and join us. We were just talking about the Christmas program—and the wedding, of course."

Great, he thought. Of course, he'd had to invite the Zooks

to the wedding since Lilly had wanted the whole of her class to attend—and the younger Zook children were some of her favorite students. Nothing like their big *schweschder*, he considered. He was not comfortable with the predator-like intensity of Kate's gaze when he slid onto the bench, but that was youth at nineteen. He remembered it. You had the irrational belief that you could have anyone, anything, if you just wanted it bad enough.

"So, you'll be attending the program, Jacob?" Mrs. Zook's tone was as casual as a mother rattler's.

He blew on his coffee before answering. "Yes, ma'am. That's my plan."

"*Wunderbaar*. I wanted to thank you too, Jacob, for bringing Kate home the other night. She most likely would have frozen without your care." As though it were an afterthought, she added, "You'll have to take her riding again sometime soon."

Jacob chafed under how the words sounded and resisted the urge to reiterate his announced and impending wedding. He shot a sidelong glance at his mother who looked back with a blank expression. *Definitely Seth's* mamm, he thought. But he had sidestepped determined girls for years while he'd been waiting for Sarah. He pinned both Kate and Mrs. Zook with an imperturbable gaze.

"Well, while I, as a soon-to-be married man, cannot have the pleasure of Kate's company, there is someone who might. You see—I haven't wanted to nose it about the community . . ." He spoke in a conspiratorial whisper so that the Zook women leaned in like frogs to a fly. "But I've made a promise to my brother. You see, he's incredibly lonely, a tortured soul you might say, and I've promised to try and help him find a love of his own, so maybe he could take Kate for a drive sometime."

"Seth Wyse?" Mrs. Zook snorted. "The boy's at every gathering there is. Why I've seen him with as many girls on his arm as I've seen—"

Jacob shook his head in sober consideration. "All a front, Mrs. Zook. A sad, sad front."

"Is this true, Mary Wyse?" Mrs. Zook's considerable bosom heaved beneath her blouse.

Mamm stared into her teacup. "I cannot say what goes on between these two boys; they're best friends."

"Never mind Seth. *You're* not even married yet," Kate wailed.

Mrs. Zook looked with horror at her daughter, and Jacob choked on a laugh. It was one thing to allude to your desires and quite another to expose them to the full light of day.

He caught Kate's eye. "I'm sorry, Miss Zook, but I must honor my bride-to-be—and my brother."

Kate gave him a sour look. "Bride-to-be, huh! Everyone's suspicious of why you're really marrying her, why I know—"

"Kate!" Again, Mrs. Zook could not contain herself and Jacob ignored the curious feeling of anger at the younger girl's barb against Lilly.

"We'd best be leaving," Mrs. Zook said, sidling from the table and giving Kate a firm shake on the shoulder. The girl rose with reluctance but hadn't lost her determined eye, which made Jacob wary. Still, he saw them to the door with his mother, then waited for his *mamm's* response to the whole conversation. To his surprise, she just hummed and went about clearing up the dishes.

"Not going to lecture me about setting up Seth?" he asked, depositing cups in the sink.

"*Nee*, did you? I thought you might have been telling the truth; Seth is such a—how did you put it—tortured soul?"

"*Mamm*," he groaned. "I'm engaged and that girl is desperate! And besides, I promised—" He broke off, and now his mother looked very interested.

"Promised what?"

"Nothing."

"Promised who?"

"*Mamm*," he exclaimed, exasperated.

She lowered her gaze to the table as she wiped. "*Ach*, I'm sorry, Jacob. I don't mean to intrude."

"*Jah*, you do, but I love you for it." He put his arm around her shoulders. "I especially promised Lilly I'd be there."

"But you usually go—though I doubt you've paid much attention standing outside with the young men."

"Well, this year will be different."

"*Ach*, I see."

He eyed her with suspicion. "There's nothing to see, *Mamm*. She'll be my wife in three days' time."

His mother smiled up at him. "Indeed she will, Jacob. Indeed, she will."

Chapter 14

*O*n the morning of the program, Lilly hurried through her routine and prayed her mother would be cooperative. Lilly had reminded her of the program the night before but had gotten no response, so she knocked with faint trepidation on her *mamm's* door, surprised that she hadn't been summoned already. When her mother didn't respond, Lilly opened the door.

"*Mamm?*"

She peered into the shadows and saw that the bed was made, an unusual thing since it was her responsibility to make up her mother's bed after school each day. Her heart started to pound and she tried not to panic. Of course her mother could be anywhere about, but Lilly recalled the one other time that she'd been gone before dawn—she had driven into Lockport and had indulged in her desire to buy things, spending their meager savings before Lilly had been able to find her.

"*Ach*, not today, dear Lord," she breathed aloud as she began to methodically search the house.

"*Mamm? Mamm?*" Her pleading calls received no response and

she flung her book satchel on the kitchen table before heading out to the barn. She saw, before she ever got there, that the wide doors gaped open and Ruler and the buggy were gone. She glanced at her brooch watch. School was to begin in half an hour. She caught at the railing next to the porch steps and tried to regulate her breathing. She might have gone to the Planks', but she knew that Alice and her family had been gone for a few days visiting an ailing aunt in another county and weren't due to return until the afternoon.

"Think, Lilly Lapp. Think." Her words were caught by the cold wind as one face came to mind. *Jacob*. Somehow she knew by instinct that he'd help her and would be discreet in doing so, and not just because he was her betrothed, but because he was that kind of person.

The thought warmed her as she raced back inside, caught up her books, pulled on an extra wrap, and began the mile-and-a-half run to the Wyses' farm. She slipped twice, falling hard against the icy ground, but got back up, propelled by worry for her mother and what the children would do if she weren't there to greet them.

She arrived panting at the Wyse door and pounded with an ice-cold hand. Samuel Wyse opened the door.

"Lilly, what is it?" He took her satchel of books.

She shook her head, trying to get her breath. "Jacob, *sei so gut*."

Both Jacob and Seth had risen from the kitchen table when she entered and now bumped into each other in an effort to come to her. She saw Jacob glare at his brother and Seth step back. Then Jacob came forward to catch her shaking arms in his hands.

"What's wrong?"

Her bottom lip quivered at the concern in his tone but she kept stalwart focus. "My *mamm* . . . Ruler's gone. I think she went to town, but I can't be sure. I'm going to be late for school and the children will be cold." She broke off, stifling a half sob. He ran his large hands up and down the cold wraps on her arms.

"It's all right, Lilly. We'll help you. I'll find your *mamm*."

He pulled her against his broad chest and she listened for a few intense seconds to the steady beating of his heart. Remembering that his family stood about, she moved away. He let her go. She looked at the faces of the Wyse men and Mary Wyse, who'd come in from the kitchen, but saw nothing but concern in their eyes. She thanked God for bringing Jacob to mind.

"*Mamm*, will you make some hot tea for Lilly?"

Lilly shook her head. "Oh, I can't, Jacob—the children."

He waved at her to be silent.

"Seth, go over to the school and get the woodstove going. Tell the kids to come in when they get there and have them run through their practice for the program. Then come back and get Lilly, please, once she's had a chance to warm up. I'll take Thunder and ride into town to find Mrs. Lapp."

"I'll search the other areas nearby, son." Samuel pulled on his overcoat and left as everyone was galvanized into action with Jacob's words.

"Don't worry, Lilly." Mary Wyse stood by her side.

"*Danki*, all of you," Lilly whispered.

"Come, child. Take your wraps off for a minute to warm up."

Lilly obeyed, then startled at Mary's sudden cry.

"Lilly! Your arms are bleeding through your blouse."

Jacob got up from where he was putting on his boots. He caught Lilly's right forearm and turned it over with gentle firmness. Her blood made bright red stains through the snow-white of her sleeves around her wrists and forearms.

"Did you fall?"

She nodded. "Twice."

He frowned, looking angry, though she wasn't sure why.

"It's nothing," she assured him, but he was rolling back her cuffs to expose the abrasions made from landing on the ice. He grunted, then pulled her by the hand over to the pitcher of water on the table.

"*Mamm!*" he bellowed.

"Jacob, honestly, I'm right here. I'll take care of her arms. You're just going to upset her more."

Lilly knew he was staring at her but couldn't return his gaze for more than a second. She felt stupid and clumsy and very cold. But she melted inside when he lifted her chin with warm fingers. "I'll find your *mamm*, Lilly. Don't worry."

She swallowed and nodded. "I know you will. *Danki*, Jacob."

He stalked out the door with Seth at his heels, and the kitchen was quiet.

Mary Wyse urged her to sit down as she brought strips of linen to clean and bandage her arms.

"*Danki*, Mrs. Wyse. I appreciate your care."

"Call me *Mamm*, and *nee*, thank *you*."

She looked up in surprise to meet the woman's warm smile. "For what?"

"For waking up my son."

Lilly wrinkled her brow in confusion as a vivid image of her shaking Jacob's shoulder while he slept crossed her mind. "I . . . don't understand."

"Jacob's been asleep for years, lulled by a dream. I think that you might be the one to show him that a heart awake to real life might be better than any dream."

Lilly flushed, and though she couldn't fully understand all of what Jacob's *mamm* suggested, she knew it was praise.

"I'll do anything I can to help him."

Mary patted her bandaged arm with tenderness. "I know you will, Lilly."

CHAPTER 15

*T*hunder took the miles toward Lockport without even becoming winded, and despite the urgency of his ride, Jacob, too, enjoyed the freedom of the powerful horse moving beneath him. It was only on a horse or around horses that he felt confident and competent. Horses didn't judge, or question intellectual abilities, or care about appearances. They were creatures of *Derr Herr's* hands, His craftsmanship and glory. Unbidden, the image of Lilly came to him. And, as he half-closed his eyes against the glare of the sun on the snow, he saw her in a rain of images, slender and poised when a teacher at the head of the class, determined and strong when she was angry, forlorn and broken when she worried for her *mamm*, and standing still in the fold of his arms.

He blinked as he realized his train of thought. He hadn't been lulled by the image of any girl but Sarah for as long as he could remember. It almost seemed a betrayal somehow to Sarah, to his way of thinking, of existing, over the last months since Sarah's engagement. But a small glimmer of an idea began to form in his heart, an awakening to the thought that the Lord might be doing something new in his life, in his world. It felt both freeing and scary at the same time.

He broke off his wandering thoughts as he entered Lockport. The small town was just beginning to come to life for a new day of business. He reined Thunder in to a slow walk on the muddy slush of the downtown main street. Several cars and buggies tooled along beside him as he began to scan the area for Mrs. Lapp or Ruler and the buggy. He didn't have to go far. A police car had parked sideways next to the Lapps' buggy. The shrill sounds of Miriam Lapp came to him from the sidewalk. He looped Thunder's reins over a nearby post with a low admonishment to the horse to stand, and he approached the policeman. He almost groaned aloud when he recognized the young officer as the one who'd broken into the quiet of Sarah's wedding. He hoped the young man would not remember him.

"Good morning, Officer. Is there a problem here?"

The police officer turned, truly young under close inspection, freckle-faced, and clearly frustrated. "Do you know this woman?"

Jacob nodded.

"*Ach*, you hush, Jacob Wyse! I am waiting here until this store opens and that's it!" Mrs. Lapp announced. She glared at both men with determination.

"I offered to let her get inside the cruiser to warm up, but she wouldn't."

"I'm just waiting to shop—that's all."

Jacob looked aside. "What has she done exactly?"

"Nothing. I mean, I just need her to move her buggy from the parking space over to the hitching post. The parking meters are for cars only."

"I'll move the horse."

"Great. Thank you." The police officer turned toward his car, looking relieved, then swung back to Jacob.

"Hey, do I know you?"

"I don't believe so—I'm Jacob Wyse." He extended his hand. The officer slowly returned the handshake. "I guess all you Amish look alike . . . kind of . . ."

"That was a rude statement, young man," Mrs. Lapp said.

The officer flushed. "Yeah, right. Sorry. I don't want any trouble with you Amish. I've got to move along." He went to his car without looking back and pulled away.

Jacob looked down at Miriam Lapp. "I'll move Ruler and then wait with you until the store opens."

"Well I doubt you'll enjoy that. So don't trouble yourself."

"It's no trouble."

"*Nee*, probably because Lilly put you up to this. Did she send you after me because she was concerned about my spending?"

Jacob tried to thrust aside the image of Lilly's shaken face and the fresh blood on her arms. "Lilly worries for you."

"Lilly worries for herself sometimes too—all this work on the Christmas program; she wants to put up a good image like her father."

Jacob shook his head, realizing that Mrs. Lapp's problems ran deeper than what he could understand. Right now he just needed to get her home in one piece and ease Lilly's mind. He turned and went to move Ruler, speaking to the horse as he maneuvered him around a car and then to the hitching post next to Thunder. He prayed as he walked back to the woman on the sidewalk, wondering how to pass the time with her until the store opened.

Dear Lord, this is Dr. Lapp's wife, a widow, and my future mother-in-law. You've promised to be a husband to the widow and a father to the fatherless. Oh, Lord, help Lilly's mamm; *help Lilly. Give me wisdom beyond myself to know what to say and do here and now to get her home safe.* His prayer brought him to a few footsteps from Mrs. Lapp. He decided not to mention Lilly or going back to the farm.

He gazed in an absent fashion at the dressing of the store window, not noticing it before. Now his mouth twisted into a wry smile. Of course, Mrs. Lapp would choose "Emily's Mystery"—the one store in town that boasted women's undergarments of all kinds.

He looked down at the ground, pretending not to notice. But Mrs. Lapp must have sensed his discomfort and pounced on him like a cat. "So, you're going to wait with me to shop, are you, Jacob Wyse?"

He lifted his gaze and regarded her with a calmness he didn't feel. "*Jah*, I am."

"Outside or in?"

He sighed. "Inside. It's a bit too cold out here." And there was no way he was going to let the woman sneak out a back door for further shopping and out of his hands.

"Well, I don't know what kind of son-in-law it is who's willing to come shopping at Emily's. I wonder whether to be pleased or worried." She narrowed her eyes at him.

A young *Englisch* woman wearing long black boots, a flowing colored skirt, and a short denim jacket walked up to them before he had to reply.

"Excuse me, folks." Her voice was casual but Jacob noted the appraising look she threw his way and he had a sudden desire to go back and sit with Ruler. The woman jiggled some keys she lifted from a leather purse, then opened the door. "Come on in. I'll turn on a few lights."

Mrs. Lapp waited while he caught the door and held it open.

"If the deacons hear of this, you're sure to get a long talking to," Miriam warned as she passed under his arm.

"Well, so will you," he muttered.

"What was that?"

"Nothing."

Jacob took a deep breath and plunged into the velvety carpeted store, trying to ignore the strange, exotic smell of the place and the multitude of half-clad mannequins that stared at him with empty eyes. He remembered daring Seth once to take a peek into Emily's when they'd been boys, and *Daed* had tanned both their hides when they'd been caught. Now he felt like an utter fool but there was no help for it.

While Mrs. Lapp went muttering among waist-high clear bins of colorful scraps of undergarments, the saleswoman approached Jacob and he removed his hat.

"It's so nice—you bringing your mother here," she whispered.

"I'm not his mother!" Mrs. Lapp announced.

Jacob gave a pleading glance heavenward as the saleswoman giggled. "So, do you make this a habit, bringing the ladies to Emily's?"

"*Nee*. Uh, no." He shifted his long legs.

"So, is there anything that you're interested in personally? Something for your wife maybe?"

He shook his head and met her gaze. "I'm not married. I mean—I will be, the day after tomorrow."

"He lost his first love, so he's settling for a different girl," Miriam offered.

Jacob cringed and the saleswoman waved off Mrs. Lapp's words.

"Oh, well, maybe I could show you some of my favorite items—for your lucky bride, of course." The *Englisch* woman let the suggestion end in a purr and Jacob thought about how much Seth would be enjoying himself right now—at his brother's expense.

"No, no thank you, ma'am. I'm fine."

She was about to speak again when a quiet bell announced the arrival of another customer. Mrs. Zook waddled into the store with a comfortable air, and Jacob had to make a conscious effort to keep his mouth closed.

⌒ 100 ⌒

Mrs. Zook looked like she might faint on the spot when she glanced from a mannequin toward him. And, for a brief second, he might have feared for her heart, had he not been so intent on struggling not to laugh. Miriam Lapp noticed her too and called out in a tone that echoed in the intimacy of the shop. "Esther Zook. This is the sales bin. Come back here and ignore Jacob Wyse. He's lost his mind."

Jacob gave a sedate nod to the quivering Mrs. Zook. "Ma'am. *Guder mariye*. I hope you're having a good day."

"My day has just begun, young man. Does your *mamm* know you're here?"

"Uh, probably not, but my soon-to-be mother-in-law does."

Mrs. Lapp gave a surprising laugh.

Mrs. Zook turned with a swirl of her cape and marched past the saleswoman toward the door. "I'll return late—I mean, good day to you. I clearly am confused this morning and entered the wrong establishment." She tossed a searing glare in Jacob's direction, then hurried out the door.

The saleswoman laughed. "She'll be back; she comes here all the time."

"All the time," Jacob repeated in disbelief.

"There's more to women than you know, Jacob Wyse, much, much more," Mrs. Lapp snapped.

The saleswoman nodded, and Jacob told himself that he had to agree.

Chapter 16

After the class had snacks, Lilly turned the children loose for an early recess at ten thirty. She followed them, wrapping herself against the cold. She'd had to borrow another of Mrs. Wyse's blouses. The cuffs were again too short, revealing the bandages on her arms, but there was nothing that she could do about it now.

She admonished the students not to get too wet while she anxiously looked up the icy road, praying and hoping that she might hear something of her mother soon. Then, almost like an apparition of her desires, a lone horse and rider came fast and free down the road to the school. Jacob jumped down, asking John Zook to mind the horse, and took Lilly's arm.

"Can we talk inside?"

"Of course."

Lilly hurried to keep up with his long strides as they entered the schoolhouse. Jacob pulled out a chair near the woodstove and asked her to sit down. He set a chair up across from hers and absently took one of her bandaged wrists in his hands.

"Is everything all right?" her voice trembled.

"*Jah*, I found your mamm in town. She's home now. Mrs. Loftus is visiting with her; she said not to worry. She'll stay the whole afternoon."

"*Ach*, I'm sorry she has to do that. Maybe I could go home for just an hour or so."

"Mrs. Loftus wants to do it. You concentrate on the program." He stared down at her wrists and Lilly asked the question that she dreaded. "What was my *mamm* doing when you found her?"

"She wanted to—shop. I let her go. I tried to reason with her, and she just started getting upset. I thought it better to let her have her head and do what she wanted."

Lilly nodded, drawing a deep breath. "I'm so sorry that you had to deal with her, Jacob, so embarrassed really. She just seems to want to fill up her life somehow—with things. I don't expect you to understand."

He stroked the bandages on her wrist. "Lilly, I do understand. Not why she is the way she is, but I have seen horses wild with fear and pain, beyond reason. I think your *mamm's* in a lot of pain somewhere in her mind. It makes her do things, maybe say things that she doesn't really mean."

Lilly's eyes filled with quick tears at his words. If only he knew how many times her mother's words had lacerated her feelings, her heart. But perhaps it was true; perhaps, deep inside, her *mamm* didn't always mean what she said.

Lilly realized that tears had spilled onto her cheeks and chin, and she tried to wipe them away. Jacob leaned close to her and she became confused by his nearness, the scent of his skin, and the enticing thickness of his eyelashes. "Lilly, don't cry."

She nodded, trying to swallow her tears, only to find that the movement brought her cheek brushing against the dark fall of his hair. Time seemed to stand still as she looked into his eyes. She recognized the kindness there, but also confusion, a searching that made her feel as though he tried to see inside her soul.

"Teacher!" Reuben Mast bawled, banging open the door. "I got a nosebleed from a snowball."

Lilly jumped up and Jacob tipped backward with his weight on the rear legs of the chair so that she could rise and slide past him.

"Shh . . . Reuben. Stop crying." She tilted his head and squeezed the small nose with her handkerchief.

"My *mamm's* gonna tan my hide for getting blood on my shirt for the program!"

Jacob laughed. "I have a *mamm* like that. Come with me. I'll ride you to my house on Thunder and let my mother get that stain out. No one will ever know the difference."

Reuben stopped his crying. "I get to ride on Thunder? Really?"

"Sure, if you hang on—"

"I will. *Ach*, I will, Mr. Wyse."

Jacob held up his hand. "And your teacher agrees?"

Lilly smiled. "Just be back in plenty of time for the program."

"No problem, Miss Lapp."

She walked out with them, Rueben still clasping her handkerchief to his nose. The other children grumbled in disappointment that it wasn't one of them who got to sit in front of Jacob on the beautiful horse. "All right, children. That's enough excitement for this morning. Let's go back inside and run through everything one more time." She ignored the collective groans of the students and gave one last backward glance to the now small image of horse and rider. She realized that Jacob Wyse would be a good father one day. She absorbed the thought with haste as she entered the school.

Jacob was true to his word and Reuben returned to class with his shirt clean and his hair slicked. The boy wriggled with suppressed excitement and Lilly knew he needed a chance to tell them all about the ride, but parents were beginning to slip in and deposit food items on the narrow benches along the walls of the school as was the custom each year. Christmas treats were a reward for the children's performances, and the whole community enjoyed them as well.

Jacob came to stand near her desk and bent to whisper to her. "Lilly, there's a mare that's having a bit of trouble foaling. I plan to go check on her. *Daed* says he'll stay with her so I'll be back in plenty of time before the program starts." He cleared his throat. "That will also give me the chance to get the horse and buggy so I can escort you home afterward, if you'd like."

"I'd like that very much, and please, go and check on the mare, Jacob. And don't worry about being late—my *daed* used to arrive at events by the skin of his teeth."

He smiled. "Thanks."

*L*illy read to the children with soft authority, keeping their attention and hoping to calm them as the hour approached for the program. The room began to fill with the tantalizing scents of cinnamon bread pudding, ginger cookies, peach patty pies, and a delectable mix of other sweet scents. Soon it was time for the *naer-fich* students to line up along the blackboard while mothers with infants took the available desks, leaving Lilly's desk open until the bishop sat in her chair. Others began to crowd into the room, spilling out the back door and peering in through the windows. And though she spotted Seth Wyse standing outside with some other men, their breath making frosty puffs of air as they laughed and talked, she didn't see Jacob or Samuel Wyse anywhere. Maybe the mare was having more trouble than they'd thought.

Deciding that she could still be missing him in a crowd, or that he'd possibly be late, she rose promptly at two o'clock to welcome the bishop and all the families. Then she slid onto a small bench up front, with her back to the crowd. She smiled in reassurance at Carrie Mast, the youngest student, as she came forward to recite a short poem. The little girl stood no taller than the chalk well of the blackboard, and Lilly had to urge her twice to focus before she began in a stuttering singsong voice.

"This Christmas Day is cold and wet,
But I know,
It's the best one yet.
Because we're here,
Just me and you—
And Jesus Christ for His birthday too."

Although Carrie's tiny voice hadn't carried past the fourth row, the applause was deafening in response, and the child popped a thumb into her mouth to the delight of all. Next came Matthew Mast, and Lilly bit her lip as the boy took his time getting into position to recite the story of Christ's birth from the gospel of Luke. It was unfortunate that, by the time he got to the angels and the shepherds, something in his little pug nose had begun to disturb him. So, two-thirds of the gospel message was delivered with one pudgy finger jammed in his nostril. While Lilly made desperate gestures to try and get him to stop, the crowd laughed outright and then grew solemn again as he ended his digging right before he finished the beautiful traditional passage.

Then Lilly rose and, as was customary, begged a concession of not speaking English for a few minutes. She asked the bishop to lead the children in singing "Silent Night" in German.

The bishop rose and began to sing off-key, yet in the proper monotone, as everyone struggled to keep up. There were no instruments, just as there were none at Meeting, but the sweetness of the children's voices, rising in unity, made Lilly's eyes fill with tears as they sang the traditional song.

Stille Nacht! Heil'ge Nacht!
Alles schläft; einsam wacht . . .

When it ended, the bishop nodded to the crowd, encouraging them to sit down.

Lucy Stolis was next, her face pale and strained, her hands clutched in front of her when she began to tell a story she'd written about the class quilt. Lilly nodded at her with a bright smile, and the child's voice gained confidence.

"This year's theme for our class quilt was 'Trees.'" She gestured with one thin arm to the quilt, and the crowd shifted to see it better. "To me, though, this quilt means a lot more than just what it looks like. Yes, it is made of stitches and cloth and color and time, but this year, doing my quilt square helped me feel better about losing my *grossmud*—I mean, my grandmother who died in the summertime of pneumonia. My grandma taught me how to stitch my first quilt square and always let me climb under the big quilt frame to catch the needles that fell through when the ladies were having a quilting. But my grandmother also loved to be outside. She loved the air and the flowers and the trees." Here, an audible sniff or two came from the listeners as they remembered Grandmother Stolis. Lucy went on, smiling a little now. "I think my grandmother would have loved my quilt square because I made my tree show its roots, its beginnings. My grandmother was like those roots to me, strong and deep, and the most important part of the tree. By making this quilt, I learned that my grandmother will always be part of me." Lucy bowed her head to signal that she was finished. There was a long pause before the community began to clap in earnest approval. The bishop blew his nose in a blue hankie and stood up to show his enthusiasm. Others stood to follow suit, not attempting to guard against vanity in the child's clear-hearted and humble affirmation of her family's history.

After that, the rest of the program followed in a blur. The Christmas program was one of the few times that Amish parents did not worry about vanity and made a visible fuss over their children's performance and progress in school, and this year was no exception. Soon, the last child had finished and Lilly felt she could finally breathe. She rose to face the crowd and was surprised and touched when John Zook brought forward a bouquet of assorted fresh flowers for her from the class.

The bishop came to stand next to her and said, "I think we'd all like to thank Miss Lapp for the *wunderbaar* job she's doing with our children." He clapped. Lilly flushed as the applause continued from the crowd; the faces outside the windows smiling with good cheer.

Soon, everyone was jostling for the snacks. Lilly circulated first inside the schoolhouse and then out, all the while trying to keep a casual eye out for Jacob.

Seth came up to her and caught her hand. "That was great, Lilly. A lot of fun and a lot of hard work on your part, I can imagine. How are your arms?"

"*Ach*, fine. *Danki*." The truth was, in the rush of the program she'd forgotten all about her scraped arms and even her fear over the events involving her mother that morning. Now she wondered whether she might ask Seth where his brother was without appearing too forward. But Seth seemed to read her mind.

"I don't know where he is, Lilly," he said low. "Honestly. I know he was going to come; the mare started to make progress and *Daed's* not here, so they both must have stayed. I'm sorry. The program was wonderful, really."

Lilly nodded, touched by the sincerity in his voice and his

willingness to apologize for his brother. And his attentiveness provided a balm to her spirits that she couldn't deny.

$\mathcal{L}$illy had just decided to go back into the schoolhouse when the sounds of a horse and buggy, moving fast, came to her. She, and everyone else, glanced at the passing buggy, wondering who had missed the program and who wasn't even stopping now. Lilly's heart fell when she recognized Jacob driving and Kate Zook as his passenger. The girl smiled and waved at the crowd, while Jacob stared straight ahead. The Zook farmhouse lay beyond the schoolhouse and he was obviously taking her home. Lilly ignored the murmured speculations around her from the groups of various families and went back inside. She accepted a plate from someone and ate without tasting a thing.

CHAPTER 17

"Are you out of your mind?" Seth growled as they hunched in the cold between the cover of several buggies.

Jacob sighed. "Look—the girl's horse was lame, in distress. What was I supposed to do?"

"And you're sure of that. Sure that Kate Zook didn't plan this just to set another snare for you?"

Jacob stopped. He tried to think. He'd come out of the lane and hadn't gone more than a few hundred feet when his sharp eyes caught the glare of a buggy wheel just off the road. He'd pulled over and found Kate Zook standing huddled next to her horse and buggy, stroking the horse's mane.

"I don't think so, Seth. Her horse was obviously in distress. Favoring his right front. He had an abscess. He can't be pulling a buggy with an abscess."

"You could have sent her down to our house. *Daed* would have seen to the horse."

"I did, but I was already so late."

"You waited until the last minute with that mare, didn't you?

You could have let *Daed* take care of her. It's not like he doesn't know what he's doing."

Jacob hung his head.

"You still might have been able to make it. What did you do?"

"I was waiting for Kate. She had gone inside to warm up."

Seth said nothing, just continued to glare at him.

"I was trying to be nice. I certainly couldn't let her walk home in this weather. I didn't know what to do."

"Something else, Jacob. Anything else. Do you know how great that performance was by those kids? How long it probably took Lilly to get it ready—and with planning her wedding besides?"

"I know."

"*Nee*, you don't. You don't think, and that's what's got you into this mess in the first place. But worse than that, you're dragging Lilly into it with you too. And she deserves better."

"Seth, I've seen you go through girls by the dozen."

"This isn't just any girl, Jacob. She's going to be your wife— your *wife*—in two days. And you just humiliated her in front of everyone."

Jacob had had enough. "All right. I get the point. I'll go and see her."

"And she'll forgive you, because that's who she is. Well, *bruder*, I'll tell you the truth, you don't deserve that forgiveness. None of it." Seth turned and walked off, leaving Jacob struggling to contain his emotions.

*L*illy gave a forlorn tug at the paper chain of red and green, breathing in the silence of the schoolroom now that everyone had gone. She always stayed behind for a few minutes to tidy up the decorations. She found it made the class ready to move on after the turn of the New Year and Second Christmas when the students returned. She tried to concentrate on a clump of dried white paste that had fallen to the floor and bent to scratch it off with her fingernail. Her nose began to run as her eyes welled with tears. There was no denying it; the image of Jacob's set face and Kate's triumphant smile had robbed the joy from the afternoon's program. She had so wanted him to come. And for him to miss the performance because of the awful Kate Zook. She rose and tossed the paste and paper into the waste, remembering that Mrs. Loftus was waiting with her mother. She turned to find her cape, prepared to go home, then recalled that she didn't have a ride.

"I missed it. I'm sorry, Lilly."

Her breath caught in her chest as she looked up to see Jacob standing in the doorway.

"*Jah*, you missed it." She kept her voice steady and wiped at her cheeks.

He sighed aloud and closed the door behind him, walking into the room.

"So, Seth's a little protective of you. He took me to task for not being here."

She shrugged. "It seems to be his nature. He's caring."

"And maybe I'm not?"

"That isn't what I meant. Look, Jacob, please just go." She concentrated on stuffing her satchel with books.

"Lilly. Kate's horse went lame. I had to stop and help her. The animal was in pain. I had every intention of being here for you."

"It seems like Kate Zook has a lot of pressing needs where you're concerned."

"I know that . . . I know she probably arranged to be there, waiting for me."

"With a lame horse?"

He shrugged. "Maybe. Maybe she's foolish and selfish enough to drive an animal that way."

"To get your attention?"

He sighed. "I don't know what to say. I thought I was doing the right thing. The horse needed help either way."

"Well, it might have done you better to have helped the horse and let the girl get lame—walking."

"I know." His boot steps echoed in the stillness of the room as he approached her desk.

"I find that hard to believe. You don't know how I felt. I was embarrassed and furious—and jealous."

"Well, of course you'd feel that way." His voice was soothing but she was not in the mood to be placated. "I make you a promise, to a special invitation, and then I go gallivanting past with another girl in my buggy—two days before we're to marry."

She lifted her eyes to his. "It's not my business who rides in your buggy. You don't owe me anything. We both know this wedding is just a—just a sham. It's still not too late for you to back out."

"I thought we were becoming friends." His voice was low, questioning, vulnerable.

For an instant, Lilly almost gave in. She really did want to become his wife. She blew out a breath of frustration. "What do you want me to say, Jacob? That you're forgiven for rescuing Kate for the second time? Fine, you're forgiven."

She moved to step past him, but he blocked her way with the bulk of his body. She almost ran into his chest and caught the fresh scent that seemed to drift from the skin of his throat. She arched her neck to meet his eyes and found them gold and intense. She took a step back.

"I didn't want to help Kate. I told you; she bothers me, like fleas on a dog." He sounded so glum that the urge to smile at him bubbled up inside of her. She ducked her head, but not before he'd seen her face.

"*Ach*, don't smile, Lilly Lapp. That would mean that you believe me, that you trust me even." He reached out one large hand and skimmed it along the sleeve of her blouse, past the bandages on her arm, to catch at her hand.

She stared down at her hand in his. His touch was warm, strong. She struggled to guard her expression, then gave in fully to the smile. "I believe you," she said, her voice low and quiet.

He let go of her hand to lift her chin so that she was forced to look up at him once more. She felt nervous and jittery, and she wet her lips as she tried to think of something else to say.

"*Danki* for trusting me. And, I am not backing out of our marriage. You've got me, Lilly, for all our lives, as *Derr Herr* allows." He bent his head and kissed her forehead; a casual, almost brotherly kiss that somehow left her frustrated and tense.

He stepped back and she watched him look around the classroom. The only thing that remained from the program was the class quilt, strung across the windows.

"I missed the program. So, give me my own performance, Miss Lapp. Tell me about the quilt. Or you can sing to me. I like 'Silent Night.'"

"There can be no performance without the children."

"Is there anything you can show me?"

"Well, I'm especially proud of the quilt this year. The students did the top and several of the mothers finished it."

He smiled as he stared at the profusion of trees. "Do you remember making a class quilt when we were in school?"

Lilly tried to concentrate and recollect what square he might have made for a quilt. He laughed when she didn't speak.

"Maybe I should ask if you remember me from school."

"*Jah*, of course I do." She paused, hoping he wouldn't ask about her thoughts of him then.

"I bet you thought I was a wild one, a little on the bad side, maybe?"

She flushed. "Well, understanding what I do now about your reading, I know why you acted out. Besides, Miss Stahley was a bit on in years and was not the most pleasant of teachers."

"She was an old bat."

"Jacob!" A giggle rose in her throat despite her admonishment. Miss Stahley had been especially hard on him.

"She kept me out of the class quilt my last year in school. Do you remember that?"

Lilly lost her smile, appalled at what he'd said. "*Nee*, how could she do that?"

He turned from her, still studying the tree quilt. "*Ach*, I wouldn't recite what she'd asked, *couldn't* really. She threw me out of class when she passed out the quilt squares, then told me later that I didn't deserve one, that I wasn't really part of the class."

Lilly drew an indignant breath. "That old bat!"

He laughed, turning back to her. "All things come full circle though, don't they? Here I am, standing in the same schoolhouse where I once was not welcome, with my own private tutor."

Lilly felt a nervous sensation of excitement at his words. She knew then just how much she wanted to teach him to read, to try and heal the old wounds caused by a tormenting teacher.

"Well, I think our tutoring will have an additional purpose then."

He gave her an intense look. "Perhaps it will."

"*Gut.*"

He seemed at a loss for something to say, then spoke quietly. "I'll take you home if you're ready."

"All right. *Danki.*"

She gathered up the last of her books and then had a sudden inspiration for the primer she'd promised to make him. She decided, with a secret smile, that it would be one he wasn't likely to forget.

CHAPTER 18

*D*o you want some help?"

Jacob looked up as Seth lounged in the doorway, his casual pose not matching the emotion in his voice. They hadn't spoken since the schoolhouse.

"I've got little to pack."

Seth sighed.

Jacob folded a blue shirt, then glanced again at his *bruder*. They'd never been separated before, not for any length of time. He realized it would be strange and sad to not have his best friend right across the hall, but then, marriage was supposed to be a chance for a new best friend.

"I'll miss you," Jacob admitted.

"*Jah*, but we always knew it had to come to this—marriage, I mean. I just didn't expect you to move away, but I know Mrs. Lapp needs you both."

"You'll marry as well one day soon."

Seth frowned. "Who? Which reminds me—I've heard it nosed about that I'm a 'tortured soul' of sorts, just looking for a *fraa*."

"Sorry."

"Somehow I don't think so."

"No, I'm not."

They grinned at each other, then Seth's face took on a more serious expression. "This thing you're doing tomorrow, the wedding. Lilly seems like the kind of person who expects forever to be a given in a relationship."

Jacob straightened his spine.

"And I don't?"

"It's not that. I just—well, things happen in life. People die. Suppose Sarah was left alone. Then what?"

It was as if Seth had seen into Jacob's mind and heart the past few weeks. He shivered—if he knew for certain . . .

He shook his head as if that would clear his mind, wiping it free of impossible possibilities.

This time Seth misread him. "It could happen."

"Of course it could!" Jacob's anger at Seth, at Grant, at Sarah for loving Grant—but especially at himself—poured out through his words and into his clenching fists.

"Then why drag Lilly into this . . . this—"

"This what?" Jacob demanded, pretending he didn't know what his brother wanted to say.

"This ugly thing you're daring to call a marriage. This thing that uses Lilly. For what? For your own selfishness?"

Jacob turned away so that Seth wouldn't see his face blazing with shame.

"That girl deserves more than that."

Jacob's breath came fast and hard. Seconds of charged silence ticked by.

Then Seth spoke. "You still haven't answered my question."

Jacob turned back to him. "Fine. If Sarah were alone, she'd stay alone—at least as far as I'm concerned as a married man."

Seth looked doubtful. "So you'd want to be with Sarah if she were left alone and you weren't yet married?"

Jacob took a step round the bed.

"All right, Seth. What do you want? Do you need me to say that I still love Sarah? I do. Do you want me to tell you that I'm going to put everything I've got into this marriage? *Jah*, I am. Is that good enough for you?"

"Maybe it's not good enough for Lilly."

Jacob was in front of him in seconds, his voice tight. "Do you think I don't know that? Do you think it doesn't matter to me that I can't get over Sarah? That I can't give Lilly everything?" His daily rationalization surfaced. "But she knows what she's getting."

"Does she? Really?"

"She's willing to build with what there is, what there can be. That takes guts. I respect her for it. The rest will have to come."

"And if it never does?"

Jacob narrowed his eyes, studying his brother. "Why all this worry about Lilly?"

"She's going to be my sister-in-law, part of the family."

"I know you, Seth. There's something else. You wanted to knock me one at the school. Why?" Jacob's head swam as a sudden realization crashed over him. "You care for her, don't you?"

Seth's eyes glowed like blue flame. "Of course I care for . . . my brother's bride."

"You do. That's what this is about."

"You're *narrish*, Jacob. I want you to treat her right, that's all. To realize that what a woman needs is passion as well as kindness. She needs a whole, devoted heart."

"I will give her my whole, devoted heart. That's what the marriage ceremony begins."

Seth blew a breath out in disgust. "If you think you can fool her—why, you can't even fool yourself. You can't go through the motions of being a husband when it's another man's wife that you want."

"Your concern is admirable," Jacob bit out, not knowing how to respond to the conviction of the provoking words.

"Somebody's got to keep up the idea of honor around here."

*E*ven those who hadn't been invited showed up to help Lilly the day before the wedding. She was pleasantly surprised at the number of women who gathered to help cook and clean. Lilly's *mamm* had tried to join the bustle of activity but had soon wearied. Lilly found her crying in the pantry of the kitchen.

"*Mamm*, what is it?"

"It's just—I know I should be helping, should have helped you with your dress and all. But . . . I just feel so bad. I can't face all those women and their energy."

Lilly slid her arm around her mother's thin shoulders. "*Mamm*, it's all right. I'm just so glad you'll be here tomorrow. You don't have to do anything. *Derr Herr* has blessed us with many hands to help. Let me take you upstairs and you can have a nice nap. I'll be up later to try my dress on for you. Come on, we can go up the back stairs so no one will notice."

She shielded her mother's face against her shoulder and led her up the steps. Then she tucked her comfortably beneath a mound of quilts and slipped back downstairs.

Ellie Loftus, the bishop's *fraa*, met her in the kitchen. "The Lord sees how well you care for your mother, Lilly. He will bless you for it." Her voice was low. "But I know how hard it is to not have a mother's help at this time. I want you to know that if you ever need anything—advice, comfort, or just a *gut* word, that I will be glad to help."

Lilly smiled. "*Danki*."

"Good. Now, we've got the creamed celery and the roasting chicken cooking. The rest of the food will be arriving throughout the day. Ruth Loder and Alice Plank have made good headway on cleaning and dusting. You'll want to do the master bedroom, I'm thinking—Edith said she'd help you."

Lilly swallowed, not really wanting to dwell on the master bedroom, when the kitchen door opened and Mary and Samuel Wyse bustled inside. Mary caught Lilly's hand as Samuel stood with his arms full of something large and covered by a patchwork quilt.

"It's a present, Lilly," Mary whispered with excitement.

"Ach, danki!"

Lilly gestured to the master bedroom as the place to put it as the other women tossed greetings to the groom's parents.

Lilly felt a surge of excitement at wondering what gift could be beneath the quilt. They entered the master bedroom where Samuel eased his burden to the floor with a muffled thump. He rose and bent to kiss his wife's cheek and then Lilly's in a warm salute that left tears in her eyes. He left the room, closing the door behind him.

Mary Wyse smiled at her. "Samuel and I are both so happy to welcome a daughter to our family. I have to confess, Lilly, that there were a few years that went by when I longed for a little girl, but the Lord saw fit to send me two wild colts instead. So . . ." She knelt down and slipped the quilt off the gift, revealing a beautiful hand-carved trunk. "So, I waited. For my first daughter-in-law— you, Lilly. I've been waiting and praying for you for a long time. And for quite a while I've been collecting pretty things from here and there, keeping them to give that special woman. You, Lilly." She tapped the top of the trunk. "Will you open your gift?"

Lilly dropped to her knees, placing a hand on the trunk. "You have no idea how much your words mean to me . . . *Mamm*." She ducked her head shyly. "To think that I've been cherished in your prayers is plenty of a gift."

As Lilly lifted the metal latch, the trunk opened to reveal the fresh smell of cedar that wafted from within. Lilly gasped at the beauty of the crocheted tablecloth that lay folded on top. The workmanship reminded her of the delicate intricacy of the summer flower—Queen Anne's Lace—and she marveled silently at its beauty. Below that, there were doilies and fine linen handkerchiefs, as well as smaller quilts that Lilly knew to be baby quilts. She couldn't help the blush that stained her cheeks and was grateful for the warm hug her soon-to-be mother-in-law gave her.

"*Ach*, Lilly, please forgive me for adding those, but I do hope the Lord blesses you with a lap full of *kinner*."

Lilly nodded, trying to resist the enticing image of a multitude of small Jacobs running about the place.

She ran a hand over the curved inside of the trunk's lid and was surprised when her fingers grazed a small notch in the otherwise perfectly smooth surface. Instinctively, she curled her fingertip into the groove and the trunk lid gave way to reveal a hidden hollow carved into the lid.

Lilly smiled at Mary. "Another surprise?"

Mary looked confused, her head tilted to better see.

Lilly eagerly felt inside the space and withdrew a beautifully carved length of wooden links, almost like a very short chain. She pulled the wood toward her and saw the initials *AW* burned into the curve of one of the links.

"I'm sorry," Mary Wyse said, her face set into unfamiliar, stern lines. She held her hand out for the item.

Lilly put the carving into her outstretched hand. "A child's toy?" she asked with pleasure.

"*Nee*, this is no toy." Mary covered it with the folds of her apron as Lilly looked on in surprise. "I'm sorry, my dear, but this belongs in the family. I didn't realize it was there or I would have removed it beforehand. Please forgive me."

"But there's nothing to forgive."

Mary's face relaxed and Lilly suppressed the curiosity in her that longed to question the wooden chain links. But, if her new *mamm* wanted her to ignore its existence, then she would. "I love all of these beautiful treasures," she added quickly, hoping to relieve Mary of any doubts about her sincerity.

A sudden knock on the door broke into their conversation and Edith Miller poked her head round the door. "You ladies done in here? We've got some cleaning to do."

"*Jah.*" Mary Wyse rose to her feet and Lilly joined her, bending to receive the woman's warm embrace.

"*Danki* so much for all of this," Lilly whispered. "You've equipped me with a lifetime of beauty."

Mary kissed her cheek. "You're welcome, my daughter," she said before leaving the room with a smile at Edith.

Edith Miller was the thin, wiry Amish postal woman of Pine Creek, and she had a sharp tongue and a quick wit. Lilly loved talking with her and wasn't disappointed now when Edith waved some dust rags at her.

"Come on, Lilly, time to clean the most important room in the house."

Lilly blushed as the other women laughed together, then went to join Edith in the familiarity of what was once her parents' room.

Lilly paused at the door to thoughtfully survey the place with its well-carved furniture and long windowpanes. She avoided looking at the bed. She'd already gone over her brief conversation with Jacob about sleeping arrangements a hundred times in her mind. He'd come over late one evening and there had been a suppressed energy about him that had made her feel like he'd come with more purpose than just discussing the ongoing wedding plans. He'd circled the kitchen like a caged cat and finally stood still and looked her square in the eye.

"Lilly, I've . . . uh . . . been thinking about it some, and I wanted to talk with you about the wedding night. Our wedding night."

She hadn't been able to control the blush that stained her cheeks and assumed a practical manner, her best defense in awkward situations.

"*Ach*, well, go ahead then." She sank down at the kitchen table and tried to keep her voice casual, despite the growing lump in her throat.

"Right. I'll go ahead. It's like this. We talked a bit the night of the engagement about taking time to court, to get to know each other . . ."

"That is correct." Her stomach flipped in *naerfich* anticipation of what he was trying to say.

"Well, I just wanted to be clear about all that. I know that things . . . uh, plans have been moving fast and I don't want you to think that I've forgotten. No *real* wedding night until we've . . . courted." He appeared relieved that he'd got it out and let one lean hip rest against the counter.

"So who will sleep where? There's only the one bed." She couldn't believe she'd asked that oh-so-practical but oh-so-embarrassing question that set him to pacing once more.

He had a stranglehold on his hat and stopped once more to slap his thigh with the twisted object.

"In the bed. We sleep in the bed. It will be—fine. You'll see." He seemed like he was trying to convince himself as much as her, and she'd nodded mutely in return. But now, the reality of cleaning the bedroom brought the whole feeling of discomfort rushing back once more.

"Might as well have another gift now before we tackle this very important room," Edith said, snapping her from her reverie.

The thin woman handed her a large package wrapped in brown postal paper.

"*Ach,* Edith . . . what is it?"

"Open it and see!"

Alice entered the room and came up behind Lilly, trying to peer over her shoulder.

Lilly tore the wrapping with trembling fingers. She always loved having gifts to open. When the paper fell to the floor, she gasped with pleasure at the mound of quilt she held.

"It's wonderful," Alice said in her ear. "Put it on the bed."

Lilly settled the mound onto the bed and began to unfold it.

"I know it's not a wedding quilt, but it's a Christmas one all right. Me and some of the girls worked on it down at the back room of the post office this past summer. I've been praying about who to give it to—and the Lord brought you to mind when I heard about the engagement."

The three women unfolded the thick spread, heavily quilted with thousands of tiny stitches. In the center was an appliqué angel, blowing his trumpet in proud announcement.

"Edith—it's so beautiful! Thank you so much!" Lilly's eyes filled with tears of joy and she moved to embrace Edith's thin shoulders. Edith patted her hard on the back, then stepped away.

"*Ach,* come on now, let's set this room to rights. Alice, would you help? I think the quilt is just the right amount of cheer that's needed in here."

Lilly tried to concentrate on the feeling of the even stitching beneath her hand as she helped Edith smooth the beautiful quilt atop the bed. But there was no getting around the swamping sensation of loss that she felt when she realized that she'd probably have no real wedding quilt of her own. Gifts like Edith's were priceless in thought and beauty, of course, but there could be nothing like sitting with a community of women and making your own stitches on a quilt that was meant to symbolize a generation of time.

Lilly knew what those stitches would have meant to her, a

yielding, a pacing of self and energy that would serve as reminders of even temper, conscious decisions, and thoughtful words. To have laid her own hand to fabric that would perhaps see new life brought into the world, nurture the sick, and cover Jacob in his old age would have been something that she would have dearly loved and cherished. But she thought as she smiled at the angel on the quilt, perhaps the Lord would bring forth a different means of comfort besides a quilting, and with that she had to trust and be content.

CHAPTER 19

*L*illy rose far before dawn on the day of her wedding. She turned up a lamp and dressed in work clothes, glancing once to the sky-blue wedding dress that lay pressed and perfect over the chest at the end of her bed. She studied it so often as she and Mrs. Stolis had worked on it over the weeks that she felt she knew every line and crease by heart, but there—such thoughts seemed like vanity. Although she did hope that Alice liked her matching dress as Lilly's sole attendant. Some Amish brides had up to three attendants but both she and Jacob thought it seemed a bit much, so she'd chosen Alice alone. She glanced in the bureau mirror, gave an impatient tug to the bundle of her hair, and set her *kapp* in proper order.

The wedding service was to begin at nine a.m. and would last a good three to three-and-a-half hours, as was custom. The size of the wedding, its numbers of guests or attendants, did not change the sanctity and process of the ceremony. But there was still a great deal of work to be done before then. Thankfully the neighbors would be arriving soon to help with the food. And, although the bride would normally not be expected to help overly much on her special day, Lilly wanted to spare her mother as much stress as possible and felt no qualms about doing the preparation work.

Lilly slipped from her room and tiptoed down the steps. She knew what she wanted most of all before the day began—a few moments alone to pray with *Derr Herr*. She pulled on her wraps and a head scarf and eased open the kitchen door to go out onto the porch.

Though it was still dark, the *munn's* glow provided enough light for her to see the crystalline branches of the trees. The shapes of the mountains sprawled endlessly, comforting her with their bulk against the still star-strewn sky. She sank down on the snow-dusted cold of the wooden step and bowed her head in her hands to pray.

"Dear Lord, I thank You for the peace and stillness of this morning. I praise You for giving me a husband such as Jacob. *Sei so gut*, let me know how to be a *fraa* to him, the kind of person he needs as a helpmeet, as Your word says. Please help me with *Mamm*—please change my attitude, give me more grace to love her as she is now. Help me to not miss *Daed* so much. Help Jacob to know how much he means to You . . ."

She lifted her head, blinking back tears as she considered how *Derr Herr* worked to lay even hidden needs on her heart—like the need Jacob had for love. She realized that she didn't, in actuality, know all that much about him, only what she saw. But her heart whispered to her that he was lonely, lonely from his feelings of inadequacy over the inability to read, lonely because he was so strong, lonely for Sarah. But *nee*, not on her wedding day would she consider his feelings for another. *Derr Herr* was working out something new, and she had to believe that.

She rose with a deep sense of inner peace as she saw Alice coming across the field and the first of the buggies full of helpers coming down the lane and felt her heart beat with excitement as her wedding day began.

"*W*ell, you two look like fine dandies," Samuel Wyse spoke from the kitchen table as Jacob and Seth entered the room in their new black suits, white shirts, and polished black shoes.

"*Danki, Daed*," Jacob replied, running a finger between his tight collar and neck. He felt jittery; there was no help for it. And, he felt foolish for last night's words with Seth; yet his brother teased him with good humor.

"So, this is it—the elusive Jacob Wyse finally meets his destiny." Seth sat down at the table and swigged from a glass of milk. He waved a hand at their *mamm's* admonishments not to get anything on his suit. "Of course, I'd be as *naerfich* as a colt, if it were me."

Their *daed* lifted his mug of coffee to him. "It may well be you soon enough, son."

"*Ach, nee*. I, for one, plan to stay one step ahead of the pretty face, the well-turned ankle, and the scheming hearts of *mamms* everywhere."

Mary Wyse cuffed him on the head. "Let your brother be. And let him get some food into his stomach at least."

"*Mamm*, I don't mean any harm. I'm just giving Jacob the chance to talk about how he feels. I mean, he could be a tortured soul in disguise."

"All right, all right. That's enough," Jacob muttered, eating his scrambled eggs in three gulps. "Why I ever chose you as my attendant is beyond me."

Seth smiled and took a bite of toast. "Of course, Lilly may have to take the schoolteacher's switch after you now and then, but no doubt you'd deserve it."

"Son," Samuel Wyse admonished. "Give your brother peace."

Jacob reached across the table and shook his father's hand, then smacked his brother in the shoulder. "Let's go. We've got to be there to greet the guests."

Seth grinned at him conspiratorially as he rubbed at his shoulder. "Watch it big *bruder*, or I might give you a smack of your own back—wouldn't want you to be in pain on your wedding night."

Jacob gave him a warning frown as his *mamm* came forward to embrace him. "We'll follow shortly, boys." Then she sniffed and turned away. Jacob caught her back against him. "*Mamm*, I love you. *Danki* for all that you've ever done for me."

Seth hustled him away from their *mamm*. "Yes, yes . . . lots of love. Why not save some for your bride?"

*L*illy tried to relax as Alice ran a brush through her long dark hair and began the intricate process of coiling it into a mass that would stay put. She looked at herself in the small bureau mirror and saw what she was—pale, anxious, and exhilarated. It was combination enough to make her feel vaguely like throwing up. She clutched the embroidered hankie that her *mamm* had thoughtfully given her just a few moments before; a token of love and times past that meant her mother gave her blessing to the day.

"It's *gut* to see your *mamm* up and dressed for the wedding," Alice murmured, her mouth lined with hairpins. "How do you feel?"

Like I'm about to jump off a cliff. "Well, there's no going back now," she said with a note of cheerful humor.

She saw Alice's frown in the reflection of the mirror and watched her snatch the pins from her lips. "You can call it off, Lilly. Right now, even. Sure, folks would be put out, but they'd get over it. You don't have to settle for anyone . . . not even a prize like Jacob."

KELLY LONG

Lilly swallowed and wondered where the composure from her early morning prayers had gone. Her composure had vanished, but her confidence had not. "He might consider me second-best, Alice, but I'm not settling with Jacob. It's what I want. Truly." *I want this . . . I want to be married to Jacob . . . I do.*

Alice sighed and resumed pinning. "Then I'm happy for you. I guess there's no marriage that's easy right off—though I'm hardly an expert." She gave her plump hip a rueful pat. "I doubt I'll ever have to fret about a man's attentions, no matter how much I'd love to be married." Lilly met her friend's eyes in the mirror. "You will know sometime."

"We'll see." Alice smiled. "But today is about you." She tucked a final pin into the intricate coil of hair and reached for a *kapp*. "There, you're beautiful. Pinch your cheeks a bit to bring out the color."

Lilly reached a hand to her face, watching herself in the mirror with surreal fascination. Then she pinched herself and the pain reminded her that today was very real, with its nerves and nausea. But she had never felt so excited in all her life.

The house felt overly warm to Lilly as she sat in the straight-backed chair and tried not to think about the fact that she was probably perspiring under the arms of her blue wedding dress. After the guests were seated, she'd entered with Alice in attendance, her hands folded tightly before her. And she'd deliberately avoided looking at Jacob until she was properly seated opposite him. Then she took a quick peek from beneath her lashes and had to catch her breath at his handsomeness. He'd caught her gaze back too and winked one warm eye, and she'd felt happy and secure for the moment.

The bishop rose to give some words of advice—or perhaps

it would be a longer sermon—to encourage she and Jacob, as was the custom.

Lilly never knew what was going to come out of Bishop Loftus's mouth. He was always wise and right, or so it seemed, but he always got to things in a funny way. Now he paced briefly, then looked to the slatted wood ceiling and back again at the small gathering.

"I'd like to raise the point that God doesn't care if you're happy."

Oh, great, Lilly thought. *Perfect for my wedding day.*

"Nope, He doesn't care if you're happy, but He does care, very much, if you have joy."

Lilly looked up.

"Now some of you will say that the two are one and the same—happiness and joy—but this is not so. Happiness is a feeling. Happiness is fleeting, dependent on the moment, the circumstances, even the weather. Joy is transcendent, enduring, and, in the biblical context, is not an emotion. Joy is an attitude of the heart. Joy brings us peace, a refuge in the midst of troubles. God gives us joy through His Spirit. But the enemy tries to steal your joy and give you temporary happiness instead. Now, is there anything wrong with being happy? *Nee,* but it cannot last. So, you may wonder why I bring up the difference between these two—it is simple really." He fixed Jacob and Lilly with his dark, raisin-like eyes.

"I bring it up to advise you, because marriage—in its true, everyday, working, living, dying state—is not easy and not much fun."

Jacob coughed abruptly into his fist.

"No, marriage is sacred before the Lord, a decision for a lifetime, but too often I think young people look upon it as a source of happiness. Do not look at marriage this way. See it as a reservoir of joy, a deep, welling spring that endures the icy blast of temper, the bite of an angry word, the void of loneliness in a heart hungry for talk when there is no response."

The bishop positively inspires one to want to be married, Lilly considered ruefully with nervous humor. She wondered what Jacob was thinking.

The bishop spoke again earnestly. "Seek joy in each other, not happiness. Amen." He stopped with his customary abruptness.

Lilly tried to ignore the stiffness in her limbs while the bishop went on to bellow out supporting scripture. Finally, he made a motion with his small, wrinkled hand, and Lilly rose to walk forward before the assembled guests to join right hands with Jacob. She took a deep breath.

It was time for the bishop to ask questions of each of them, similar to the vow questions asked at *Englisch* weddings. But Ezekiel Loftus was either too old or too wise to ask the normal questions regarding obeying, sickness, and health. Lilly had sat through many a wedding when the old man had the couple squirming with embarrassment and the guests gathered suppressing laughter—which was why she'd been dreading this. She hoped that today he was in a sober frame of mind. She held her breath as he began to pace in front of her and Jacob, his wizened arms behind his back. Finally, he turned to Jacob, and Lilly felt her groom's hand grow warm in her own.

"Jacob Wyse?"

"Yes, sir?"

The bishop stroked his long gray beard and peered up at Jacob.

"Do you promise to love Lilly Lapp more than you do those horses of yours? Because it's a known thing that you might tend to your horse before your *fraa*, and that simply might not do in the case of childbirth or fire."

Lilly felt the small crowd shift behind her and heard a sudden stifled chuckle.

Jacob spoke with complete seriousness. "I do promise, sir."

"To what?"

"To . . . love and care for Lilly . . . more than horses and whatever you just said, sir."

"Uh-huh. And do you promise, my son, to love Lilly Lapp beyond all others, beyond any other—as long as *Derr Herr* gives you life?"

Lilly resisted the urge to look at the floor as the crowd stilled behind her.

"I do so promise, sir," Jacob said steadily.

The old man nodded in apparent satisfaction, then swung his gaze to Lilly who met his eyes without flinching.

"Lilly Lapp?"

"Yes, sir," she murmured.

"Hmmm . . . well, let's see, you're the schoolteacher, which means you're honorable, trustworthy, and loyal . . ."

Lilly felt vaguely like he was likening her to a dog.

"And you care for your *mamm*, show love for your neighbors, and are, I believe, of excellent character. Why are you marrying this man?"

The guests tittered, but the bishop's dark eyes were steady, penetrating. Lilly took a deep breath and half-turned to Jacob.

"I marry him because I've always had respect for him, since we were *kinner*. He loves the creatures made by *Derr Herr's* hand; he loved my father—" Her voice shook a bit.

"Go on," the bishop ordered.

She wet her lips and saw that Jacob was looking at the floor, not at her, almost as if he felt he didn't deserve her words. She spoke louder and he lifted his eyes to her own. "*Derr Herr* has provided this man as a proper and fitting husband for my heart and home. I marry him of my choice and of my privilege. He is—my friend and completes my life like the pieces of a quilt are worked to complete a whole."

Jacob's eyes gleamed golden green and she felt lost in the moment, as if they stood alone.

The bishop cleared his throat and spoke in High German as he enclosed his wrinkled hands about Lilly's and Jacob's own. "Well then, before the Lord, these two make a vow to wed. And I give my blessing upon their union, that they may live long and joyfully together, with laps full of children and hearts filled with love."

Lilly came back to the moment at the sounds of benches creaking and people beginning to talk, which made her realize the wedding was over. She was Lilly Wyse now, and though the bishop had dropped his hands after his blessing, she and Jacob still stood staring at each other with hands clasped.

"Come now," the bishop snapped. "It's time for turkey and dressing. It's near starving that I am. Jacob, you've got all your life to look upon her. And Lilly, go and talk to those school *kinner* who behaved so well throughout the service."

Lilly loosed her hand to go and obey the bishop but she was conscious of Jacob's eyes as she moved about the room, embracing and being held in both congratulations and joy.

Alice gave her a kiss on her cheek. "Some things won't change between us, Lilly Wyse. You can always come to me for any support you need."

Lilly rejoiced as her mother hugged her, then moved on to tentatively embrace Jacob. Lilly thought it might be a good beginning for the future between her *mamm* and husband.

Chapter 20

*T*he last of the guests left at dark, having stayed to help clean up and wish the couple final farewells, even though it was customary for the bride and the groom to clear up alone. Mrs. Lapp had gone to bed much later than usual, doing Lilly the honor of greeting everyone and participating in the day's celebration, even though Lilly could tell that the event was a strain. It hadn't been particularly wondrous for her either, she realized. She'd felt uncertain at moments when guests had teased good-naturedly about her and Jacob's hidden courtship, yet there was nothing hidden before the Lord surely. Still, she now stood uncertainly in the quiet kitchen, fingering one of her *kapp* strings.

Jacob leaned against the sink, sipping from a glass of water he'd poured himself. "Well, Mrs. Wyse—what shall we do now?"

Lilly went to the desk in the sitting room. "I've got your wedding gift." She pulled a thin, simply wrapped package from the desk and slid the drawer closed. She brought it to him with a hesitant smile. "I hope you like it."

He put the water glass down and accepted the present. "I'm sure I'll love it."

She watched his tan fingers work at the wrapping and waited with *naerfich* anticipation for his reaction. He pulled out a primer she'd made and held it closer to the light of the lamp.

"The cover's pretty," he observed, studying the pencil sketching of the mountains in winter.

It wasn't the cover that she was worried about, she thought, then held her breath as he turned to the first page.

She waited while he moved closer to the lamp. She knew what he was looking at, the delicate fingertips of a woman's hand pressed against the strength of a man's open palm, a gesture of consent, yielding . . .

"I don't know what the word is," he said, his voice husky as he indicated the letters at the top of the sketch.

"Touch."

He swallowed and turned the page.

Again, she forgot to breathe. She'd drawn him as she remembered him the day at the sink when she'd helped change his bandage—his broad back bare, his dark head bent, as if he waited in a posture half taut, half yearning.

"Back?" he asked, and she nodded, noticing that a flush stained the strong bones of his face. She hoped she hadn't gone too far.

The opposite page displayed a couple in a kindled embrace. Her hair was undone and fell over the strength of his arm, while his mouth hovered a mere pencil stroke from the parting of her lips.

Lilly watched as Jacob shifted on his long legs and noted the pulse that beat in the strong line of his throat. "Kiss?" he queried, then looked at her fully. His eyes glowed like golden embers and she suddenly wanted to run. She snatched the primer from his hand and took a step backward, clutching the booklet behind her back.

"I . . . I suppose that's enough for one lesson. Three new words." "Words I'll never forget," he confided. "When's my next lesson?" "Well—sometime?" she asked, rather helplessly.

He reached behind her back and gently pried the primer loose from her fingers. "Fine, but I'll keep my wedding gift, if you don't mind."

She felt a mixture of gratitude and disappointment when he let the moment pass without fuss.

Then he caught her hands.

"Come on. Put on your cape. We need to go outside for your gift."

She smiled in pleasant confusion, but allowed him to help fasten her cloak and settle a shawl about her head.

She drew a deep breath of the crisp mountain air then took his arm as they slipped and crunched across the snow-covered ground. He led her to the barn, and she felt her heart begin to sink as she realized what her gift probably was. *But I don't want a horse.* She immediately squelched the ungrateful thought and kept a smile on her face as he slid the door open.

The barn seemed to have taken on a new appearance. It had been ruthlessly cleaned and stacked with plenty of fresh bales of hay and bags of seed. Stray cobwebs were gone and the mellow light of a kerosene lamp played across a new worktable where unfamiliar tools were arranged in careful order. Even Ruler had obviously been groomed well for the day, a black ribbon cleverly threaded through his now silky mane.

"The barn is one of my favorite places." Jacob smiled at her. "Seth came over sometime before the wedding. He probably worked for hours to do all this."

"It looks beautiful," Lilly replied, amazed at the transformation from what had felt like a dark and gloomy place since her *daed's* passing.

"Well, I hope you'll find your gift beautiful too." He walked to the far end of the barn to a newly framed stall. He snapped a lead on a horse, but Lilly could only glimpse the head. All horses looked alike to her somehow and she curled her toes inside her shoes at her disappointment over the present.

But then Jacob led the animal into the light of the lamp and Lilly blinked in realization. "Why, it's—it's the mare, from that day."

Jacob brought the gentle beast close and put the lead in Lilly's cold hand.

"Her name's Buttercup. She looks much better now."

"*Ach*, she's a beauty." Lilly admired the now-healthy sheen of the reddish coat and the bright yellow ribbons which trailed from a few braids in her mane. She looked deep into the animal's dark eye and knew that this creature was one who'd suffered much but had come through with dignity and quietness. She felt her fear melt away and reached a tentative hand to stroke the mare's forehead.

Jacob cleared his throat. "I thought—well, that she was sort of our matchmaker, in a way, and she's truly gentle, Lilly. I think she suits you and will be a great horse to work with while you're learning to ride."

Lilly slowly slid her hand away from the mare and glanced away from Jacob's warm eyes. "Do I have to keep that promise— to learn how to ride?"

He stepped closer to her, so that she could feel the warmth of his long legs even through the thickness of her cloak. "Lilly," he whispered. "Look at me."

She darted a glance up at his face and then let her gaze drift to the clean, swept floor. She felt him move. He caught the edges of the shawl wrapped under her chin and worked the knot with gentle fingers, lifting the cloth up and away so that she felt the chill of the air on her ears. He bent his head and put his mouth close to her neck. She shivered with the curious sensation of his warm breath competing against the cold.

"Lilly," he murmured, "you're so strong, but there's so much more to you than just strength. There's passion. And because of that"—he trailed his lips along the line of her throat and she raised her hands to touch his chest, the lead still in her hand—"you can learn to ride; you can do anything. I believe that of you, but you don't have to do it alone anymore. I'm here."

Her eyes filled with tears at his words; it was like he could see inside her heart. "*Ach*, Jacob," she whispered. He caught the tear that spilled over the curve of her cheek with his mouth and moved as if to kiss her lips when the mare gave a sudden snort. Lilly startled, dropping the lead and moving away from his warmth.

Jacob laughed. "There's a jealous girl." He bent to pick up the lead. "She just wants a little attention too." He made odd deep sounds from the back of his throat, and the horse shifted with visible good humor, as if he'd actually touched her. Lilly pressed her hands into the folds of the cloak as she realized that this was Jacob's element, his classroom. She found herself watching him with intense interest.

Jacob moved abruptly, reaching a hand to rub Buttercup's neck. "I'll put her back. Go on in—it's too cold out here for little seashell ears like yours."

She nodded, feeling unaccountably dismissed, and caught up her shawl, hurrying out of the barn and into the night air.

Jacob moved mechanically as he led the horse to the stall and swung the door closed after ushering Buttercup inside and removing her halter and lead. It was so easy—in a way—to do and say the right things, the things expected of a husband. A casual caress here, maybe a kiss there, but his eyes burned as he acknowledged the truth to himself. When he touched Lilly, thoughts of Sarah still came to him. Even with the incredible primer that had so stirred him, he couldn't help the passing thought of what it would be like if it were Sarah who longed for his touch instead of Lilly. He put the heels of his hands to his eyes and bent his head. The two women had become tangled in his mind like knots in a chain, and Seth's words came back to haunt him. He couldn't fool himself. He drew a sobbing breath and started to pray. *"Please, Father. Help me not to sin by coveting another man's wife. Help me to choose. To choose my wife's love. To decide to love her.* Sei so gut, *answer that prayer I said at my wedding today and sweep the past away; drive it away. Make my heart new.* Ach, *Lord, please."*

CHAPTER 21

*L*illy startled a bit when he opened the master bedroom door a crack.

"Can I come in?"

"*Jah*, of course."

She'd taken off her cloak and shoes, and now she stood in the light of two lamps, surveying the wedding gifts which lined the bed and decorated the floor of the room.

"So, what did we get?" he asked with a smile, hoping the residue of his tears didn't show. She returned his smile. "Many *wunderbaar* things. I especially love the painting . . . no guessing who that's from." She lifted a small watercolor of the schoolhouse in winter from the foot of the bed and held it out for his admiration. None of the gifts had labels on them; they were meant to be given to the bride and groom as representations of the goodwill of the community as a whole. But the painting could have been done by no one else.

Jacob nodded at the art. "I guess you're officially in the family now if Seth's letting you see his work."

"I'm honored."

Jacob bent to admire a new leather bridle on the floor while she put the painting back and fingered the clean steel of a teapot. "There are linens too and a lot of canned goods. And I'm not sure, but I think that the leather tooling kit is from Sarah and Grant Williams. I saw her entering the bedroom before the wedding with something about its size."

Jacob nodded, not speaking, and she went on in a hurry.

"*Ach*, and the schoolchildren, or perhaps their mothers, made this." She held up a square of fabric.

"A square?" he asked with good humor.

"No . . . not just a square." She moved closer to him and displayed the quilt square which had all the children's names embroidered on it with a delicate border of hearts and vines and the wedding date. "There was a little note with it. I'm to use it when I have my wedding quilting . . . I mean . . . if I do."

"Is a wedding quilt that important to you? Isn't this one beautiful enough?" he asked, placing his hand on the quilt Edith had brought the day before.

"Well, yes, but . . ." Was it wrong for her to long for a wedding quilt? For something made especially—and only—to cover her and her husband on a cold winter's night? Something done together with other women as a gift of love for her and an encouragement for the marriage?

"I guess we missed some things in all the hurry. If it's really that important . . ." He looked at her with seriousness.

She shook her head. "*Nee*, I have everything I need." She realized, as she spoke the words, that she badly wanted for them to be true. She wanted to find complete contentment in the belief that *Derr Herr* had given her Jacob to stand by her in life. For what more should she ever want? She was ashamed that she longed for the validation of a wedding quilt. How could it be so important? She swallowed and glanced at the bed.

"I guess we should clear things off so that we can get some sleep," he remarked casually.

"*Jah*," she agreed and moved to help him start placing the gifts on various bureaus and side tables. When the bed was clean, and Edith's angel quilt folded back, they both stood and stared at what now seemed like a very small space of pillows and linens. Jacob cleared his throat and then regarded her directly.

"All right, so we've talked about this before. No expectations of a real wedding night until we've had some time to—um, court. I think I can trust myself to stay on my side of the bed. What about you?" He grinned and she flushed, looking away.

"Of course," she said in a prim voice.

"*Gut*. I'm tired." He reached for the opening of his wedding coat and slid it down his long arms while Lilly tried to concentrate on the stitching of the quilt's edge. *Did he mean to simply undress in front of her? What was she to do?*

"Just my shirt, Lilly. Is that all right?"

She turned at his question to see his suspenders about his waist and his fingers poised at his collar. She nodded and watched him from the corner of her eye, unable to contain her curiosity. His chest was well tanned and deeply muscled. She let her gaze slip up to his shoulder and was surprised at the minimum of puckered red skin left from the gunshot wound. He must have felt her watching because he half turned.

"It's worse on the front—the exit wound, you know. Grant Williams took out the stitches awhile ago."

She was once more amazed at his perception and looked fully at his broad chest, marred only by what looked like a starburst of sore tissue on the splay of his arm. He moved toward her to give her a chaste kiss on the cheek. She longed to turn her head to meet his lips.

"Goodnight, Mrs. Wyse. I'll turn off the lights and you can do whatever you usually do for bed. I'm so tired that I'll probably be asleep before you're done. I'll take the side nearest to the window."

She watched as he walked to the dresser and extinguished the lamp, then sensed him as he felt cautiously for the bed and slid in. The room lay in utter darkness; she couldn't even see her hand in front of her face. She stood frozen, not sure what to do, until the deep, even sound of his breathing told her that he was asleep. She put her hands out to feel for the edge of the bed, stubbing her toe on something and swallowing a squeak. She decided she'd sleep with her hair up and her clothes on and make sure that she was awake before him so he wouldn't know. She didn't want to appear overly shy, but she wouldn't have been able to find her brush or nightgown in the deep dark anyway.

She slipped beneath the mound of linens and quilt and turned away from him, but it was difficult not to feel the warmth that seemed to radiate from his body. She closed her eyes with reluctance, not wanting to accidentally touch him, and certain that she'd get little to no sleep on her wedding night.

Jacob turned in the bed, still half asleep. He wondered how far he could actually stretch out without touching his wife. He let a cautious hand trail across the bed and came in contact with her hip, then jerked his hand back. Stifling a sigh, he fell back to sleep. Soon he was dreaming, and it felt comfortable and familiar.

He was walking across a newly plowed, sunlit field and Sarah was beside him. They were talking, just like always, easy talk that came as naturally as the rain. But something pulled at his conscious-ness, an awareness that across the field there was a deep copse of trees. He felt drawn to it for some reason, but when he turned to go there, Sarah walked on ahead without him. He stopped in confu-sion, then returned his attention toward the trees. A tall, slender girl with long dark hair danced in the shade of the woods. He could only catch glimpses of her. He hurried his steps, drawn with irresistible attraction to the dancing girl. He turned back to call to Sarah, wanting her to know about the beauty of the dancer. But Sarah kept moving ahead, and he let her go.

CHAPTER 22

*L*illy came fully awake when she heard him call out the name . . . *Sarah*. She rolled over and looked at him in the half light of predawn. His hair was ruffled against the white pillow, his lashes thick crescents against his flushed cheeks, his breathing rapid and uneven. He was dreaming—about Sarah.

Lilly felt a chill deep inside as if he had struck her with an icy hand. She moved away from him in silence. She didn't try to check the tears streaming down her cheeks, and she clenched her hands together beneath her pillow. Somehow, last night in the barn, she had thought that he was interested in her as a person. As someone to share his life with. The idea of him still harboring his love for Sarah had foolishly never even entered her mind.

Now she knew the truth; his subconscious mind revealed where his heart truly lay, and she must never, ever forget it. She decided that allowing him to get too close to her would only hurt her in the end. She wondered if she'd been a fool to go through with a wedding to someone who was so in love with another woman that he dreamed of her on his wedding night. She swallowed a sob, then jumped as she felt his hand on her shoulder.

"*Guder mariye*, Mrs. Wyse." His voice was deep, lulling. She thrust the sound from her mind.

"You slept in your wedding dress? Why didn't you change?"

She wiped hastily at her tears, then hoped her voice would come out steady. "I couldn't see in the dark. So silly of me."

"Are you all right?"

She felt him shift in the bed, moving closer to her.

She nodded hard. "Allergies—in the morning. I need to get a drink of water." She wriggled from beneath his hand and slid from the bed, keeping her head turned. She hurried across the wide fir boards and slipped out the door and into the safety of the kitchen.

She knew she had to go back to him, if only to grab clean clothes and change before her mother awoke and started to ask questions. So she splashed icy cold water on her face from the sink again and again, then dried herself with a tea towel. She straightened, smoothed out the wrinkles in her wedding dress, then headed back to the bedroom.

She had made her vows before *Derr Herr* and man, and she had no intention of forsaking her words—no matter whom he chose to dream about.

Jacob allowed himself the rare luxury of lounging awake in bed while the first streaks of dawn played across his chest and arms. He folded his hands behind his head and closed his eyes. His father had insisted he take the day after the wedding and Christmas day off from his normal chores and work. He hadn't wanted to, but now he considered that it might be nice to spend some time getting to know his bride. The *Englisch* idea of a honeymoon was not something practiced by his community. Instead, couples would usually spend the remainder of the winter months with the groom's family, visiting relatives here and there, and then move into their own little place, usually on the groom's family property. But there was always the possibility for differences in living arrangements, like in the case of Lilly's *mamm*.

He opened his eyes as Lilly reentered the room, her head still down.

"Feeling all right?" he asked.

She nodded, and he watched as she began to gather clothing from the neat row of nails along the wall, then picked up her brush from the dresser. There was definitely something wrong, but he couldn't put his finger on it. Perhaps he'd accidentally touched her in his sleep and made her feel uncomfortable.

He pulled his hands from behind his head and played with the sheet tangled along his hip for a moment. Then he cleared his throat.

"Lilly, before you go dress, I was wondering if there is . . . uh . . . some husband's privilege that you'd like me to exercise?"

That made her look up. She stared at him with eyes as round as a hoot owl's and stood frozen at the end of the bed.

"A husband's privilege?" she whispered in a tight voice.

He watched her from beneath shuttered lids as she appeared to be gathering the resolve to bolt.

"*Jah*, I thought there might be something that you wanted . . ."

She looked like she was considering as she put a slender hand up to feel for her *kapp*, which was askew from the night's sleep. Stray tendrils of rich brown strands fell in wisps around the fine bones of her face and neck.

"You think I want something from you?"

"Mmm-hmm."

She put her hand down and clutched her clothes in front of her like a shield.

He watched in some confusion as myriad expressions played across her face—anger, sadness, and then, reluctant determination.

She dropped the pile of clothes to the floor and stepped closer to where he sat.

"You want to know if I want something from you—something for the little wife to keep her feeling happy?" Her voice trembled with suppressed emotion.

"*Jah?*" He wondered where he'd made his mistake.

"Very well, Mr. Wyse."

She used her schoolteacher tone and he had the feeling that he'd just grabbed hold of the wrong end of a rattlesnake.

Did she want something from him? She wanted to give him a firm kick somewhere. Her tears had given way to a definite flame of anger, and she was furious with herself for even now letting her eyes stray to his bare chest. She dragged her gaze upward and saw uncertainty mingled with concern in his eyes. She dropped her arms to her sides and stood stiff and still.

He stood up and caught her close, then bent to kiss the tip of her nose. "You're riled about something, my *fraa*. I wonder what?"

She shrugged her shoulders and looked at his sock-covered feet.

"What have I said?" He reached to touch her hair with a gentle hand. "May I help you brush your hair?"

"What—do you mean?"

He smiled as she peeked up at him. "I'm a hand at grooming horses, but your hair is altogether different—it's so soft and smells like summer. It's like something from a dream—" He broke off, seeming to lose his train of thought, and she frowned.

But his hands were already at her hair, feeling for the pins that held her *kapp* in place.

"How many hairpins do you use?"

She tried to concentrate on the unusual question while his clever fingers began to find each pin in its hidden place.

"I don't—I mean, it doesn't matter."

"Sure it does," he coaxed, locating a pin behind one ear and bending to brush his lips against the spot.

She stared fixedly at his chest, trying to remind herself where his heart truly lay. She recited in her head the proper anatomical terms for the bones and muscles that moved and flexed in perfect symmetry before her. *Thorax . . . sternum . . . trapezius . . .*

With a flick of his wrist he tossed her *kapp* backward onto the bed, and she felt more of her hair begin to come loose. He bent his face close to hers, so that his own dark hair brushed her hot cheeks. "Well, teacher, you're trying to be a million miles away. Why is that?"

Her breath felt funny in her chest, like the time she'd raced some students to the top of Elk Mountain and had won. She couldn't help but meet his warm eyes and she tried once more to focus. *Iris . . . cornea . . . mouth . . .*

She pulled away from his arms, feeling confused and absurd, with one part of her hair up and the rest down. She hugged her arms protectively across her chest and knew she had to get things out in the open with him or she'd probably always feel consumed with the raw emotions he seemed to inspire. "You ask me what I want? Fine. I want truth between us, Jacob Wyse."

"Truth?"

"*Jah.*" She turned to face the window, not wanting to see his face when she spoke. "Do you still love her?"

There was a distinct quiet in the room that did little to reassure her.

"Sarah?" he asked finally.

"*Jah*, Jacob—Sarah." Her voice trembled and she clenched her hands into fists. "I must know." She turned to face him.

He shook his head once as though to align his thoughts in order to speak. *"Nee."*

"Truth!" she demanded.

"Why do you ask—"

"This morning you cried out in your sleep. You called for her. You said Sarah's name."

CHAPTER 23

$\mathcal{J}$f she'd struck him a physical blow, it couldn't have shocked him more. He sank down onto his marriage bed—the bed where he'd spoken the name of another woman. He had no doubt that what Lilly said was true. He frantically combed through his mind to catch the dream, but it eluded him. He was never much at remembering his dreams; they'd never seemed to matter. Though he knew the Bible said that sometimes the Lord would speak to one of His own in dreams. Yet now—now, something from his stupid mind had hurt his new bride—and badly. He couldn't imagine how he'd feel if Lilly had cried out the name of another man, but he knew it had to be the intense pain of a knife blade cutting. He stared at her bent shoulders and dropped his head in his hands.

"Lilly . . . I can't even begin to imagine how you feel. I'm so sorry."

"That's not good enough, Jacob."

"No, I know." He looked at her, feeling his face burn with shame. "I don't remember dreaming of Sarah."

"But you were. Admit it. To yourself. To me. You really do

love her still, maybe more than you even guessed. More than I could have guessed . . ." There was painful resignation in her tone, and it made his eyes sting.

He tried to think, to search his soul and mind, then remembered his fervent prayer of the night before.

"Lilly . . . I want to love you. To choose you."

"Choose me? You did that already, Jacob. It's called a wedding, remember?"

He rubbed his hand across his eyes. "Choose you first. Consciously. I-I've prayed about it. I don't want to have feelings for Sarah. I'm trying."

The room was quiet and he watched her think, his breath held. At last, she turned from the window, her slender body in silhouette from the sun's first rays.

"All right, Jacob. I knew what I was getting. I knew it. This is my fault too, for going forward, for believing that you could forget."

"I can forget. I will."

"No. Your will can accomplish nothing on its own." She took a deep breath. "The Lord must work this out between us. I . . . I forgive you though I cannot promise to forget."

He bowed his head at her words, then listened as she gathered her things and slipped from the room.

Lilly went about her morning chores examining her own heart. There was no sense being mad or keeping secrets in a marriage that she'd vowed to honor all of her life. She'd accept his apology but remember to keep him at a distance emotionally.

She rolled back the wine-colored sleeves of the blouse she'd changed into and smoothed her white apron over her black dress. Then she set about making a big breakfast, hoping that Jacob would enjoy it; she might as well proceed with an attitude of goodwill.

She'd have to get up earlier on school days now too, she considered, as she made potato cakes out of the wedding's leftover mashed potatoes. Tending to both her mother and Jacob's meals would probably require a little more time.

She looked over her shoulder with a tight smile as the master bedroom door creaked open and Jacob walked into the kitchen. He'd changed into an aqua blue shirt and dark pants, and his hair looked freshly combed.

"Scrambled eggs, fried ham slices, potato cakes, and tomato preserves for breakfast," she said low, attempting to be pleasant.

"That sounds *gut*." He clasped his hands behind his back and moved to look out the kitchen window where snow fell in thick flakes.

"I have to make some Christmas cookies after breakfast—for all the guests who are bound to come round."

"*Ach*, sure. That's fine."

She set a platter of the delicately fried potato cakes on the table.

"I forgot to mention," he spoke. "My *mamm* invited us over this afternoon. She said to bring your *mamm*, of course."

Lilly grimaced a bit as she turned the tender ham slices. "We must go—I'd love it, but I don't know if my mother will come or not."

"Do you mind leaving her for a bit at the holiday?"

"*Nee*, she'll be fine. And, like I said, the bishop makes sure people always drop over, but I suppose more will come today because of us—*Mamm* just won't answer the door if she's not feeling up to visitors." She brought the rest of the food to the table and surveyed the settings. "There—would you like to eat? *Mamm* will probably be up later and take something in her room."

He came to the table and then bolted through his food so fast that she'd barely had the chance to begin on her eggs. He rose and took his plate to the sink, rinsing it, then depositing it on the counter.

"I have the outside chores to do—the horses and the firewood. You needn't worry anymore about those things. I'll be back in a bit." And he was gone out the kitchen door with his coat half on and his scarf trailing loosely about his neck, dangling to his lean waist. As her eyes filled with unshed tears, she noticed he'd even left his hat behind.

Jacob walked rapidly to the haven of the barn and slid the door closed behind him as though he were being pursued. The horses nickered in greeting, but he couldn't think straight enough to respond. Instead he leaned his back against the support of the wooden door and closed his eyes.

His head swam with half-worded prayers. He'd asked for *Derr Herr's* help to choose to love his wife and then he'd called out for Sarah—on his wedding night. He tried again to grasp the dream, to rally his subconscious into some kind of obedience. But he couldn't remember, and Lilly had said she couldn't forget.

He expelled a breath of surrender. What had she said about his will? It was not his will that could work in all of this, but the Lord's.

He opened Buttercup's stall and greeted her with the back of his curled hand. Then he touched her gently on her withers. And she yielded to his touch. His *gentle* touch. *Yield.* He needed to learn how to yield to the Lord in the same way his horses learned to yield to the touch of his fingers—even those secret parts of his mind that seemed so far out of reach. Even his dreams needed to fall into the trust of the Lord.

CHAPTER 24

*D*espite how the day began, Lilly was having more fun than she could remember in years. She and Jacob were at the Wyse home for Christmas Eve supper. Mr. and Mrs. Stolis had been some of the many guests she'd received at her own home during the day, but they'd also offered to stay with her mother a bit, who actually seemed like she was up to having visitors. Lilly didn't ponder this shift in her *mamm's* moods; she'd grown used to their unpredictability. But she considered every moment of the time at her new in-laws' a blessing and smiled with determined warmth at Jacob when he glanced up from a chattering Kate Zook. He returned the look and she chose to interpret the intensity in his gaze as goodwill. Then she found herself in the cheerful embrace of her brother-in-law.

"Having a *gut* time?" Seth asked, dropping his arms about her waist.

"*Ach, jah.*" She smiled up into his handsome face, thinking to herself once more how different the two brothers were—like light and darkness.

She leaned close to Seth and whispered low. "I loved the painting. *Danki.*"

"Ah, my secret's out."

She shook her head. "I'd never tell anyone, but I would love to see more of your work."

"Would you?" he asked with a smile.

She nodded with sincerity and he caught her hand. "Then come with me, sweet *schweschder*, and I'll be glad to indulge you— away from this crowd."

She followed happily as Seth led her upstairs.

"I've been working on something a bit different. It's for Jacob's birthday. The motion is difficult to get right." He flung open a door and she entered the room, clearly seeing that it was more of an art studio than a bedroom, with paints, brushes, canvases, and tools in great abundance. He turned up a lamp, then held it before an easel. She gasped with pleasure at the half-formed image of a herd of horses running free across a vast plain.

"*Ach*, Seth! It's beautiful. It's like they're running toward me. I can hear their hoofbeats. You've been blessed with such talent."

He smiled with obvious pleasure. "*Danki*. I haven't been sure of this one."

"Jacob will love it. But, tell me please, when is his birthday?"

Seth set the lamp on a table. "Not until February—Valentine's Day, in fact."

I should have remembered, she thought. She'd once sketched him a valentine when they were in school but had never had the courage to give it to him. It had ended up in the waste bin. She glanced back at the painting.

"Seth, I know you don't want anyone to know about your talent, but it would be so wonderful if you'd teach a class on art, maybe to the schoolchildren?"

He held up paint-stained hands. "Whoa, little *schweschder*. That is not my kind of doings. *Kinner* scare me. I never know what they're going to do."

She laughed. It was so easy to be with him, so simple and comforting. With Jacob, she always felt like she was walking blindfolded, always taking a misstep with him.

"What are you thinking?"

She lifted her shoulders. "Just how different you and Jacob are."

"Are we?"

"Surely."

She watched him run an absent finger around the rim of a paint container.

"How?"

"What?" she asked.

"How are we different?"

"Well, you're fun and cheerful, but you've got this whole other serious side to you in your art. And Jacob—Jacob's like a storm, unpredictable, moving. I guess you'd know even better than me."

"I know my brother; he's part of my heart. But he can be distant as the *munn*. Sometimes too far away to touch."

"*Jah*," she agreed, her smile tight.

"But touch matters."

His tone was level but she felt drawn by his words. It was as if he understood the struggles she had—her insecurities and her fears about whether she'd ever truly be able to be close to her husband.

But there was something else—a flash of intensity in his blue eyes—as he half turned from her.

She stepped closer to him, laying a hand on his white sleeve. "Seth?"

He drew a deep breath. "Don't listen to me, Lilly. I think I'm half crazy. I love my brother."

"Of course you do," she soothed, watching him swallow, the strong line of his throat tan against his white collar.

"Of course I do. But he can be hurtful sometimes. Even if he doesn't mean it."

She sighed. "Well, *jah*, I guess you're right about that."

"Has he hurt you, Lilly?"

She had to turn away from him and blink at the sudden tears that filled her eyes, but she shook her head. *"Nee."*

She felt him touch her shoulders gently. "Lilly?"

She wanted to turn at the tenderness in his voice, to press herself against him and cry for what she was—insecure, wounded, and second-best. But to allow herself even that comfort would be disloyal to Jacob, so she stood, frozen.

His hand stroked the length of her back, tangible warmth she could feel and trust.

"Ach, Seth," she whispered in misery.

He moved, quick and fluid, to encircle her with his long arms and to press her against his chest. She heard his heartbeat and smelled the fresh cotton of his shirt as he reached his hand to find and soothe the tenseness at the back of her neck.

"I thought I could do it," she sobbed after a moment.

"Do what?"

She felt him begin to rock her in his arms, his dark clad legs steady and sure.

"To accept it . . . you know? That Sarah was . . . is . . . his first love. But I can't. He warned me the night of the engagement that it would be hard, but I didn't listen and now—" She lifted her tear-stained face to look at him and he bent his head to brush his mouth against her cheek.

"Shhh . . . Lilly, don't. Don't do this to yourself."

She swallowed, feeling foolish that she'd been so happy one minute and had now turned into a watering pot. "I'm sorry, Seth." She sniffed and would have drawn back when Jacob's voice arrested her from the doorway.

"Hiya. Do I interrupt?"

CHAPTER 25

*J*acob watched his brother holding his wife with a detached fury that surprised him in its intensity. He leaned against the doorjamb and spoke in a soft voice.

"Seth, I ought to whip your back raw for this. Go downstairs. Now."

"She needed comfort, Jacob. Something you're not willing to give."

"You've got about five seconds."

Seth slid his arms from around Lilly with visible reluctance. "Fine. You work this out, Jacob—if you can." He brushed past and Jacob had to restrain himself from laying hands on him.

He closed the door quietly, then turned to face her. She didn't look guilty, only sad, and he felt a renewed stab of self-recrimination and anger that he couldn't give her the easy comfort that Seth could. Then his prayers came back to him, and he felt *Derr Herr* speak deep inside. *Choose. Decide. Decide to give.*

He pushed off the wood of the door and came to stand in front of her. She had her arms crossed protectively against her chest and her blue eyes swam with tears.

He drew a deep breath. "My brother can gain anyone's admiration; he's quick-witted, even-tempered, talented—but, sometimes, in a way, he makes me feel like an old man. I've always thought that I had to be stronger, more cautious, and more serious—to protect him somehow."

He reached out to thumb away a stray tear that spilled down her cheek.

"I don't want to be all those things with you, Lilly. I want to be alive, to breathe, to be real." He trailed his hand down to rub the fine bones of her wrist, her tears dampening her soft skin. "Oh, Lilly . . . what was it your primer said? Touch?" He drew his finger across her stiff arms, then back up to trace the gentle curve of her shoulder. He stepped closer, thankful that she didn't retreat.

He used the back of his hand to cross her damp cheek, feather across her brows, then come back again to test the delicate bones of her arms.

He thought how small and refined she seemed for all of her slender height. She was a lady in so many ways, and she would, of course, be drawn to culture like Seth's art. He broke off the thought and gently reached both arms around her, not holding—waiting.

"I'm not Seth, Lilly. But I can give," he whispered.

He watched the indecision in her eyes, the haunting drift between his betrayal and her want. Then she spoke clearly and broke the circle of his arms.

"And I'm not Sarah, Jacob."

She wiped her sleeve across her eyes and made for the door, the sound of her footsteps echoing in his mind like stones thrown far away.

She hadn't taken more than five steps into the hall when she felt her heart convict her for crying out to Seth, and not God—nor to

Jacob. She remembered the quilting vision she'd had the night of the engagement and thought how far she'd drifted from that message in her life. And she knew she was trying to get away from that message when a dark part of herself began to whisper that she'd not even had a wedding quilting. Her feet found the top of the stairs of their own accord and she gripped the carved banister. What did a wedding quilt matter? What did it prove? That she was legitimately married? Well, she knew she was, and she'd just dishonored her husband with his own brother, no matter what her intent. The Lord had given her the idea to work to create something in life with Jacob. She felt like running back to the room and letting him hold her, but she couldn't. Not when she remembered his hoarse cry of Sarah's name and her resolve. She prayed that God would help her release her insecurity and found herself at the bottom of the steps.

If Mary Wyse knew there was something wrong, she gave Lilly no indication as she caught her arm and encouraged her to walk with her into the main room.

"Uncle Sebastian is telling stories—he's Samuel's uncle, really. He runs a logging outfit deep in the mountains and normally only comes down to have a visit at First Christmas. He's a character, but we all love him. You'll have to see."

Lilly smiled, hoping her face wasn't blotchy from her tears. She didn't see Seth anywhere and wandered in the direction her mother-in-law pointed her.

$\mathcal{L}$illy gathered close with other visiting *aentis*, uncles, and cousins, who listened with merry enjoyment as Uncle Sebastian regaled them with tales from the woods. The man was probably about seventy and, to her surprise, appeared to be partially blind in his foggy blue eyes. But his gnarled hands moved with certainty to accept the glass of milk and plate of gingerbread cookies that a cousin brought him. Lilly knew that here was a man who had experienced much of life and had endured, like the mountains he came from.

He wiped his mouth with the back of his hand, smiled, and recalled another tale. Lilly could see that everyone around her waited with pleasure for his words, even the adolescents who would normally keep to their own side of the room. Insolent Kate Zook also seemed momentarily transfixed.

"*Ach*, I was just reminded of the time one summer that me and the boys took a trip away to the Ice Mine . . . but you all probably know this one."

He was met with a chorus of protests and Lilly began to listen, loving the oral storytelling traditions of her people. Uncle Sebastian stroked his beard.

"*Jah*, it's always a wonder to me to visit that place. Now the *Englisch*, some of them call an ice mine a freak of nature, but that's not quite right because it is not an actual mine. It's really a deep shaft, put there by the Lord, I guess. When the ice formations appear during the spring of the year and continue through the hot weather, folks around can have fresh ice. But it's a funny thing— the shaft goes dry in winter; perhaps *Derr Herr* figures we've got enough ice on the ground then. The last time I went, me and the boys saw huge icicles measuring about as big around as a strong man's arm. The ice is real pretty too, clear and sparkling . . ."

"Oh," Lilly spoke up from back in the group. "How was this place found? It sounds lovely."

"*Ach*, well, a new voice . . ." He paused, then raised his voice. "And Jacob, you grow stronger every year. When will you leave your horses, eh, and bring that broad back up to the timber?"

Jacob laughed as Lilly noticed that her husband had drifted close. "I give my word we'll come for a visit this summer, sir," he said.

"*Ach*, I forget so easily—it's 'we' who'll be coming, but I hear that your Sarah married another man."

There was a distinct pause in the conversation around them, and Lilly tried to look normal as Jacob caught her eye in the sudden stillness. "I've recently come to realize that each woman is her own . . . not a man's to be had."

Lilly tried to ignore the feeling of chagrin his words produced and pulled nervously at her *kapp* string.

Uncle Sebastian pursed his weathered lips in thought. "So, did I miss a wedding or not?"

The family moved as Jacob reached his long arm through the small group to catch Lilly's hand and pull her forward, directly in front of the man.

"My bride, Uncle Sebastian, Lilly Wyse."

Lilly had to ignore the warmth of Jacob's hand on her own and focused instead on the strange feeling that she was being studied deeply . . . not just by the bleary eyes of the older man but somehow further. The expression "sight beyond sight" drifted across her consciousness as she stood in patience.

Uncle Sebastian put down his milk and cookie and held out a hand to her. She took it readily as Jacob let her go.

"Ahh," he murmured. "Now, here is one who is like my Rachel was. Hair dark as the shadows of a glen, eyes like hidden pools, and strong, *jah*, but a strength that yields—bends, but never breaks. You have chosen well, Jacob, but she lacks one thing."

Lilly had colored under the pointed remarks and hoped he wouldn't comment on her need for children. But he laughed, and she stared at him.

"*Nee*, my daughter, it is not the *kinner* that you want for, because I can see that they dance about you like drops of sunlight through the pines. *Nee*, you lack for something else, something even more precious. Do you know what it is, Jacob?"

Lilly felt the eyes of all turn to her husband, and she watched, knowing he was mentally sifting through answers.

Uncle Sebastian laughed again and tugged on her hand with remarkable strength. She leaned forward and bent close to him, breathing in the smells of the mountains and fresh air. "I will tell you, my beauty, because perhaps the Lord has not revealed it yet to you."

Lilly caught her breath and bent closer as the old man whispered a single word in her ear. She drew back a bit and stared into the wise eyes and felt tears come to her throat.

"*Nee*, no crying now, not on the eve of the Savior's birth." He patted her hand. "But you remember and perhaps let your Jacob know when you've found it, will you?"

She kissed his weathered cheek. "*Jah*, I promise." She wondered if the man could see her heart and knew how distant Jacob seemed to her.

But Uncle Sebastian let her go and began another tale.

She slipped away from the group. Jacob followed and caught her arm as she moved toward the kitchen to help *Mamm* Wyse.

"What did he say?"

Lilly shook her head. "I cannot tell you."

Jacob frowned. "He didn't say that."

"*Nee*, but I know it just the same. I've got to go and help your *mamm*."

She slipped from him, knowing he stared after her, and went to the fragrant and bustling kitchen to join the other women of her new family.

*L*illy concentrated on stirring the pot of cider to circulate the many good spices that had been added to the fragrant brew. She was lost in her own thoughts until the familiar sound of a girl's voice cut across her consciousness with sharp tones. She glanced over one shoulder to see Mrs. Zook hustling Kate into the adjacent pantry, and tried not to listen. But it was difficult when both mother and daughter's voices were so loud and strained.

"I told you, Kate, keep your voice down. You'll make fools of us as you make a fool of yourself by taking up with this *Englischer*."

"I don't care what you say, *Mamm*. Tommy Granger is nothing like his father. He hates his father, and I'm tired of playing second fiddle to a bunch of whey-faced girls who have no right to be married at all."

Lilly noticed the other women out of the corner of her eye and saw that they, too, overheard. She stirred harder, blinking back tears of frustration. Kate's whey-faced comment was not-so-subtly directed at her.

Her mother-in-law had obviously had enough and marched through the group to the pantry to speak in low, fast Penn Dutch. Then, there was a sudden silence and Kate ran from the small room to snatch her cloak from a peg and disappear outside. Mrs. Zook emerged, appearing as though she'd aged, and Lilly felt a moment's compassion for her. It could not be easy to manage a headstrong girl like Kate.

The women soon bustled back to various chores while Lilly handed Mrs. Zook a fresh cup of cider and the atmosphere drifted back to one of goodwill. But Lilly's heart still smarted from the younger girl's barb. She knew Kate's words stung because they were laced with the unfortunate truth.

CHAPTER 26

$\mathcal{T}$hey sat together in silence in the moving sled. Jacob held rein on Thunder as the horse sought to gather speed and slide the cutter along in the brisk night air. But Jacob was in no hurry to get home and face his marriage bed once more. For one thing, he'd told himself that he absolutely would not go to sleep, not if there was any chance that he'd make a fool of himself as he'd done the previous night. He didn't need that much sleep anyway and could always catch a nap here and there when he was back working at the horse farm. It seemed that a long life of dreamless nights sprawled before him unless he could put a bit and bridle on his *dumm* mind.

Then he thought of Seth and his throat ached. His fury had burned down to a gnawing hurt, and he had to concentrate on the road to keep from reliving the moments in the bedroom all over again.

"Your home is so alive, Jacob. You're blessed to have such a family," Lilly said.

"*Jah*, the Lord is *gut*." He searched his mind for something else to say, wanting to bridge the wide gulf that seemed to stretch between them. "Are you cold?" he asked, wondering if she'd just think it was an excuse to get her closer to him. He had to admit that was part of it. But he really was concerned about her. She finally scooted across the seat of the small sled and he thought he could feel the sweet warmth of her against his side, even through the thickness of his coat.

"I hope my mother was all right," she said. "But I suppose if she hadn't been, we would have heard. Your *mamm* sent a whole baking pan of sticky buns home to tempt her appetite."

"That's nice."

"Jacob, I'm sorry about Seth. I—didn't mean anything, but I was wrong. Please forgive me. It will never happen again."

He looked down at her face, pale with concern even in the darkness.

"You're forgiven. Don't worry about it. I mostly blame myself anyway."

She was silent and he strove once more for some balance of conversation. "It must be going to snow again tonight; my shoulder's aching."

"*Ach*, I'm sorry." She patted his gloved hand, then drew away, taking a deep breath. "I felt sorry for Mrs. Zook. Did you notice how tearful she looked at supper? I was really surprised at the argument that she and Kate had. Did you—could you hear them?"

"*Jah*, it was difficult not to."

"Do you think Kate will be all right? I mean . . . I know I've never been that fond of her—I've actually been quite jealous of her at times. But Tom Granger's son? It just doesn't seem right—even if it is her *rumspringa*."

He shrugged. "*Englisch* or not, the son may be different from the father, and we cannot judge."

She made a soft sound of agreement.

"I guess I feel like a person's got to make choices," he said. "And maybe I'm prejudiced, but it seems to me that women tend to get involved with other people's choices a lot more than men do."

Lilly gave a quick sniff. "Well, I hope you'd be involved if it were your daughter . . ." She broke off and he remained silent, unsure of what she wanted him to say.

She drew a small breath. "I guess the truth of why I'm interested in Kate Zook running around with an *Englischer's* son is because that jealousy hasn't really gone away. I'm still jealous of her—or something. And that sounds bad, like I want to be the one running around or having *rumspringa*—I mean, after tonight with Seth . . ." She trailed off anxiously and he decided to have mercy on the tangle of words she'd gotten herself into.

"Did you have a *rumspringa* or were you always sure about being baptized and joining the church?"

"*Jah*, I was sure; I didn't need a time of running around to know." There was a faint, wistful tone in her voice that belied her words and surprised him. Lilly, who seemed so steady and calm and logical, perhaps wanting to experience the outside world. It just didn't seem to fit with what he thought he knew of her.

"Tell me about your *rumspringa*," she ventured.

He half-laughed, remembering. "You don't want to know."

"But I do, really."

"*Ach*, it was . . . a mess, really." He let his mind drift back over the wild year when he'd been nineteen. Time stolen from the *Englisch* world came to him in a rush of flagrant images—baseball games and beer drinking, blue jeans and T-shirts hidden for quick changing in the back of his buggy. But also . . . the girls.

"Did you . . . I mean . . . you were waiting for Sarah, so you probably didn't . . ." Lilly broke off but he knew exactly what she was getting at.

"Didn't see other girls? *Englisch* girls?"

"Well, *jah*."

His mouth tightened with regret as he thought of the count-less times that year that he'd gone past what he knew was proper, nuzzling and kissing girls without any particular concern. It didn't matter how willing and eager the girl had been. It had been wrong. He'd rationalized his behavior with juvenile male pride that he was "practicing" for Sarah, so she'd get no bumbling fool for a husband. Now, he just felt cold by the meaningless moments and wished he could take back his behavior despite the fact that he'd confessed it in vague terms before he'd joined the church.

He sighed aloud.

"So—there was a girl . . . other girls?"

"*Jah*. I was young and stupid."

"Well, it was your time to choose. To experiment with the out-side world and its values."

"Yes, but sometimes experiments are not worth the cost."

She said nothing, but her intense expression showed she was working through something. He spoke with sudden intuition. "You want to be free sometimes, Lilly, don't you?"

She took a long time to answer. "Maybe. I'm not sure. Why do you ask?"

"Because you went from nursing your father to teaching school, to caring for your *mamm*, to marrying me."

"But those were all choices that I made."

"Those were choices you thought you *should* make—to do what was right, what was honorable."

"And so we're called to do. It's as we're instructed by *Derr Herr* and His Word."

"And Christ's declaration that He came to give abundant life . . . here and now, not someday—what about that?"

"My life is abundant," she said quietly.

He shook his head. "And that's what you still think you're

supposed to say. I want you to tell me what you'd like to do if you had absolutely no responsibilities. No mother to care for, no father to mourn, no job to work, no husband—just you. What would you do?"

He waited, feeling like he could virtually hear her sorting through answers, searching for the right one, the dutiful response.

"I don't know," she said finally, carefully.

"Why don't I believe you?"

"You don't have to."

"Lilly, *sei so gut* don't hide—even though I know you have a right to with me. Tell me what you'd like to do."

She blew out a frustrated breath. "All right—silly things I guess. I'd like to take my *kapp* off and dance in the first spring rain, eat candy instead of breakfast, see what an *Englisch* woman's magazine reads like." She paused, shaking her head. "See? This is a senseless conversation."

"Because I'm getting too near the hidden Lilly?" he persisted gently, watching her swallow in delicate profile.

"I . . . I don't usually allow myself to think about me, inside, that much. It's easier to keep walking forward."

"You're worth thinking about, Lilly Wyse."

She shrugged. "Well, it's foolishness to speak of anyway, Jacob. I have what I need."

Her answer was simple yet so complex in its layered meanings to his ear. He chafed at his inability to say what he wanted, what he thought she deserved to do—to have.

They turned in silence down the lane to the Lapp house, where the single lamp burned in the waiting darkness.

*W*hen they entered the house, Lilly slipped off her outer clothes and then tiptoed upstairs to find that her *mamm* had gone to bed early again. She came back down and put the still-warm sticky buns on top of the stove for a morning treat. Jacob hadn't taken off his coat, and she looked at him questioningly.

"I've . . . uh . . . got some late chores in the barn. Go on to bed. I'll be in later."

She watched him go back out into the darkness and sighed. Christmas Eve had set in with a swamping feeling of squelched expectation for Lilly, although she wasn't exactly sure what she had expected, especially after a morning and afternoon like they'd had. She sat at the kitchen table by the light of the kerosene lamp and crumbled a sugared Christmas tree cookie with her listless fingers, not feeling the least bit sleepy. Then she decided that she would not wallow on the eve of Christ's birth.

She and her mother hadn't decorated a Christmas gift table in the two years since her father had died, and Lilly decided that perhaps the traditional round table, decorated and ready for Christmas Day, might lift her mother's spirits. She pulled on her boots, extra wraps, and gloves, and caught up a kerosene lamp to make her way out to her father's small toolshed. The night was crystal clear, with the *munn* casting a yellowed gleam over the crusted snow. She saw the light between the crack in the barn doors but decided to let Jacob have the alone time he seemed to want. She reminded herself that she shouldn't care anyway.

She opened the small door of the shed and held the lantern high, peering inside at the jumble of tools and veterinary equipment that had not been disturbed for a long while. She would have to bring Jacob out to go through her father's things, she decided, and let him see if there was anything he might want.

She located the small hatchet, latched the door behind her, and set out in search of some pine boughs to place around the table's edge.

The *munn's* glow was almost so bright that she didn't need the lantern. She kept it lit anyway as she prowled along the land behind the barn, looking for a small pine tree suitable for surrendering a few fragrant branches.

As she crunched through the snow, she thought about Jacob's comment in the buggy that his shoulder ached. Although she'd patted his hand in a comforting gesture, she realized that she hadn't truly felt compassion for him—at least not heartfelt compassion. She gazed up at the moonlit sky and realized that she wasn't being very forgiving, especially at the time of Christ's birth when God brought his Son into the world to make provision for forgiveness and reconciliation. She became so lost in the consideration of the idea that she nearly walked into the small-needled pine that was just about her height and perfect for boughs.

She set the lantern down in the snow and knelt to reach where the lower, longer branches connected with the trunk. She should have gotten a hacksaw, she thought with irritation, as she tried to angle the hatchet in through the snow-laden limbs. Already the cold was seeping through her skirt as she awkwardly began to chop.

"What are you doing out here?"

She jumped and twisted on her knees to find Jacob towering over her, his shadow stretched long in the light of the lantern.

"Jacob! You scared me to death. I thought you were busy in the barn."

"I'm finished. Give me that." He dropped to his knees beside her. "You should have gotten a hacksaw."

She handed him the hatchet without a word and watched while he made short work of trimming off a few branches. Then he rose, put the hatchet under his arm, the boughs under the other, and reached down to haul her to her feet. They walked in awkward silence back toward the house and were almost there when Lilly stopped, convicted again about his shoulder.

"*Ach*, I forgot something in the barn."

"I'll go. What is it?" he asked.

"Horse liniment."

"What?"

"Liniment . . . you know . . . to tend the horse after it's been running."

"I know what it is. Why do you want it?"

She shrugged. "I just do."

He rolled his eyes. "All right. Take the branches and go in. I'll be there directly."

She turned to watch him trudge toward the barn through the snow, determination building in her heart.

CHAPTER 27

*L*illy had just finished smoothing a patchwork cloth over the small circular table she'd dragged into a prominent place in the sitting room when Jacob returned to the house, setting the large brown bottle of horse liniment onto the sink counter.

She entered the kitchen with resolve as he took off his hat and coat.

"*Ach, gut.* Will you please slip your shirt off your shoulder and sit down at the kitchen table?" *There. Her voice sounded detached and calm, with just a hint of wifely concern.*

Jacob turned from putting his hat on a nail. "What?"

She was not going to repeat herself. "Come on, it's late, and you'll feel ever so much better. It's an old trick of Father's—using the liniment, I mean."

She grasped the big bottle and uncorked it. The distinctive pungent odor of mint and other herbs spread through the air. She looked at him expectantly.

"I don't—what are you doing?"

She began to tap her foot, watching as he seemed to take an unwilling step closer to the table.

"Your shoulder, Jacob—you said it was hurting. I'll put some liniment on and it'll help. I want to help you as your wife should."

She saw myriad emotions cross his face. He was probably wanting to laugh at the idea of using a horse medicine and no doubt didn't savor the thought of her willing hands against his skin. She squelched the insecurity she felt and held to her purpose. He hurt; she was going to fix it.

"*Danki*, Lilly, but I'm fine, really. It was just a twinge."

"Slip your shirt down and sit."

"I said I'm fine."

"And so you may be." She stopped her foot tapping and turned her back to him. She did not want him to see the tears of frustration and hurt rising in her eyes. Perhaps there was only one woman he wanted to be there for him. "Will I not be your *fraa*, Jacob?" she asked.

Then she remembered the look on his face when he saw her and Seth in an embrace. It might be that hurt that kept him distant now. She sighed, the truth weighing heavily upon her. She needed to forgive him as much as she needed his forgiveness.

She heard the surprise in his voice. "Lilly, I'm sorry. Here, I'll do as you ask. Thank you for your help and concern."

She turned around in time to see him ease his suspender down and had to catch her breath. She frowned. She was not going to be moved by his nearness. She concentrated on moving the end of the kitchen bench for him. She watched as his reluctant fingers pulled one side of his shirt from the waistband of his pants and then reached for his collar.

She waited while he slid the fabric from his arm, and when an unaccounted flush burned her cheeks, she decided that the fire must be built too high in the woodstove. She clenched her teeth as he exposed his shoulder and bent his head. *I might as well get used to his undressing*, she told herself, reaching to adjust a stray tendril of hair from the side of her *kapp. He is my husband, after all—even if in name only.*

He sank onto the corner of the bench and put his elbows on the table.

"*Nee*. Just let that arm relax," she instructed.

He obeyed, dropping his left arm to hang down straight. She stepped over the bench, lifting her skirt in a bunch to sidle next to him. She tried not to notice his nearness and the scent of pine that clung to his skin.

"You don't have to do this," he muttered.

Oh, yes I do, she thought, angling closer to him.

"It's not a problem, Jacob."

She poured a handful of the liquid into her cupped palm, then put the bottle on the table.

"Is it very bad?" she asked, her hand poised near the scar.

Yes, her own mind whispered. *This whole idea is very, very bad somehow because it wasn't just about helping him any longer; it had become a hazardous intimacy.*

"No. Go on."

He jumped when she laid her hand against the back of his arm, causing her to startle as well, so that some of the liquid spilled from her palm and ran down the tanned length of his arm.

"Sorry," she choked. "Are you all right?"

"*Jah*."

Of course he was. It was only she who had these absurdly sensual thoughts.

Yet, perhaps he wasn't as unaffected as she thought. His breathing was shallow and he stared fixedly at the wood grain of the table.

She began to move her fingers in a circular motion against his skin, first soft, then with increasing pressure, watching his pulse throb in the line of his throat with each seeking pass of her hand.

"It's funny how your scar is beginning to look like a star in front here." She kept her tone conversational.

"I . . . I can't talk now," he confessed in a rush, and she felt a warmth radiate along her shoulders at his admission.

"You don't have to, Jacob. Just relax."

She sought to deepen his comfort. She moved her palm to the back of his arm, finding different nerves and tendons. Then she raised her other hand to brace against the back of his shoulder so that she might gain better pressure.

He made a choked sound from the back of his throat.

"Does it feel good, Jacob?"

He nodded and she allowed herself to smile, trying to ignore the whisper of her mind. She wanted him to be unable to recall the ache of the wound. She wanted her hands to become an anchor for him, a rock thrown in the center of a pond—with him part of the resonance, the rippling outlay of wet and warmth and . . .

She stopped and rose, putting the cork back in the bottle. *That was quite enough.*

He let his head fall forward on the table atop his other arm.

"Now just sit there a moment, and I'll put a cloth round your shoulder, so you needn't get your shirt stained."

He didn't move until she'd finished her ministrations. Then he lifted his head and looked at her with distant eyes and a faint smile on his face.

"Jacob, are you falling asleep? Why don't you go to bed? I'll show you the Christmas table in the morning."

He agreed, brushing past her with murmured thanks, then moving to the bedroom, leaving her behind with her hands tingling from far more than the burn of the liniment.

He sprawled facedown across the bed and felt the pull of deep sleep, something he'd thought to deny himself. But he was shaken, rattled to the core, by the touch of his wife, and sleep seemed like the least problematic way to handle the situation.

He looked so deeply asleep when she entered that she decided not to disturb him despite his domination of the bed space. She hastily changed into her nightgown and took down her hair, extinguished the lamp, and curled up in the rocking chair with an extra quilt.

Happy Christmas, Lilly."

She woke slowly, unsure if the brush of Jacob's lips against her mouth was real or part of a dream. She opened her eyes to find that the sun's rays were beginning to climb the frosted window, heralding the day of Christ's birth. She stretched beneath his gaze, feeling stiff and sore from her night in the chair, but smiled up at him just the same—before she caught herself.

She wondered if he'd dreamed of Sarah again last night.

"Happy First Christmas, Jacob."

He was already fully dressed, wearing a green shirt that she remembered from Meeting that especially brought out the color of his eyes.

"Why the chair?" he asked.

"*Ach*, you were sleeping so soundly that I didn't want to disturb you."

He nodded and turned away from her to face the bed. "I . . . uh . . . I've been thinking, Lilly. I decided that it might be best if I slept on the floor for a while." He went on in a rush while she felt her heart drop. "I think I'm used to a bigger bed—or something. And, when we both go back to work, we'll . . . uh . . . need a good night's rest. I believe the floor's a *gut* idea. What do you think?" He turned back to her.

She struggled to reply, feeling bereft somehow. "That's . . . fine, but surely you'll be cold?"

He gave her a cheerful grin, and she sensed his relief. "I'm as hearty as a horse. Throw me a couple of quilts and I'll be right as rain."

She nodded, and he clapped his hands together as if marshaling his thoughts. "All right. I did the chores already. I'll leave you to dress and I'll peel the potatoes for lunch. I don't think your *mamm's* up yet."

She wet her lips. "I'll check on her in a bit. I'll hurry."

He was already at the door. "No hurry. Take your time, teacher. I know how to start getting things ready for the noon feast." He left the room with a whistle, and she sat still beneath the quilt, feeling the desperate urge to pray.

Well, Lord . . . he can't even sleep next to me. He loves Sarah so much—maybe I was wrong, Father. Wrong about everything. Maybe I tried to convince myself that this wedding was Your will. Maybe it was my own.

She half-sobbed aloud at the thought, then had the sudden desire to talk to Alice. She decided to dress and run over to the Planks' for a few minutes, rising with determination, wiping away her tears.

CHAPTER 28

*A*lice was in the midst of food preparations and alone in the kitchen when Lilly peered briefly through the back door window, then gave a quick knock. If Alice thought it was strange that she was not at home with her new husband on their first Christmas morn together, she gave no indication.

Lilly hugged her friend, then sank down at the kitchen table.

"What's wrong?" Alice set two mugs of steaming cider on the table and waited. Lilly wet her lips, unsure of where to begin.

"*Daed* and Jonah are outside doing chores," Alice prompted.

"Everything is a mess. I . . . I think maybe I made a mistake. That I was trying to say I'd heard God's voice in marrying Jacob, but maybe it was just my own desire. And, I know you asked me about this before the wedding. Maybe I should have listened."

"Did you have a fight?"

Lilly shook her head, realizing she couldn't explain about the bed or Jacob calling Sarah's name without feeling like she was betraying him somehow. She let her head fall into her hands.

Alice patted her arm. "Lilly, I've known you since we were

kinner. Don't try and second-guess yourself. You made a decision and went through with it. God doesn't abandon us, even if it is our own plans that we're seeking. He always takes us from where we are. I guess it just takes awhile longer sometimes, when we decide to break our own path instead of using the one He lays before us."

Lilly lifted her head and wiped at her nose with a handkerchief she'd pulled from her sleeve. "*Danki*, Alice. I needed a place to run to for a few minutes."

Alice laughed. "Run away here anytime, my friend."

Lilly slipped back into her house like a wraith. Jacob still stood at the stove, but he looked up with a hesitant smile to greet her. "Is Alice having a *gut* holiday?"

"*Jah*. I'm sorry, Jacob, for just running out like that. I . . . I've got to check on my *mamm*. I'll be down shortly."

He tried not to watch her go up the stairs, but he couldn't help himself. Somehow, everything was wrong and it was all his fault. He felt a pang of homesickness wash over him—homesickness for something he couldn't describe. A sure place in the world. A true heart. He swallowed as his eyes blurred and he longed to touch Lilly, to give her comfort and wipe away all the pain his words and thoughts had caused her. He wanted to wrap her in a wedding quilt, a real wedding quilt, patterned by hands that loved and nurtured. He thought about her against the imaginary fabric, her dark hair loose and flowing—

A soft knock on the back kitchen door startled him from his thoughts and he ran a hand across his eyes and left his cooking. Surely it wasn't a neighbor so early . . .

He opened the door and saw Seth and his heart filled with a rush of emotion.

"Jacob?"

His younger *bruder's* eyes were deeply shadowed and he stood as though he carried an impossible weight on the breadth of his shoulders, wringing the circle of his hat through his hands.

"Seth, come in."

"I . . . can't. I've been such an idiot and I wanted you to know how sorry I am. I hurt you—and Lilly. I've been up all night, praying. I don't know. Maybe I was jealous because you had someone wonderful, and I didn't think you were treating her right. Maybe I thought your marriage would come between us. I've tried to figure it all different ways." He drew a shuddering breath. "Anyway, that's all. I wanted you to know." He turned as if to go and Jacob caught him by the shoulder.

"Come in here, little *bruder*." Jacob struggled to keep his voice from shaking.

Jacob caught Seth in a strong hug, squeezing him until he heard his back crack. Then he laughed, yanking his brother's cold coat sleeve.

Seth entered with his head down and Jacob closed the door behind him.

"Lilly's upstairs with her *mamm*. Look, I could have wrung your neck when I saw you with her, but you made me aware of something I think. I was so mad. I don't get that mad if I don't care, Seth." He lowered his voice and met Seth's anguished but hopeful blue eyes.

"*Nee*, you don't."

"So you're not in love with her?"

"I love her because she's yours, Jacob, but I'm not *in* love with her. And I don't blame you if you don't believe me. I don't even think I know what real love is anyway."

Jacob smiled. "Someday you will. And then—I owe your wife a hug."

Seth punched his *bruder* on the arm, then returned the embrace that made the world right once more between them.

CHAPTER 29

*L*illy crossed the upstairs hallway and knocked on the door with trepidation.

"*Kumme* in, Lilly."

Lilly was amazed at the warmth in her mother's voice and opened the door in some confusion. Her *mamm* was dressed and seated on the edge of her made bed, concentrating on braiding her long, grayish-brown hair. She turned to look at Lilly over one shoulder.

"Happy Christmas."

"Happy Christmas, *Mamm*, what . . . I mean . . . it's so good to see you up bright and early."

"I thought we should prepare for guests today. You know the bishop always makes sure that the widows are visited properly . . . although, now, with your marriage, I'm not really without a family any longer . . ."

Lilly sagged against the door, unsure of what to think. It was one thing to see the occasional lifting of her mother's spirits, the fleeting good mood, but to have her seem so vital was confusing.

"Are you . . . all right, *Mamm*?"

"*Jah*, I'll be down shortly to help with the meal preparations. Run along now and help your husband . . . I can smell the stove going."

"All right."

Lilly walked down the stairs, rubbing her forehead. She went into the kitchen and leaned against the counter.

"What's wrong? Is your *mamm* poorly?" Jacob put down a wooden spoon and came closer to her.

"*Nee* . . . she's better . . . or something."

"Now that's a Christmas miracle, *jah*? Great!"

She shook her head and met his eyes. "No . . . it's . . . there's something wrong. I don't know what it is, but I can tell. I can feel it. I'm scared, Jacob."

He put his hands on her shoulders and looked at her with concern. "Maybe you're overtired, Lilly. Surely your *mamm* feeling better doesn't scare you, does it?"

"I don't know . . . I guess it sounds strange."

He smiled and bent to kiss her cheek just as they heard her mother coming down the stairs.

"Go on and sit down a minute, Lilly," he whispered. "I'll put the teakettle on."

She did as he instructed, watching in amazement as her mother joined them at the table to make conversation and to talk with excitement about the coming day.

Later, with a rare smile, *Mamm* accepted Lilly's gift of crocheted snowflakes. Then she gave them a small cedar box which Lilly knew had been a gift from her father to her mother, one she held especially dear. "I want you both to have it . . . a keeping box, Hiram called it. You both can keep your memories inside."

Lilly smiled and started to relax as she caught glimpses of the woman she knew her mother could be. She decided that she'd been silly in her fears and that *Derr Herr* was perhaps giving them a very special Christmas gift indeed.

$\mathcal{L}$illy's mother retired at a much later hour than usual, after a day of visiting with company and more pleasant talk than she'd uttered in a lifetime—or so it seemed to Lilly. Now she and Jacob sat in chairs near the gift table and he smiled at her in the warm lamplight.

"I forgot to tell you that Seth came by this morning. He . . . wanted to apologize."

"I bet that was the best Christmas gift you got today," she said, thinking how much Jacob loved his *bruder*.

"And I bet the best gift you had today is how you must be feeling about the change in your mother."

"Well," she said, lowering her lashes, "I'll treasure your present always." She lifted the folded piece of leather from the table and realized how much time it must have taken for him to make the book cover. It was detailed workmanship of the finest quality, with intricate vines and flowers intertwined in abundant patterns etched into leather.

He laughed. "*Gut.* I'm glad you like it."

She laid the book cover back on the table, then reached into her apron pocket for his gift. She'd debated for half the day with herself as to whether or not she should actually give it to him. It had seemed like a good idea at the time, but perhaps he'd find it silly. She sighed and passed him the simply wrapped small parcel.

"And here's your gift, Jacob."

"*Danki.*" He smiled, clearly pleased. She watched him open it. He pulled out the square of plain cotton fabric and held it closer to the light of the lamp.

"It's a square," he observed.

She laughed. "I'm sorry. It's not just a square. It's a quilt square.

Your own. I remembered what you told me about Miss Stahley, and I thought, well, maybe you'd like to make a quilt square during one of our tutoring sessions, and I could add it to our class's spring quilt."

He was quiet for so long that she feared she'd offended him somehow, but when he looked up, his eyes were golden-green and full of emotion. He shook his head and the lamplight caught on the stray blond strands of his hair. Lilly thought he'd never looked so serious, nor so handsome.

"Lilly . . . it's so . . . nice. And *gut*. You make me feel like you can see inside of me, like you listen to me . . . thank you." His chair creaked as he leaned forward to embrace her with warm arms, then folded the square carefully and tucked it into his pants' pocket.

She gazed at the present table once more, where handmade decorations of clay and paper trimmings nestled among the pine boughs. He began to ask her about each clay ornament until she slowly began to reveal forgotten parts of her life.

"The Christmas tree is from second grade year," she recalled as he carefully held the faded green dough.

He turned the tree in his palm toward the light of the lamp. "I can still see your tiny fingerprints in the dough."

She took it from him, smiling; it seemed an intimate observation. And she wasn't sure how to respond.

"You still have small hands," he said as she placed the tree back among the aromatic pine branches.

"Do I?" she asked, extending her hands with innocence toward the light. He touched her then, soft strokes of one callused thumb over her knuckles. And she stilled, like a rabbit in the snow, until the moment was broken by the sudden intonation of the clock and a brief clicking noise, like the closing of a door.

"Did you hear that?" she asked, glancing over her shoulder and drawing from him.

"It was probably just the house creaking." He looked back to the table. "Tell me about this material here. It almost looks like a quilt top."

She smiled in memory and caught up an edge of the gay patchwork fabric. "*Ach*, this is my favorite. My father and I sewed it together when I was a little girl."

"Only a real man and a *gut daed* would not be ashamed to quilt with his daughter," he said with warmth.

"I know. That's how he was."

He caught her hand against the fabric. "I miss him too, Lilly. He taught me so much when I was young."

"I used to watch you come over to the barn from my window." His eyes gleamed at her confession.

"Did you now? I should have paid more attention . . ." He trailed off and she kept from mentioning the fact that his thoughts had probably been occupied by Sarah.

"I remember once that Father had a large, unbroken black gelding out in front of the barn and he left you holding the horse's lead to go and get something from his shed. The horse must have spooked or something because it started to toss its head and prance around, obviously very agitated. I was terrified for you. But you just stood there, relaxed and calm. I don't know what you did, but he seemed to quiet some. And then you reached out and touched him. And he just stood still. The more you touched him, the calmer he became."

"I remember that. I was scared out of my mind that the horse would rear or kick, or completely take off. But I knew if I could be calm and relaxed, he might take cues from me. So, I just breathed into his nostrils and did the rest on intuition."

They were silent for a moment, then Lilly drew a deep breath. "Do you think *Derr Herr* gives us intuition at times, to help us do His will?"

"If you mean the way we stepped into our engagement and wedding, then yes."

She moistened her lips in thought, then rose from her chair. "We should go to sleep. *Danki*, Jacob, for a *wunderbaar* first Christmas." She bent as if to hug him, then simply touched his shoulder and hurried to their room.

*J*acob sat for a while, perplexed at the emotions that seemed to rush past him whenever Lilly was near. His arm ached and he longed for another dose of liniment—especially if it could be anything like the last time. He sighed aloud, wanting to give Lilly time to change her clothes and get into bed before he took up his self-imposed place on the floor. He knew she wasn't all that happy with the idea, but he couldn't trust himself—in more ways than one. In that moment he realized he wasn't worried about saying Sarah's name in his sleep again; he just didn't want to risk touching his *fraa's* white skin while he dreamed . . .

CHAPTER 30

*J*acob moved to turn off the lamp. He paused, feeling a compelling urge he couldn't ignore. He lifted the lantern, walked through the room to the kitchen, and then to the back door. He slipped on his boots, opened the door, held the lamp up, and stared outside into the bitter cold, unsure of what he looked for. He almost went back inside, when once again he felt that he shouldn't. He paused. Turned. Walked across the back porch and down the steps, feeling the wind bite through his shirt. He told himself that he'd just go check on the livestock, then go back inside. He felt he must surely be tired or too occupied with thoughts of Lilly to think straight.

He almost tripped when his boot came in contact with something. He swung the lamp in front of him and the shine caught on the bluish white of Mrs. Lapp's face and closed eyes, then on her exposed arms, summer nightdress, and pale, bare legs and feet. He almost choked as he tried for a second to process the image, and then he was down on knees, scrabbling in the snow to slip his arms beneath his mother-in-law. The light tipped and went out as he caught her against his chest. He rose and began to run with her slight weight to the shadow of the kitchen door.

*L*illy came out of a sound sleep to hear Jacob calling her name. She ran from the bedroom to see him bending over the kitchen table, lamps lit, his arms moving feverishly over what appeared to be a bundle of quilts.

"Jacob, what's wrong?"

She ran to his side, then saw her mother's white face and blue lips in waxen relief against the wood of the table. She sucked in her breath and put her hands to her mouth in horror.

"She's alive, Lilly. She's breathing, but we've got to get her warm . . . better than this . . . We've got to get her to the hospital . . ." He muttered frantically as he rubbed her mother's arms beneath the quilts.

"What happened . . . *ach*, what happened?" Lilly thought she might vomit. Instead she moved in a daze to rub her *mamm*'s ice-cold leg.

"I found her . . . outside, lying in the snow . . . Lilly, I've got to go and get Grant Williams right now. He might be able to warm her up better . . . an ambulance might take too long . . . Can you stay here? Rub her arms and legs . . . try some warm cloths . . . I won't be long." And he was gone, coatless and hatless out the still-open kitchen door before she could say a word.

She sobbed aloud and ran to close the door, then took a deep breath. *Think*, she told herself, and began to pray. She snatched the bottle of liniment from the counter and spilled some of its contents into her shaking hands. She set about reaching beneath the quilts, spreading the herbal warmth across her *mamm*'s chest and down her arms.

"Help me, *Gött* . . . help her . . . help me, help me."

Finally she lifted the quilts to climb upon the table and lay her body across her mother's. She closed her eyes, listening to the faint heartbeat. She slid her hands to clasp at the body that had given her life and prayed that Jacob would hurry.

She became aware that strong, gentle hands lifted her. She sobbed, not wanting to move.

"It's all right, Lilly . . . it's all right . . ." Jacob cradled her against him and her eyes snapped open.

"My *mamm* . . . ?"

"Grant's here now. It's all right."

She struggled in his arms and he set her down. She leaned against his cold bulk as Grant Williams bent with a stethoscope over her mother.

"Heartbeat's fairly steady . . . but there's no way for me to accurately measure core body temperature. I've got the basic equipment but I won't take the risk of running fluids to warm her—not in this setting. We've got to get her to the hospital." He lifted his blond head and nodded briefly at Lilly. "You probably saved her life with the liniment and the external warming, but there are still some risks. Get me all the tinfoil you have. Jacob, bring the buggy round; we have no time."

They both scrambled to obey. Lilly ran in confusion to the pantry and brought out the large roll of tinfoil.

"Great." Grant grabbed the roll and flung back the quilts. He glanced at Lilly. "I've got to take her gown off . . ."

"Yes," she said.

He was quick and gentle, wrapping her mother's limbs close to her body with the foil. "It acts as a heat conductor," he explained. "Keeps heat in as well." He continued the foil wrapping all the way up around her head, leaving room for her face, then he piled back on the quilts and picked her up.

"You're coming, of course. Put a coat on over that gown and let's go." Lilly pulled on her cloak and bundled her hair down the back of her neck, inside the wool. She rammed her feet into a pair of boots, then realized that she still clutched her mother's nightgown of summer cotton. She followed the doctor out to where Jacob waited with the buggy.

CHAPTER 31

*H*ere, drink this."

Jacob slid a Styrofoam cup into Lilly's hands and watched until she took a sip of the hot chocolate. They were in the Lockport Hospital's ICU waiting room and had been there for an incredibly long two hours without news.

Grant Williams paced the hall, obviously not wanting to disturb them, and Jacob was grateful for his consideration.

Lilly sat still and straight, her slender hands still holding her mother's nightgown. He tried to hug her, but she wouldn't relax, so he just sat beside her. They were alone in the room, and he prayed the passing time would not bring bad news. Grant had mentioned something about possible organ damage.

"She must have been walking in her sleep," Lilly said.

"What?" It was the first full sentence she'd said in an hour, and he stared into her blue eyes, huge in her white face.

She looked at him and spoke matter-of-factly. "My *mamm* . . . somehow she must have been walking in her sleep."

He took a deep breath, then turned away from her for a moment, slowly shaking his head. "No, Lilly."

"What do you mean, no?" she snapped.

He looked back at her and watched as her cheeks filled with angry color.

"Lilly . . . I don't think this was an accident."

"Of course it was." Her bottom lip quivered. "Of course it was."

He felt his eyes well with tears and reached to draw her close. She yanked herself away from him. "Don't touch me."

He let her be, just once brushing her hand. He waited.

She drew a shuddering breath. "Her gown . . . it's a summer one."

"I know."

"It's just so silly . . . her choosing a summer gown on Christmas day . . ." Her voice broke and she curled into herself, drawing her knees up and rocking slightly.

He moved to gather her to him, and this time she collapsed against his chest. He ached to absorb her pain, to take it from her somehow.

"Lilly, it's going to be all right."

She pulled back to stare up at him. "How could she do that? How could she . . . I should have known. I thought something was wrong earlier . . . I might have stopped her."

"*Nee*, this has nothing to do with you."

"She seemed so happy—"

She broke off when a man cleared his throat.

"Mr. and Mrs. Wyse . . . I'm Doctor Parker."

Jacob rose to shake the *Englisch* man's hand while Lilly visibly composed herself and straightened upright on the couch.

"Would you mind if I pull up a chair?"

Jacob grabbed a plastic-backed chair. "Here, doctor. Please sit down."

"Thank you."

Jacob sat back down and caught Lilly's hand in his own.

"Mrs. Lapp is going to be fine . . . physically," Dr. Parker began.

Lilly stiffened next to him, then spoke.

"*Physically*, doctor?"

"Yes, her vital signs are good. There is no organ damage that we can find. She's come around a bit. We'll have to watch her, of course, but, as I said, I believe her to be out of danger at the present."

"That's good news, Doctor," Jacob said, waiting for the rest as he studied the concern in the other man's eyes.

"Do either of you happen to know why she was outside? Dr. Williams said she was wearing a summer gown." He glanced at the fabric Lilly clutched in her lap.

Jacob squared his shoulders. "We understand that this was not a mistake."

"*I* don't understand," Lilly said firmly. "She was *gut* today . . . eating well, talking . . . ."

Dr. Parker nodded. "Yes, unfortunately that is sometimes the case when someone has made the decision and come up with a plan. They almost feel relieved, released somehow that their pain will soon be over."

"My mother had no plan. We'd just entertained visitors."

"Mrs. Wyse, how long has your mother been depressed?"

"She . . . she's not been the same since my father died. That was two years ago."

"I see."

Jacob exhaled. "Doctor . . . we . . . we just thought that she was changed by her husband's death. Feeling poorly, you might say. Is there . . . is there something else we might have done, that we could do to help her?"

Dr. Parker spoke gently. "Please, don't blame yourselves. I've lived in this area for nearly twenty years and I have a great deal of respect for your people and your ways. Because of who you are and how you live, clinical depression doesn't typically occur in your community at the rate that it does in the outside world. But it does occur, and it's a very real illness. Yet it's one that responds well to medicine and to proper counsel."

"To medicine?" Lilly asked. "I . . . I don't know . . ."

"Mrs. Wyse, please don't be afraid of the medications. They are very effective and can make all the difference in someone's life—sometimes the difference between wanting to live and wanting to die. And, in addition to that, medicine can help improve a person's quality of living, their daily life."

"I see."

Jacob felt her turn to him and he looked down into her tear-stained face. "Lilly, we've got to try and help her. *Derr Herr* gives a doctor wisdom and medicines that work. Should we turn our backs on that blessing?"

She shook her head and then faced the doctor. "Please do whatever you can . . . I . . . I want my mother to have a better life."

Dr. Parker smiled. "We'll keep her here in the hospital for a time. Our fourth floor houses an inpatient mental health care unit. She'll stay for two weeks so that we can stabilize her medication and provide her with therapy before you take her home. I appreciate your support, Mrs. Wyse, Mr. Wyse." He shook their hands and then walked from the room. He paused briefly to talk with Grant, then continued down the hall.

Lilly sighed aloud and her voice quivered. "I pray this is right, Jacob."

"It is, Lilly. You will see."

CHAPTER 32

To Lilly's great surprise, over the ensuing two weeks, the community arose as one gentle, palpable force to bring help and solace and hope to her family. She was greatly humbled by the outpouring of visitors, food, and compassion. It wasn't that she did not expect the best from her people, but issues of mental health seemed seldom discussed or even heard of. She hadn't thought anyone would understand.

Bishop Loftus, for all of his age and distinct ideas, was of a particularly progressive frame of mind when it came to mental health. He made sure that Lilly could feel good about not having to visit the hospital each day by making a schedule of other women to go in her stead. And he contacted a mental health organization in Lancaster, established by and created for those Old Order Amish who struggled with depression and other mental health issues. A representative would come to the area and provide counseling at the hospital for her mother and then find similar lay support in the community.

In all of this, Lilly gave thanks. Especially for Jacob's stalwart presence and openness to talk and be supportive about her mother. His responsiveness revealed a depth and reservoir of grace that she'd only seen before in her father.

Jacob smiled when she'd confided this one evening after dinner. "You have the heart of grace, my *fraa*, which is why you can see good things in me."

Lilly had felt her cheeks glow with pleasure and kissed his handsome cheek.

*I*t was just before Old Christmas, or the observance of the Epiphany, when the community began to circulate word that a new family was moving into the small, vacant Stahley farmhouse less than a mile north of the schoolhouse. Grace Beiler, a widow, and her seven-year-old son, Abel, were coming from Ohio to Pine Creek to live. Mrs. Beiler's husband had drowned in an ice fishing accident that winter.

Grace Beiler was a first cousin of the King family, and everyone in the community strove to prepare the house to make her feel welcome. Early one Friday before school was to resume, Lilly finished some chores that she had at the schoolhouse, then drove the buggy over to help with the cleaning of the place while the menfolk saw to the roof and other repairs.

When she entered the small kitchen, it was already a hive of activity. The women were having a *vrolijk*, a time of working and socializing together, and they welcomed Lilly with warmth into their midst.

Mrs. Stolis was painting the white drywall of the kitchen a soft peach color. She handed Lilly an extra brush. "How's your *mamm* these days, child?"

Lilly was aware of the interested but kind ears listening for her reply so she gave a noncommittal shrug. "Better. *Danki*. She should return home in a week or so."

Mrs. Stolis smiled and nodded as Lilly focused on her brush-strokes and trying not to get paint on her apron.

The sound of someone jostling through the front door of the house came through to the kitchen, and Lilly heard Seth Wyse's voice. She wondered where Jacob was in all the busyness and was surprised by her desire to drop the paintbrush and go have a look for him.

Seth stood in the kitchen archway with a thin piece of wood in his hands.

"Ladies. Peach paint and all as pretty as peaches, I see." His grin swept the room, and Lilly focused back on her painting. Despite the peace that now reigned in the relationship between her husband and his brother, she thought it wise to remember that she had not been immune to Seth's empathetic charm and she never wanted to make that mistake again.

"I need to set up a quilting frame, ladies."

"Going to take up quilting, Seth?" Mrs. Stolis asked while the others laughed.

"*Nee*, not just yet, but Mrs. King sent me over. It seems the Widow Beiler makes her living quilting, so we've got to have a *gut* frame ready for her."

"You'll have trouble fitting it in the front room," one of the women remarked.

"Well, we'll give it a try. Jacob's bringing in the other pieces now."

Mrs. Stolis laughed and tapped Lilly's arm. "Do you wonder where Jacob is at every moment, Lilly? That's what it is to be newly married. I only wonder where James is when he's late for supper."

All the women laughed, and Seth cleared his throat.

"Ladies, I'll be leaving before this conversation gets any more questionable on the value of men and where they are in your lives."

Mrs. Stolis turned to Lilly when he'd gone and whispered,

"I've heard it said that he's a tortured soul . . . longing for true love . . ." She waited expectantly and Lilly struggled not to laugh.

"*Ach*, so it's true, I'm afraid, and all his cheerfulness is but a ruse . . ." She let the idea dangle as the women gave a collective soft sigh, and Lilly knew Jacob would have been proud of her.

*C*ome here," Jacob whispered in an urgent voice.

"What do you want? I'm busy," Seth said.

"Just get in here."

Jacob had finished fitting the quilt frame into the front room of the house and now stood outside the small barn, motioning to his brother before anyone might notice.

Seth finally ambled over and Jacob grabbed his arm, hauling him inside the dim interior and sliding the door shut. The men had just finished refitting the barn's structure and were doing a general cleanup. Jacob turned up a lantern and took a deep breath of the sweet smell of baled hay.

"All right, what's the big secret? I'm supposed to be helping Father with the upstairs windowsills."

Jacob reached into his coat pocket and withdrew the primer that Lilly had given him as a wedding gift. He held it out to his brother.

"What's this? Hey, these sketches are great—and a bit suggestive!" Seth turned the small booklet to better see the pictures, and Jacob smacked his arm.

"Lilly made it for me for our wedding."

Seth smiled. "No wonder you wanted to strangle me on Christmas Eve. If I'd have known that this is what you two were sharing . . ."

"We're not sharing any—I mean, she's supposed to start giving me reading lessons soon."

"They never had books like this when I was in school."

"Hey, I'm serious. I really want to try. But I don't want her to think that I'm completely *dumm*."

"Only a little then?"

Jacob sighed and snatched the book back. "Never mind. Go on and help Father."

"All right, all right. I'm sorry. What do you want me to do?"

"I just thought that if you could teach me some of the words first, that I could memorize them, and then when she tutors me, well, I wouldn't look like a fool."

Seth was quiet for a long moment. "You never look like a fool, Jacob." His voice was serious.

"Right—that's why I write like a *boppli*, and can't read, and steal horses, and let girls marry me without any consideration for how they really feel."

"I mean it. I look up to you."

Jacob lifted his eyes to meet his *bruder's*. "Thank you, Seth."

"All right, then let's give this a whirl. You'll surprise that smart wife of yours and maybe get a few kisses in the process."

Jacob cuffed him on the shoulder. "You're a *gut* little *bruder*."

"And don't you forget it."

CHAPTER 33

*L*illy felt weary but happy at what she and the other women had been able to accomplish in the little house. Once she finished the kitchen, she'd gone on to scrub the hardwood floors, wash the windows, and work at stocking the small pantry to bursting with contributions of canned and dry goods.

She'd been so absorbed in the work that she hadn't realized that several hours had passed. She slipped on her cloak and went outside. There were still some men working here and there on the porch railing and steps, but there was no sign of Jacob. Then a light from the crack in the barn door caught her eye.

She walked over and would have entered when Seth's voice, raised in unusual frustration, gave her pause. She glanced over her shoulder, then leaned her ear closer to the door, the better to hear.

"Look, just memorize it already! I am not going to teach you to sound it out first. You'll just look like a fake. Let her think that you can grasp the whole word! And, Jacob, come on, with these drawings it's not too tough to figure out the word!"

Lilly nearly jumped when her husband's voice growled in

response. "I know how she thinks. She's not going to buy it unless I—"

"Unless you what, Jacob?" Lilly stood still in front of the now open barn door as the two brothers scrambled guiltily to their feet from where they'd been sitting on stools near the workbench. They both had their coats off and their sleeves rolled up, and each was flushed with angry color. She watched Seth slip something behind his back.

"What are you two doing?" She used her teacher's voice and had to struggle not to laugh; they both obviously looked like they expected to get into trouble.

Seth smiled, and Lilly suddenly recalled that his charm was usually how he'd gotten out of things when they were in school. She arched an eyebrow and waited.

"Are you through in the house already, sweet *schweschder*? I was thinking of adding some color to the boy's room upstairs . . . do you mind giving me your opinion on some different shades of blue?"

"Later, perhaps."

She let her gaze trace her husband's face and noticed that he was looking increasingly caught. Trapped somehow. She didn't like to see him that way.

"Give me what's behind your back, Seth Wyse. You may . . . I mean, please go. I'd like to spend some time alone with my husband." She deliberately infused an extra bit of warmth into her tone at the suggestion and watched Seth throw a helpless glance at his brother.

"Uh . . . all right . . . Jacob was just showing me the artwork in the book you made for him. The sketches are quite well drawn." He slapped the book into her outstretched hand and grabbed his coat. "I'll, uh . . . leave you two alone." He slid the barn door closed before she could say another word.

Lilly looked down at the creased primer, then at Jacob. He'd turned his back to her, his arms stretched wide as he clutched the edge of the workbench with white knuckles.

"I missed you," she said softly. "In the house . . . I didn't know where you'd gone."

"Sorry," he mumbled over his shoulder.

She took a few steps closer to him, admiring the broad width of his back and shoulders in his light blue shirt. She wanted to touch him but knew that he'd probably resist. She might have chosen to walk away, because she had no doubt that he'd been working on the primer with Seth. She didn't want to embarrass him, but she wondered, both as a teacher and as a woman, how far she might push him to get him to open up about his reading difficulties.

"*Danki* for showing Seth the book. I'm glad you liked it enough to share it."

He shrugged and she gazed around the barn, looking for inspiration.

"So . . . when you teach me to ride . . . what will you do to help me not be afraid?"

He turned slowly. "What?"

She wet her lips and looked down at the floor. "I know we haven't had a lot of time to think about it, but the idea of learning to ride. It still scares me, terrifies me, really. I wondered what you'd do to help me."

"I . . . I'd tell you not to be afraid. I'll make sure that you don't get hurt."

"*Jah*, but how can you do that? I'll probably fall."

He shook his head. "*Nee*, that's not true. It's often poor teaching that lets a new rider fall. With the right practice and exercises, getting your seat, maintaining the proper body line and balance, there will be less chance of you falling. And if you did . . . if you did . . . I promise I'd make it feel better fast." His voice had taken on a husky timbre that sent shivers of delight across her shoulders, but Lilly kept her focus.

"So . . . I'll have to trust you then?"

He took a step closer to her. "*Jah*, but I promise that you can."

She lifted the primer between them and he stood still. Then she looked deeply into his eyes. "And I promise that you can trust me, Jacob. I won't let you fall."

He stared at her, pain and indecision playing across his expressive face. Finally he swallowed. "I don't . . . I don't want you to find that your husband is a fool, Lilly. Not smart enough . . ."

Her heart melted at his words and she longed to embrace him but she stood, motionless.

"Jacob, you are so intelligent, so wise, and you could never be a fool. I promise. Please trust me. I will not let you fall."

He took a deep breath. "I said I'd try. I'll trust you."

She felt a thrill of exultation and said a silent prayer to *Derr Herr*, asking Him for wisdom for the moment.

"*Gut. Danki*, Jacob. I won't let you down."

She stepped to the workbench and let her cloak slide onto one of the stools. "Okay, just right now, I want to ask you one question. One tutoring question."

He moved closer to her and she could sense the tension in his body. She put out her hand to touch his, letting her fingers play over the rough calluses and long fingers, then sliding her hand up to his wrist and finding the pulse point, beating fast and steady. She sensed that he responded to physical touch, and she kept her hand on his skin until he'd inched beside her and they both stood into the circle of light from the lamp at the workbench. She put aside the primer and turned to him, moving her hand to delicately skim his bare forearm where his sleeve was rolled back.

"What's the question?" he asked hoarsely.

She let her voice drop, infusing her tone with warmth like the permeating intimacy of a fledgling nest, feathers tight and close and safe.

"I want you to tell me how you feel about reading."

He stared down at her, torn between the sensations of her touch, her voice, and her very odd question. "How I *feel* about reading?"

"*Jah.*"

He cast about in his mind for some answering quip, something to deflect what he understood to be a direct question. He didn't like to think about how he felt about reading, about how he felt about himself not reading. "I . . . don't . . ."

Her hand had skimmed past the rolled cuff of his shirt and now played along the line of his upper arm. "Do you feel the same way about reading as you do about horses?"

"No," he answered, appalled at the suggestion.

"So, how is it different?"

He swallowed hard, feeling cornered and unsure. But he'd promised to trust her. He expected her to trust him. And she touched him with such extreme gentleness—butterfly touches, but enough to send sensations tingling through his body.

"Jacob, *sei so gut.* How do you feel about reading?" She leaned closer to him until he had to blink or feel like he might drown in the deep blue of her eyes.

"I hate it," he choked.

"I know," she soothed. "Just like I hate the thought of riding—until you touch me, with your words, your hands. You said once that I didn't have to do things alone. You don't have to do this alone, Jacob. You don't have to read alone. Okay?"

He nodded, feeling torn between sudden tears and kissing her, and he wasn't sure which would have brought more relief when she dropped her hand and gave him a bright smile. She scooped up the primer and her cloak. "We'd best go home."

He nodded. "I'll be along."

He stood still, taking deep breaths after she slid the barn door closed behind her. He decided then and there that if every tutoring session was like the one he'd just had, life was going to be one endless, delicious torment.

CHAPTER 34

*L*illy was at school early the first day back after the holidays. A little more than two weeks off was always more than enough for her, although she knew she'd miss seeing Jacob throughout the day. She glanced around the classroom with pleasure as she waited for the students to arrive. The school board had made sure, as it always did, that volunteers had come during the break to thoroughly clean the small building. The windows sparkled and new corkboard had been hung in convenient spots around the room.

As was her usual custom, Lilly had decorated one of the main boards with a "welcome back" image, this time a tree and large snowflakes. She'd found the idea in the never-ending resource of Amish teachers everywhere, *The Blackboard Bulletin*. She had carefully lettered each student's name on one of the snow designs and was happy to have added Abel Beiler's name to the rest of the class.

She'd heard that Grace Beiler and her son had moved in the previous day, and she guessed that the Zook children would probably stop by and have the boy walk with them to the schoolhouse.

She'd just adjusted the world globe and was straightening some papers on her desk when steps sounded outside on the porch. She looked up as the back door opened, not expecting a student so soon.

Seth entered, hat in hands, and a strange expression on his face as a beautiful, petite Amish woman in a long cloak walked in behind him. She wore a black bonnet that framed her pale face, black hair, and, upon closer inspection, wide pansy-purple colored eyes and sooty lashes. A young boy peeped from behind her cloak folds.

Lilly stepped from behind her desk to greet them.

"Lilly, this is Grace Beiler, and her son, Abel. I . . . uh . . . was passing by and thought I'd help introduce you." Seth sounded odd despite the warmth of his greeting.

Lilly extended her hand and shook the other woman's cold fingers. She didn't try to engage the child, who was obviously too shy to come forward, but smiled at his mother. Then she looked at Seth and the word *smitten* came to mind.

"Why, thank you, Seth. I think we'll be fine from here."

"Uh, right. I'd better get back to the farm. Mrs. Beiler, Abel, a pleasure. Lilly, have a *gut* day." He slapped his hat on his head and seemed to shake himself, then made for the back door.

When he was gone, Lilly spoke softly.

"*Ach*, Mrs. Beiler. I'm so glad to meet you and to have you as part of our community. I hope you'll be happy here."

The woman smiled faintly, but Lilly noted the bruise-like shadows beneath her eyes and knew how difficult the move must have been in addition to the loss of her husband.

"Please, call me Grace. I . . . I wanted to talk with you about Abel before the other students came. I'm not sure what you've been told."

Lilly's lips parted. She didn't like discussing things about children directly in front of them and was going to suggest that Abel go to the play yard when Grace gave a slight shake of her head. "I'd prefer to keep him here," she said softly. "I don't always know how he'll react in new situations."

Lilly nodded. "Since the accident with your husband, you mean?"

"No, always. Abel has a traumatic brain injury from birth and quite a few delays because of this. We—my husband and I—took him to the best neurologists in Philadelphia. He has issues with short-term memory loss, mental processing, and handwriting. But he is capable of learning, if you can reach him." Her beautiful eyes scanned Lilly's face. "I can tell by your expression that my letter didn't get to your school board in time to explain—"

"Um . . . no . . . but that's fine. Has he attended school before?"

"*Jah*, for a year and a term in Ohio. He was making progress somewhat but then my husband . . . well . . . we had to move. Would you feel more comfortable if I put him into one of the special schools? I'm told that Elk County has one."

It was true, Lilly considered quickly, that there were schools for students among the Amish with unique needs or learning styles, but she felt convicted in her heart to give things a try with Abel Beiler.

"I'd like to try, Mrs. . . . . Grace. And please, call me Lilly." She smiled as the other woman's face cleared. *She really is remarkably beautiful*, Lilly thought. And there was no guessing her age. She somehow appeared both young and old at the same time. "Perhaps you might come in for another conference later this week and give me some more details about his medical and academic history."

"Thank you, Lilly, I will." She pulled a small metal bucket from beneath her cloak, then turned to press it into Abel's hand. "I've brought your lunch pail." She knelt beside her son, and Lilly got her first clear look at the boy's face.

He was small and as fair-skinned as his mother; his eyes, too, were hers—wide violet blue, with a feathering of dark brows. He had a worried pucker about his lips and his small chin quivered as his mother murmured to him. She kissed his cheek, hugged him hard, and rose to smile at Lilly.

"I work from home—quilting—and I'm only a half mile away. If there are any problems . . ."

"Please don't worry, Grace. We'll be fine. He'll have a good day."

The woman nodded and slipped from her son's grasp, hurrying back down the aisle and out the door.

Abel sank to the floor as if devastated and hugged his arms around himself, rocking back and forth. Lilly decided to let him be; he was obviously self-soothing and that was good.

She went about her classroom preparations, keeping up a gentle flow of conversation to which the child didn't respond. She pointed out his seat and his name on the snowflake on the wall and then went to the back of the room to greet the other students as they began to file in.

"Children, we have a new student. Abel Beiler. Please say hello."

Reuben Mast frowned as he sidled past the still rocking boy to get to his seat. "What be wrong with him, teacher?"

"What *is* wrong, and the answer is nothing. Abel will just learn differently than some of us do. And . . ." Her gaze swept the room of quiet students, now assembled. "I expect you all to give him the help and care he may need to become adjusted to being in a new school and new home. Do you all understand?" Her tone was warning, but her eyes were expectant, hopeful. She saw the older students catch on by their nods. "Good. Then let's proceed."

"Since we all made it through the Christmas program, we'll now return to our regular schedule. I'll start off this morning by reading from the Bible. Let's see . . ." She went to her desk, walking around Abel, and picked up her Bible.

"I've chosen Isaiah 45:3 to begin the New Year. 'I will give you the treasures of darkness, And hidden wealth of secret places, So that you may know that it is I, The Lord, the God of Israel, who calls you by your name.'" She closed the Bible. "Who can tell me what that means?" She waited expectantly, raising a brow at her older students.

Abel spoke in a monotone, still rocking. "It means that there are good things in life that can come out of bad—out of the dark."

All eyes swung to the boy on the floor. Lilly swallowed. "Yes, that's right, Abel. Very well done. Are there any other thoughts?"

No one else seemed to know what more to say, so she asked them to rise for the recitation of the Lord's Prayer. After the prayer they moved on to sing. As their voices began to rise, Lilly noticed that Abel got to his feet. He held onto the desk next to him with a thin arm and hummed along with the others to the traditional hymn.

In the still isolation
You find my praise ready
Greatest God answer me
For my heart is seeking you.
You're always here
Never still though silent
You rule the yearly seasons
And you set them in order.
This cold winter air
Calls with mighty feeling.
See what a mighty Lord,
Summer and Winter He makes.

The song ended and the class sat down, and Lilly breathed a faint sigh of relief when Abel did the same.

Jacob was riding fence on the border of the Wyse farm along the highway when a horse and buggy slowed to a stop near him.

He rode closer in the frosty glare of the midday sun on the snow. He squinted beneath his hat as he recognized Sarah. She leaned to the side of the buggy and smiled at him. He noticed with vague surprise that her face inspired no particular change in his heart rate, no sudden pang of regret or longing. It almost was as if he were free from a spell cast long ago, that he'd woken up and discovered that reality was more than fine—it was freedom. He smiled and reached his gloved hand out to her. She took it lightly and they shook hands over the top line of the fence.

"Where are you off to, Sarah?"

"Town . . . I've got to buy some fabric." She tipped her head shyly. "I'm going to make some baby clothes."

He raised a brow, then burst out with the first thing that came to mind. "You're pregnant? Sarah, that's wonderful." And he meant it, he realized. He could have gotten off his horse and danced with incredible joy. It stunned him. He was genuinely happy for her and Grant.

"Jacob, thank you." Her radiant smile warmed a part of his soul, but it was a distant warmth—not the flame of emotion he felt when he was with Lilly. Was *Derr Herr* making everything new?

"Now tell me, how is Lilly's *mamm*? Grant says she's making great strides."

"*Jah*, we're to fetch her home tomorrow afternoon. We couldn't have made it without Grant's help. He's a *gut* man, a *gut* doctor."

"And it's not taken you long to figure that out," she teased.

He laughed. "No, not long at all. I'm sorry, Sarah. I wish I could have seen things clearer, earlier—for everyone's sake." He reached out and touched her hand with affection and they both looked up as another horse and buggy came trotting past on the opposite side of the road. Mrs. Zook gave them a speculative look and a stiff nod.

Sarah smiled at him once the other woman had passed. "It was good to see you, Jacob."

"Good to see you too. And pass my congratulations on to your husband."

As she picked up the reins, he waved, then turned to keep checking the fence, a broad grin on his face.

CHAPTER 35

O just thought it my duty to stop and let you know, Lilly. You're not much older than my Kate and I don't want to see you hurt." Mrs. Zook gave her a forlorn look and sniffed into a large hankie.

Lilly had just seen Mrs. Beiler and Abel off a few minutes before when Mrs. Zook had marched into the schoolhouse.

"Mrs. Zook, I'm sorry that you're struggling with Kate, but I hardly think that Jacob and Sarah stopping to speak to one another should be any concern."

"Well. You can certainly choose to ignore my care in this, Lilly. In the absence of your mother, I think it's only right that—"

Lilly put up her hand to silence her. "I trust my husband, Mrs. Zook."

Mrs. Zook leaned forward as if dispensing delicious gossip. "He had his hand upon hers, Lilly—and they weren't shaking hands." Her eyebrow rose as if waiting for a response.

Lilly tried not to let the sudden fear rising in her show. "As my mother is returning home tomorrow, Mrs. Zook, I really must clean up and prepare for tomorrow's lessons. If you'll excuse me . . ."

The older woman turned on her heel, her cape whirling about her. "Very well, Lilly Wyse. And I won't say that I was the first to give you news that might save your future."

"Good day, Mrs. Zook."

Lilly sank to her desk chair as the door slammed close. She put her throbbing head in her hands and tried to ignore the venom of the so-called "duty" in the woman's gossip. It had been a difficult day as it was, knowing her mother would return home the following day, dealing with Abel Beiler, who was sweet but was obviously going to be the most challenging student of her teaching career thus far. And, she was adjusting to marriage—a difficult thing under ordinary circumstances made even more difficult by the fact that her husband was distracted by his love for another woman.

As much as she wanted to, she could not still the fear that rose stronger within her heart. She began to pray that *Derr Herr* would give her release from her worry.

Jacob inched deeper beneath the pile of quilts on the floor, then rolled over on his stomach to play with the crack in the wood floor in the darkened room. He knew Lilly was awake too. He could tell from her rustlings and her breathing. He'd grown used to waiting for the even cadence of her breath before he allowed himself to fall asleep.

Something was bothering her . . . he could tell from her pleasant but thoughtful manner at supper—clearly forced. Probably she was worried about her *mamm's* homecoming . . .

"Abel Beiler came to school today," she spoke quietly from the bed.

He rolled over and propped himself up on one elbow, trying to see something in the sooty dark.

"How is the boy? It can't be easy to have lost your father so recently."

"I don't know how he is—what troubles him and what doesn't." She briefly outlined Grace Beiler's explanation of her son's health.

"Maybe a special school is the answer, Lilly. I've heard that the teachers are kind and have more help in the classroom."

He heard her bedclothes shift. "I know, but I feel that the Lord wants me to try with him. He's really no bother, actually more of a puzzle. It's not that he disobeys or is disruptive . . ."

On his side now, Jacob propped his head on his hand. "Then what is it?"

"Sometimes he'll engage with the class and then, for no clear reason, drifts away into his own world."

"Is that so bad?"

"Well, it's distracting in a way I can't describe. Sometimes he's rocking a bit. Sometimes mumbling softly to himself."

"Have you spoken with Alice yet? Surely she'll have some ideas. How much longer has she been a teacher over in the next school?"

"Three years. Not a lot more, but I know she's had some challenges. I'd planned to talk with her soon."

She shifted again. He remained silent, sensing she had more to say.

"Jacob, I've thought about whether I might be vain in trying to teach him myself. I don't think that's the reason—truly, it's a conviction of my heart."

"It is *Derr Herr* who brings conviction to the heart. When He does, we are wise to listen." Jacob thought for a moment. "How old is he? Seven? Can he read?"

"Some. It's hard to tell, but he understands what's being said. He's insightful and can speak with high intellect when he chooses."

"You know, when I've gotten hold of a colt that's been badly or cruelly broke, or just one that seems a little slow or stubborn to other people, I often hitch him to a well-broken horse, one that can kind of act like a—"

He heard her clap her hands once. "Like a mentor! Jacob, that's perfect! But I wonder which student might be best for him."

He cleared his throat as an impulsive idea came to his mind. It was out of his mouth before he could consider. "I could do it."

"What?"

He went on slowly. "I might be able to help the boy some way. He's just lost his father—I don't know. Maybe he'd like horses . . ." He trailed off. *Probably a silly idea.*

He heard her fling back the quilts, then heard her bare feet hit the floor. Then she was leaning over him in the pitch dark, her hands on his chest. "*Ach*, Jacob. You're brilliant and so very kind. If you can spend some time with him in the evenings or maybe after school, it might give him confidence or make him calmer. I'm so proud of you that you're willing to suggest this."

She bent and hugged him, a quick, frustrating touch, and then she rose and pattered away. The bed creaked as she got back in, and he stifled a sigh.

After a few minutes, just when he thought she might be drifting off, she spoke again, her strained tone very different from only a few moments before.

"Mrs. Zook stopped by the school today. She said she saw you and Sarah meeting together on the roadside."

"What? That old troublemaker."

"She said you had your hand on hers. She said it looked affectionate. She said you weren't shaking hands." Her voice shook a bit more with each statement.

He didn't even attempt to stifle the sound of disgust that blew from the back of his throat.

"Well, did you?"

He didn't like her accusation, especially when he'd offered to help her with one of her students and she'd responded with excitement. "*Jah*, Lilly, that we were. Sarah was tired of Grant's company, despite the fact that she's going to have his *boppli*, and I decided to dishonor my bride in full view of everyone. That's what we were doing." He slammed his pillow down and rolled over, covering his head.

"How do you know?"

"What?" he snapped, yanking the quilt back down.

"How do you know she's pregnant?"

He almost groaned aloud. Could he not learn to keep his big mouth shut? But there was no help for it now. "She told me."

"Even Mrs. Zook didn't know. You must have been the first she told."

He thumped his pillow hard. "No, Lilly, I was not the first. I'm sure Sarah told her husband and her family and then maybe me. I am not first of anything with Sarah. And I don't want to be. Not even second or third. Look, I want to go to sleep. Is that all right?" He shouldered the quilt and let his sarcasm hang like frost in the chilly air of the room.

Chapter 36

$\mathcal{L}$illy plucked a clothespin from the line and dropped it into the basket. Alice had done the same from the other side of the sheet. They began to fold the sheet together, as they had done hundreds of times, like a perfectly choreographed dance.

"He doesn't love her anymore," Alice said, continuing their conversation.

"I don't know, Alice. I really don't."

"I saw them, you know."

"When?"

"Tuesday."

"That was four days ago. Why didn't you tell me?" Lilly's heart began to fear, picking up its pace.

Alice placed the folded sheet into the basket while Lilly reached for the next clothespin.

"I forgot."

Lilly stopped. Turned. "You forgot."

"Lilly. It was nothing. Really."

"Then why did you forget?"

Alice plucked her end of the sheet off the line and the dance began again. "Because it was nothing. I probably should have remembered because the most remarkable thing about it was that it was so clear Jacob doesn't love her anymore."

They moved down the line, removing trousers one at a time. Lilly looked at her, not convinced.

"Look, Lilly. The entire community has watched Jacob's eyes trail Sarah wherever she went for so many years, his face full of emotion and attraction. So when I saw him in town, walking by her, saying a friendly hello, but declaring an eager interest to get home to you, what should I think? Lilly, that connection is dead between them."

Lilly knew Alice wouldn't lie just to make her feel better. Her heart began to grow lighter.

"Besides," Alice said, happily pairing socks and dropping them in the basket, "I've seen how he looks at you."

Lilly cocked her head. "How?"

"Like he wants to spend the rest of his life with you."

Lilly urged Ruler into a trot. She'd finished the school day with a certain resolve in her heart that had been strengthened by hours of silent, ongoing prayer. She turned down the lane to the Williamses' farm and felt her heart pound within her chest. She was grateful to see that Grant's buggy was gone, meaning he was probably out on a call. Perhaps it would make things easier.

She took a deep breath as she knocked on the front door, half hoping that no one would answer. But the glass of the door reverberated a bit with the approach of hurried footsteps, and Lilly was soon met with the smiling face of Mrs. Bustle. She knew the *Englisch* Bustles, as everyone in the community did. The elderly couple was like Grant Williams's extended family and often came for visits from Philadelphia.

"Well, if it isn't the schoolteacher! Mrs. Wyse now, correct? Please come in."

Lilly stepped inside, unsure of how to proceed with her sensitive errand if the older woman was present.

"How are you and Mr. Bustle?"

"Fine. Just fine. And now we're doubly happy to visit when Sarah is——" The good woman broke off, clearly flustered by what Lilly knew she'd nearly revealed and wondered what such suppressed joy must feel like.

"Ah, I mean . . . would you like to see Sarah? Or did you need the doctor for one of your animals? He's out on a call right now."

"Sarah, actually. Please."

"Just come with me then." The woman turned and lived up to her name by moving quickly across the hardwoods. Lilly followed, feeling an increasing uncertainty as she passed through the immaculate rooms of the old farmhouse. The place had such a domestic yet cultured feel about it, something in the stray piece of furniture or muted color of the walls that was still just a little bit *Englisch* as befitting Grant's upbringing.

But there was nothing so domestically Amish as the sight of the home's mistress in flour up to her elbows as she stood at the kitchen table.

"Lilly! What a wonderful surprise. We were just making raisin-filled cookies."

Lilly looked into the beautiful face of the girl opposite her. Here was Jacob's fantasy, the shadow of his true love, both immersed in life and carrying it within her. It seemed a futile thing in Lilly's mind to even try and compete with the vitality and real beauty of Sarah Williams, a vision of the past or not. Yet that was not why she'd come. She let her eyes stray to Mrs. Bustle and wondered how she'd ever say what she needed to.

Sarah must have sensed her discomfort because she made a sudden exclamation.

"*Ach*, I nearly forgot."

"What is it, dear?" Mrs. Bustle asked with concern.

"The mail. Grant was expecting some medicine samples. Perhaps Lilly and I will walk down the drive and—"

"You'll do no such thing," Mrs. Bustle interjected. "I'll go myself this moment. I'll not have you running down the lane after some fool medicine when you could easily slip and . . ." The woman's voice faded to an indistinct mumble, followed by the sound of the front door closing.

"I'm sorry, Lilly. It seemed like you wanted to talk or something, but maybe you'll think me silly."

Lilly shook her head. "*Nee*. You're right." She plunged on before she lost her nerve. "The truth is, Sarah, that I've come to talk to you about something difficult."

"Difficult? What do you mean?" Sarah wiped her arms with a dish towel and pulled a chair away from the kitchen table. "Here, please sit down."

Lilly sat but kept her hands clenched in the lap of her cloak. She didn't know what to do with the chaotic mixture of feelings that whirled around within her. Now that she was there, she didn't know how she was even going to begin. Should she tell how she despised Sarah for showing up in her husband's dreams? For being beautiful? Perfect? Everything Jacob wanted?

Or would she say what a good Amish woman should say? That she's trying to trust *Derr Herr* with her marriage.

What she really wanted was to say—as well as believe—was what she had thought and prayed about for days.

"Can I get you some tea?" Sarah interrupted the swirl of her thoughts.

"That would be nice," Lilly said, thankful for the few extra moments before she'd have to speak. But then, maybe she'd just have a little casual visit, then leave without ever exposing her fears and sadness to this beautiful woman. Of course, Jacob would love her. Lilly could not compete with someone as lovely and sweet and demure as Sarah Williams.

Sarah placed a plate of freshly baked raisin-filled cookies in the center of the table. She poured hot tea from the kettle on the stove into two mugs and set one in front of each of them. She returned the kettle to its place and sat in the chair closest to the stove so that she could easily be a good hostess if her guest needed anything else.

"They smell delicious," Lilly said, lifting a cookie from the plate and taking a warm, gooey bite.

"My mother's recipe," Sarah said. "We often begged her to make them as we grew up."

The front door banged as Mrs. Bustle returned from her short jaunt to the mailbox. She burst into the kitchen, a large padded envelope in her hand. "Here's something," she said, moving right on through presumably to deposit it on Grant's desk. "I'll be going upstairs to have a read if you don't mind, girls. I'm sure you can visit without me."

Lilly was both relieved and distressed at the announcement. Now she had no excuse except fear and cowardice to not speak the truth to Sarah.

"Go on ahead," Sarah called to Mrs. Bustle. She smiled at Lilly. "She is so funny. Everything she does is different from anyone I've ever known. Yet you can't help but love her immediately."

She picked up a cookie and began to eat it. "You know, Lilly, I'm very happy for you and Jacob."

"Truly?" Lilly asked, searching her face for a sign that she was putting on a false cover to hide the truth. Yet all Lilly could see was an open, honest, lovely face, a happiness exuding from her.

"It took me awhile, though."

Lilly swallowed. "Why?"

"Because Jacob found his true love and it wasn't me."

"But you were already married when we became engaged."

"Yes I was. Don't misunderstand me. I love my husband dearly. There isn't a day that goes by that I am not profoundly grateful to *Derr Herr* for giving me the perfect husband."

"Then why—"

"I suppose that although I was married to Grant, I still enjoyed knowing that Jacob loved me. A silly schoolgirl idea that a nice boy desires my company." She shook her head. "Foolish, foolish. But sometimes the heart doesn't make sense, does it?"

Lilly felt much of her fear drain away.

Sarah continued. "But then he became quickly engaged to someone beautiful. Someone much smarter than me. A woman with a job and not afraid of people or what they might think. You have always been someone I've admired, Lilly. You're so different from me and so right for Jacob."

Lilly put her cookie down on a napkin. She'd placed her tea to one side, stunned. Not knowing what to say.

"Lilly, I've known Jacob all my life. We've been such *gut* friends. I probably know him better than anyone except his brother." She put her hand up. "Again, don't misunderstand me. We were never intimate in any way except our laughter and sharing."

Lilly took a bite of her *appenditlich* cookie, hoping that would help Sarah to continue.

"But somehow, I knew truly that I was never the right girl to be his *fraa*. And then, when he chose you, I felt you were so right for him."

"Thank you, Sarah. I . . . I don't know what to say. I never thought you'd felt that way about me."

"I should have told you sooner perhaps. You're not angry with me for my foolish, jealous thoughts?"

Lilly started to laugh, but only a bit, until she had to take a deep breath and confess her own thoughts. "No, Sarah, I'm not angry. I'm surprised. You see, I came to tell you that I've been jealous of you and your relationship with Jacob. I . . . I've confessed it before God and I believed it only right to confess it to you as well. I've not been much of a friend in my thoughts toward you, and I want you to know that I'm sorry."

She drew a shaky breath and saw that Sarah's face only held concern and gentleness. "Lilly, it's so funny, really—how people think. What they think when they're really honest with themselves and with each other. I think evil has its way so much in the world because we refuse to tell the truth, be brave, and speak to one another in love. If we had not spoken, we would have let evil put an unseen wall between us."

"And we would have missed the truth. I don't want to be angry with you, Sarah. That is why I came. I hope you can forgive me."

"I will." Sarah raised her mug. Before taking a sip she said, "Maybe this truth telling could become a habit between us, Lilly Wyse. I would dearly love a new best friend."

Lilly felt the glacier of her jealousy begin to melt away in the light of Sarah's obvious sincerity.

"I'd like a new friend too," she replied with honesty. "Thank you, Sarah—for listening. For helping me to see."

Sarah rose and came around the table to hug her, and Lilly found herself returning the heartening embrace.

"*Ach*, Sarah . . . there's one more thing—Jacob told me that—well, about the new *boppli* you carry. Congratulations to you and Grant."

"Oh, *danki*, Lilly. I'm so excited and *naerfich*." Sarah smiled as she pulled away.

"You will be a wonderful *mamm*."

Sarah squeezed her hands. "Thank you, my *freind*. Please come for a visit anytime, Lilly."

"You too, Sarah. Really."

*W*hat exactly is your problem today?" Seth asked in a conversational tone.

"Nothing."

"Uh-huh . . . well then, married life must not agree with you real well, because you're meaner than that cat of *grossmudder's* who takes your eyebrows off whenever . . ."

"Not today, Seth."

"All right, all right."

Jacob walked to the other side of the round pen where they were training a two-year-old Country Saddler to get used to pulling a buggy. He didn't mean to snap but he'd had no chance to talk with Lilly; she'd been gone before he was awake, leaving him breakfast warming and no note. Not that he'd be able to decipher it anyway. Truth was, he was mad at himself for losing his temper and still mad at her for not trusting him.

He glanced up at the racket. Seth had attached a tire rim to a rope fastened to the horse's harness. The clatter of the rim along the ground was meant to simulate the metal wheels of the buggy and allow the animal the chance to become accustomed to the noise.

Jacob automatically gave the horse some praise as he circled past, patting the animal's rump and muttering low in his throat. Then he tried a vocal command they'd been working on.

He yelled, "Ho!" and the horse paused, slowing, but still not stopping completely.

"Let's take off the tire rim," Jacob called. "He's not ready yet. We'll just work with the carrot stick and basic commands today."

Seth moved toward the horse while Jacob gathered up the metal garbage-can lids he'd hoped they might use to create sound once training had progressed. He took the lids back into the barn and laid them on a shelf as a realization hit him.

He needed to be as patient in his marriage as he was with his work. The irony of the bishop's wedding vow question came back to him, and he frowned. He hadn't really been as gracious and generous in spirit to his own wife as he was being to the young horse outside. And how would he have felt if he'd heard gossip about Lilly and—his throat caught—Seth. The memory of his brother holding Lilly made his throat ache, and suddenly he understood.

Lilly couldn't help clasping and unclasping her gloved hands as Jacob drove the horse and buggy toward Lockport Hospital in the light of the wintry afternoon.

Finally Jacob's hand came down to cover hers, and she looked at him.

"I'm sorry, Lilly, about last night. I shouldn't have been sarcastic. I know I hurt your feelings."

Lilly breathed a sigh of relief. She'd prayed throughout the day as to how to handle the situation with Jacob, knowing that she should never have given in to the poison of Mrs. Zook's tongue. And her visit with Sarah had helped so much. *So right for Jacob.* The words echoed in her mind and allowed her the ease of forgiveness she might not have been able to give otherwise.

"Oh, Jacob, you've done so much for me and what you've offered for Abel. Please forgive me for doubting you. And . . . I have to tell you." She paused, gathering courage to speak. "I went to visit Sarah."

"You did? What about?"

"About my feelings of being jealous. I wanted to confess that to her and to wish her well with the baby."

Jacob shook his head.

"What?" she asked.

"Lilly, you're amazing to me. I tell you that I understand how you must feel and you leapfrog over my simple answers to something so much more real. Do you know what courage you have? How you face life head-on? You might want to be free sometimes, but there is already something free and wild in you. Call it your spirit or your soul. It just . . . it calls to me."

She sat silent beneath the praise of his words, drinking them in.

"Lilly, I did see Sarah yesterday, for less than two minutes. And, you should know, I felt nothing, nothing special at all."

She turned to him with a half smile playing around her lips.

"Do you know what, Jacob Wyse? I choose to believe that—at least, I think I do."

He nodded, tightening the reins as he navigated around a slight corner. "And that is more than enough for me, Lilly. The fact is that I'm honored to wait until you'll give me more of your trust, when I've had the chance to earn it."

Lilly studied his profile; there was no doubting the sincerity of his voice. Dare she believe the whole of his words? If Jacob was no longer in love with Sarah, then perhaps . . .

"Here we are."

She looked up to find they were at the entrance to the hospital. Although she'd visited with her mother often, and had extensive talks with the counselor from Lancaster, she still felt unprepared for her *mamm's* homecoming. There were so many things that could happen. She had seen a genuine improvement in her mother's mood, appetite, and energy level. She just prayed that the transition would go well.

They took the elevator to the familiar fourth floor. When they stepped out, Dr. Parker turned from the nurses' station to greet them.

"Mr. and Mrs. Wyse. I wonder if you might come and meet with me and the visiting Amish counselor for a few minutes before you see your mother."

"Is something wrong?" Lilly asked when they'd been shown into a small conference room.

"No, certainly not. Please sit down."

Lilly sat and Jacob moved next to her, letting his heavy arm fall around her shoulders.

The Amish counselor, Julia Chupp, entered with a smile and sat down across the table.

Dr. Parker cleared his throat and looked intently at Lilly. "We've learned a few things over the years, Mrs. Wyse, about clinically depressed patients who've attempted, but not succeeded, in a suicide."

Lilly swallowed at the use of the word, having tried not to think of it directly, even as her mother had been recovering.

The doctor continued. "We've learned that it's necessary to consult with the families and involve them in the total treatment plan, including plans for the patient's discharge and aftercare."

Mrs. Chupp nodded. "And Dr. Parker understands the importance of the unique needs of your mother—her cultural needs as an Amish woman in relation to her depression. In other words, part of her healing needs to be addressed in terms of her faith."

Everything started to sound a lot more complicated to Lilly. She concentrated hard as Dr. Parker handed her a stack of papers.

"In addition to these release forms, I've included a great deal of information for your family. You will note we've made some specific appointments with aftercare providers whom Mrs. Chupp has met and approves of."

"There are other doctors?" Jacob asked.

"Yes, a psychiatrist, a psychologist, and appointment times for a small group—a support group—of other Amish women who've gone through this illness in the area."

Lilly looked up in surprise. "Others?"

Dr. Parker nodded. "Yes, and not just from your community but from surrounding Amish communities as well. A higher-risk patient, like your mother, is identified and given priority in scheduling after-care appointments to ensure her linkage with outpatient services. There's also a schedule of her medicines for you to monitor."

"Higher risk . . . you mean she could try to . . . again?"

Mrs. Chupp reached across the table and patted her hand. "That's a family's greatest fear. Although it's possible, your mother has responded well to treatment. You'll have to be aware of the risk and signs of any regression in her behavior, but you cannot sit up nights worrying about it. The medication can also help a great deal."

Lilly lifted the sheath of papers, feeling slightly overwhelmed, but grateful for the support that seemed to be so well established for her family. Nonetheless, she cast a beseeching look at Jacob and he bent to kiss her cheek.

"It'll be all right, Lilly," he whispered. "You're not alone."

She nodded, looked up, and flushed as she became aware of Dr. Parker's kind eyes.

"Shall we go and talk with your mother?"

"*Jah*," Lilly whispered, feeling her heart begin to pound.

Jacob was pleased to see his mother-in-law looking so fit. She was dressed neatly and her hair was tucked beneath her *kapp*. She'd also gained a little bit of weight and the shadows beneath her eyes seemed to have almost disappeared.

The ride home was uneventful. He was pleased to hear Mrs.

Lapp speak in normal tones with Lilly. When they entered the Lapp home and had removed their outer clothes, Jacob noticed that his mother-in-law clutched a black notebook in her arms as if it were of the greatest importance to her.

"Have you been writing, Mrs. Lapp?" he asked, gesturing to the notebook as Lilly made tea.

"Please, Jacob, call me *Mamm*. I should have suggested it before, but . . ." She gave him a shy smile and held the book up. "This is my journal from my time at the hospital. I wrote in it every day. It helped me express a lot of thoughts and feelings about my marriage and Hiram's death. I plan to continue writing in it."

"That sounds *gut*, *Mamm*," Lilly observed from the stove. "I . . . I also wanted to tell you that, upon Dr. Parker's recommendation, we changed your bedroom. It's a lot brighter and softer. Alice, Edith, and some other friends came to help."

"*Ach*, I'm so glad. I was dreading going back upstairs to that dark room. I seem to like the light more now and realize that I must have some sunshine every day."

Jacob was amazed at the change in her, but he felt cautious, watchful, especially after Dr. Parker's talk.

He waited while Lilly saw her *mamm* up the stairs at bedtime. Then she soon joined him in the sitting room.

"*Mamm* fell asleep so quickly after her medicine. The papers say we should keep an eye on whether or not she takes the medicines, especially when she starts to feel even better than she does now."

He nodded. "I forgot to ask you how Abel was today."

"Absent," Lilly said flatly. "I hope he's there tomorrow, but there's no telling."

"Well, I'll drive you there in the morning and then pick you up. If the *buwe's* about after school, maybe we can have a lesson." He paused to think. "What about your *mamm*—should she be left alone?"

"*Ach*, Mrs. Chupp and the bishop have arranged a schedule of regular visitors to minister to her for the next two months at least. She won't be alone long at all."

"*Gut* . . . that's really *gut*, Lilly." He cast his eyes about the room, not wanting to go to his bed on the floor but seeing no choice in the matter either.

He moved to brush his lips against her cheek, lingering for a moment, until he had to pull away. "Good night," he whispered, then turned to go to their room.

CHAPTER 37

Sleigh bells rang out merrily, and Lilly smiled at the spray of snow Thunder kicked up as the cutter flew along the road to school. It had snowed the night before and Jacob had surprised her by bringing round the sled instead of the buggy. They'd left her *mamm* in good spirits after seeing to her needs and knowing that Mrs. Loder was due to stop in early that morning.

Her satchel of books bounced against the sled robe and she laughed aloud with delight as they sped down one hill and up another in a stomach-lifting thrill.

She felt Jacob's eyes on her. "Do you want to drive?"

"What? Thunder? I don't think so . . . we'd end up in the field."

He handed her the reins, enclosing her small hands with his own much larger ones. Thunder sensed the change in drivers because he tossed his head and dropped his pace a bit.

"Just hang on and let him know where you want to go. You're in control. It's almost like driving the buggy."

He withdrew his hands and waited while she frowned, then

tentatively snapped the reins. "Go on," she encouraged. "I've got to get to school on time, big fella."

The horse drew to a stop and Lilly huffed at Jacob.

"A stubborn student," he observed. She wasn't sure if he meant her or his horse. She turned her gaze to Thunder's broad back, then she made an imitation of the clicking combination sound followed by the rumbling *hupp* she'd heard Jacob use. The horse pricked his ears. She did it again louder, then slapped the reins. They were off down the lane, the landscape whizzing by. She turned briefly to grin at her husband.

"Horse talk!" she shouted. "Anyone can do it."

He laughed aloud and took the reins as they pulled in to the school yard. Lilly was about to accept his praise when something caught her eye. A broken window in the side of the building, jagged with pointed glass, reflected in the sun's early morning rays. She felt her stomach drop and then saw that the schoolhouse door stood wide open.

"*Ach*, Jacob. Something's wrong."

"Stay here a minute. I'll have a look. It was probably just some *kinner* playing ball." He handed her Thunder's driving reins and went to the open door. When he didn't return within a few moments, Lilly jumped down, tied Thunder to a hitching post, and followed Jacob inside. She climbed the steps of the porch and then stood, frozen in amazement, as she stared at the interior of the classroom.

The students' wooden desks had been overturned and spray painted bright yellow and orange. Papers, supplies, and artwork were strewn and torn, some blowing forlornly from the wind that whistled in through the broken window. The chalkboards were spray painted as well. The welcome tree was torn in long strips with the snowflakes crumpled and trampled on the floor. Her desk had been upended and the wood deeply gouged. Its drawers had been flung about and emptied of everything. Even the new corkboard had been torn down and shredded, and her Bible lay facedown and open on the hardwood, treated so harshly its spine had cracked.

She automatically moved to pick up the Bible first, clutching it against her as she stood beside Jacob, who surveyed the scene with his arms crossed against his chest. Other Amish schools had been vandalized in years past, she'd known, but nothing like this had ever happened at the Pine Creek School. Her initial feeling of shock was fast turning to anger as she glanced at her brooch watch and realized that the students would be coming soon.

"The children will come. I can't let them see this. Whoever did this deserves to be—"

"Why?" Jacob turned to look down at her, his expression calm. "Why, what?"

"Why can't the students see? It's their school."

She bristled. "*Jah*, and it's supposed to be a place of safety and peace. Not this mess. "

"They can help you clean it up."

She looked at him like he was *narrish*.

"What's wrong with you, Jacob? Do you see this? How would you feel if it were your barn, your horses?"

He laid his hands on her shoulders and stared down into her eyes. "Lilly," he said softly. "Remember, forgiveness first. Then you can be angry or hurt. Don't forget the ways of our people, our history. Forgive first. Extend grace."

Something quieted in her soul as she listened to him. He was right. Whoever did this deserved forgiveness just as the Lord forgave her when she sinned. She took a deep breath. "*Danki*, Jacob, for reminding me. It is . . . not so bad. We can straighten things out and pray for those who did this. Then we'll have school as usual."

Jacob gave her a quick hug. "*Gut. Gut* teacher."

The students began to file in, their initial reactions very similar to Lilly's until she gently reminded them of what Jacob had brought to her heart. Even Abel, who at first appeared bewildered, seemed to understand as he bent to pick up some papers.

They all worked together as Lilly began to hum some hymns and Jacob rode off to notify the school board. Within two hours, things were put relatively to rights, and she was able to work through an abbreviated daily schedule, calling on the younger students to come forward to recite their arithmetic.

Jacob decided the cutter was the fastest way to travel on the snowy roads and gave Thunder his head, soon arriving at the bishop's farm. The old man was carrying a bag of feed over one shoulder with ease as the sled came to a stop.

"Jacob Wyse . . . spending time alone with your horse, hmm? How is your *fraa*?"

Jacob smiled and hopped out, wanting to take the 120-pound feed bag from him but knowing he'd only insult the man. "I'm afraid there's been a bit of trouble, Bishop. The schoolhouse was vandalized sometime during the night. I left Lilly and the children there to finish with the cleaning up."

"Bad off, was it?"

"The window needs to be replaced and desks need some repairing. The spray paint needs to be removed. The corkboards are gone and the blackboards aren't in very good shape."

"Let me put this in the barn and go tell Ellie. I'll ride over with you and have a look."

Soon they were headed over the roads and Jacob noticed that the bishop smiled at each dip and turn. "Now, *this* is *gut* for my heart, Jacob. *Danki*."

"My pleasure. And my horse's, of course."

They were about to turn down the lane to the schoolhouse

when the unfamiliar blip of a siren startled Thunder and he crow-hopped and began to gain speed. Jacob pulled him up as a police cruiser eased alongside them.

"Oh, boy—" the bishop muttered as they both recognized the face of the young officer who'd invaded Sarah's wedding.

The policeman slid down his car window. "Hello . . . um . . . uh . . . I'm Officer Mitchell. Probably you might know me from that time I acted like a fool at a wedding of yours. But, I'm trying to learn . . . uh, anyway, I got two kids in the back here. I think they might be Amish, or at least one is. I wasn't sure what to do. I caught 'em early this morning spray painting the back of the post office in town. I wondered if you'd had any incidents out your way."

The bishop cleared his throat. "*Jah*, the school's been van-dalized. But, we tend to handle these things by not involving outsi—the *Englisch* law. We have our own ways."

"Yes, sir. I've been studying on that. I . . . uh . . . can you give some advice on what to do about the kids?" The officer's face looked even younger than before against the white of the back-ground snow.

Jacob felt compassion for him. "May we see them?"

"Sure . . . oh, sure." He got out of the squad car and opened the back door. "Come on out, now."

Tom Granger's teenage son slid first from the seat, blinking from the snow glare. Kate Zook followed, her hair undone, and dressed in *Englisch* clothes. Jacob and the Bishop exchanged a brief glance.

"If you don't mind, Officer Mitchell," the bishop said, sliding from the cutter, "I'll have you give me a ride over to the school-house and you can let us off there."

"Oh, yes . . . surely."

Jacob stared straight ahead for a moment, then turned back to look at Granger's son. "I'll take the boy home in the sled."

Officer Mitchell nodded with relief. "Great. Thank you so much. I didn't fill out a report. Just figured they were kids up to some mischief is all. Not a lot to do around here for fun in the winter." He went around to open the car door for the bishop, then hustled Kate back inside. He waved as they took off, leaving Jacob and Tom Granger's son alone.

"Gonna get in?" Jacob asked after a minute. The boy wore a jean jacket and dark pants, but no hat or warm coat. He was tall and thin, probably about seventeen, with bleached blond hair and a sullen expression.

"No . . . no thanks, mister. If I go home, my dad'll beat me. Plain and simple. I've had enough of it. He told me to get out and I'm out. So, you just drive on to your nice Amish life where everything's perfect." He jammed his hands inside his pockets and glared at Jacob. "Did you ever stop to think that if you pressed charges I might have had a warm bed in jail tonight?"

Jacob closed his eyes briefly against the boy's words. To seek jail as a refuge. Images of the comfortable bed at his *mamm* and *daed's* house came to him. Even the floor of his new home sounded better than what the boy had. He took a deep breath. "It's not our way to press charges; we're called to forgive."

The boy snickered and scuffed at the ground with a dirty sneaker. "Well thanks a lot, buddy. Forgiveness is doing me a bunch of good right now." He hunched his shoulders against the wind and turned to walk away.

"I stole a horse from your father."

Jacob watched him stop and then look back.

"What?"

"I stole a mare from your dad. He shot me as I was trying to get away. I married a girl to help cover it up. My mother-in-law tried to kill herself on Christmas day. And I can't read or write much."

The boy took turned and took a step nearer the sled. "You

must be one crazy Amish guy. I thought you people's lives were perfect."

Jacob nodded. "Yeah, my perfect Amish life. You think you're the only one with problems and who makes mistakes, well . . . *hiya*, I've been doing it for a good long while."

"Yeah, but you're big. I bet no one ever beat you."

"No, you're right. But I beat myself up a lot inside."

"It's not the same."

"How old are you?"

"Eighteen."

"So, you're of age."

"My birthday was yesterday."

"Why are you still at home if this is going on?"

"I just got kicked out, remember?" He eyed Jacob as though he was *dumm*.

"Why aren't you working?"

"Who's gonna hire Tom Granger's son around here? It's all Amish, just about."

"I'll hire you. What's your name?"

The boy gave a rueful shake of his head. "Tom Jr. I hate it."

"I'll call you Tommy. My brother and I run a horse-breeding outfit. Do you treat horses like your father does?"

"No. I . . . I used to cry when I was a kid and he whipped them."

"Fair enough. You come work for me and my brother for a year, sleep in the barn, keep things straight—you'll have food in your belly and a warm place to lie down at night. Oh, and my wife'll probably try to further your education; she's the teacher hereabouts."

"Then, it was her school that we . . . Why would you help me?"

"Get in. We'll go together and tell your father."

The boy clambered into the sled and Jacob tossed him a lap robe.

"I'm Jacob Wyse, and I'm helping you because I owe your father a debt in a way, and because I've got to live out my faith in what I do for it to be real—even if it means I make mistakes sometimes." He started to turn the sled and smiled. "But I promise that helping you is no mistake."

The boy was quiet for a moment, then spoke with grim enthusiasm. "No matter what you owe him, getting my father to agree to all this is going to be one ugly fight."

Jacob smiled. "We'll see."

Half an hour later, Jacob, standing in front of Tom Granger, had to admit the boy knew his father's temperament well.

"I know you for who you are!" The older man scoffed as he studied Jacob's face. "Beard or no beard. You're the horse thief."

"That's right," Jacob said calmly. "And I've told your son all about it—with the exception of the price I paid for the mare."

Granger's face turned beet red as he glanced to where Tommy sat in the sled. "Well, you let the boy come up here and explain what you're offerin' to me. He's got an obligation to his family, to work around here, not for some stupid Amish!"

"He says you beat him." Jacob's voice was level. "And that you kicked him out. How can you speak of family obligation?"

"You mind your own business, that's what!"

"What exactly is the problem, Mr. Granger? Why the anger? The hatred? The bitterness is destroying you and your family. If you like I could—"

"You could what?" The irate man stared at him as if truly waiting for an answer. A moment later he gave a bark of laughter. "Whatever you think you could do I'm sure would be a real interesting idea. You go on now, and take that worthless boy with you. He's no longer any son of mine!" He turned and slammed the door and Jacob eased off the porch with a sigh, having no doubt that Tommy had heard every word.

He climbed into the cutter with his shoulder and head throbbing distinctly, but he smiled at the boy's pale face. "There. Not so bad."

"Yeah, right."

"Hang on, kid," he murmured as he turned the sled away from the farmhouse. "Just hang on." And he began to pray that the *Englisch* boy might have the hope of a different life.

*L*illy finished a lesson on modern geography, grateful that the world globe had only been dented and not damaged beyond repair. She was just about to have the students line up to wash their hands from the large thermos of water she brought every day when a knock sounded on the door.

The children stilled in their seats. Lilly knew how they felt. She was still a little on edge after the morning's happenings. She went to open the door and was surprised when Kate Zook entered, her eyes downcast, followed by the bishop.

"We've someone here to help with the cleaning when class is done, Mrs. Wyse." The bishop said softly.

Lilly took in the smeared eye makeup and the bright paint stains on her clasped hands. Quickly, she pulled her cloak from its nail and covered Kate's *Englisch* clothes, reaching gently to tuck her long hair in at its collar.

"John," she called over her shoulder. "Please bring me a damp cloth."

The boy obeyed, looking at his *schweschder* but saying nothing. Then he went back to his seat.

Lilly lifted the cloth with tenderness to the younger girl's face. At first Kate stiffened, but then gave a faint sob as Lilly continued to remove the makeup, revealing the fresh skin beneath. Then she put her arm around the girl's shoulders and led her forward. The bishop followed.

"Boys and girls," Lilly began, "Kate Zook has come to help us clean up a bit. And the bishop has come to hear our lessons. Kate, why not sit here, next to Abel Beiler . . . and Bishop Loftus, please take my desk."

Everyone was situated and Lilly was about to have a brief spelling bee when Abel spoke up in his monotone voice. "She has paint on her hands. The same as the board. And she looks funny." He stared out the cracked window. "She's the one who did this."

Lilly glanced at the bishop, who met her eye with a twinkle in his own and thought fast. Here was a teachable moment, and she must not lose the opportunity.

She wet her lips and clasped her hands behind her back. "Yes, Abel is saying aloud what we've all been thinking. That Kate did this to the school."

"Well, I wanna know why," Reuben Mast yelled out without raising his hand. "And why don't she get in trouble for it any. She just has to help clean up. My *mamm* would tan my hide from here to Lockport."

"Reuben . . ." Lilly's tone held a faint note of warning and then she said to the other children: "What Reuben asks is fair. But God's love and the way He commands us to love one another does not have to do with what's fair. Love and forgiveness depend on grace, on mercy—those things we cannot see but they may change the world in their giving. It is the Amish way, to go beyond fairness and to think about forgiveness first. Then we can be angry, or hurt, or sad."

"Well, my *mamm* don't think like that . . ." Reuben muttered, and the bishop choked on a laugh.

"*Doesn't*," she corrected. "Actions have consequences. Do you think Kate feels no pain about what she did? No sorrow?" Lilly glanced to where the girl sat with her head bent.

John Zook spoke up against his *schweschder*. "Maybe she's just sorry that she got caught."

"And maybe you, John Zook," the bishop said, "are tired of all the attention your *mamm's* been paying to Kate's running around, and you're a mite jealous of the whole thing. And maybe a little angry."

John's face flushed. "*Jah*, sir."

The old man looked at Lilly. "*Sei so gut*, go on, Mrs. Wyse."

"Well, I . . . I just want to remind us all—" She stopped, a motion from the back of the room catching her eye. Abel Beiler had leaned over, gently stroking Kate's hair with his thin hand.

"She's crying." He looked at Lilly. "She needs some loves." The boy moved to lay himself half over Kate, and the sound of her sobbing became audible.

Lilly's eyes filled with tears, and the bishop suddenly withdrew a large hankie from his pocket and turned to look toward the cardboard-patched window. Lilly's gaze swept over her scholars and she waited.

John Zook stood up first and walked back to where his *schweschder* sat. He awkwardly patted the side of her head where he could reach around Abel. The other students followed; each one moving to touch Kate, and when they couldn't reach, touching the shoulder of the one in front of them, forming a circle of love about the girl.

Lilly sniffed and turned to look at the old man at her desk. "Bishop Loftus, I don't think you've had the pleasure . . . our new student, Abel Beiler."

CHAPTER 38

"So, how's your time coming with the Widow Beiler's boy?" Seth said.

They were exercising two of the horses, having ridden far afield in the lessening snow of early February.

"Why do you always call her the 'Widow Beiler' like she's some crow? The woman's downright beautiful," Jacob stated.

"I hadn't noticed."

Jacob shot his brother a quick glance and grinned. "*You* hadn't noticed? Now, why do I have trouble believing that?"

"Fine. She's beautiful. All right. So what?"

"Lilly told me she saw you and the widow together and that you looked 'smitten.'"

Seth laughed aloud. "Smitten? Not me, *bruder*."

"Well, what were you doing then?"

"Being a good Amish man and helping introduce her around."

"Why not give her a chance?"

"A chance for what?"

"A chance to let her into that cold, cold heart of yours."

"I thought my heart was tortured—longing for true love. You can't have it both ways."

"I've heard she's a good woman, Seth. You've tried everyone else around here." Jacob threw him a brotherly look—as pointed and sarcastic as his words.

"I've told you before; I plan to outrun every scheming woman within a twenty-mile radius."

"Somehow I don't see Grace Beiler as scheming for you."

"Then she's a wise woman."

"So, you haven't thought of her?"

"The only thing I'm thinking of is beating you back to lunch and *Mamm's* fried apples 'n onions. Tommy'll eat 'em all if we're late. Last one back has to stable both horses!"

Thoughts at school had turned toward Valentine's Day, and Lilly enjoyed the cheerful heart decorations in the windows and around the classroom. The school board and community had come together for a few hours, along with Tommy Granger and a much subdued Kate Zook, to repair the school. And now, nearly a month later, everything held the fresh scent of new wood and paint. Even the blackboards had been replaced using similarly-sized pieces from a school that was being torn down two valleys over.

At home one evening, Lilly asked her *mamm* if she wanted to help her make traditional Amish Shatter Candy to give as a treat to the students on February fourteenth. She was happy when her mother agreed.

In truth, Lilly was developing a new way of being with her *mamm*, finding common ground to talk about things and feeling much closer as they often went to medical or therapy appointments together. The community continued to rally in support, never ceasing to provide companionship and trips away from the house for her *mamm* while Lilly was at school and Jacob at his family's farm.

She glanced into the sitting room at her husband as he half-dozed in a chair. In profile, the soft lay of his growing beard only made him appear more handsome, and Lilly had to remind herself not to stare. He worked endlessly long hours, often rising before 4:00 a.m. and not returning home until supper. And last night there'd been two foals born, which meant he'd gotten little to no sleep at all.

Lilly eased the large frying pan atop the stove and spoke in whispers to her mother.

"Remember when we used to make Shatter Candy when I was little, *Mamm?*"

"*Jah*. Your favorite part was the shattering. Your *daed's* too."

Lilly smiled. "And I remember that neither of you would let me have more than three pieces until Valentine's Day. *Ach*, I'm so glad we can talk about Father without it hurting you so much, *Mamm*."

Her mother patted her arm. "It's probably always going to be hard, but I learned in the hospital to just be in the moment instead of living in the past or worrying about the future."

Lilly measured out the granulated sugar from the large jar while her *mamm* poured the corn syrup into a cup. Both sugar and syrup went into the heated frying pan with a cup of water.

"What flavor are you planning?"

"*Ach*, cinnamon, I guess, for Valentine's. And I suppose we'll use the red food coloring."

Her *mamm* rummaged in the pantry and returned with the ingredients. The syrup was soon boiling and Lilly pulled up a tiny bit on a spoon to drop into a clear glass of cold water. A soft ball formed.

"Not ready yet," her *mamm* advised. "Just a few more minutes though."

Lilly added the food coloring as the sugar climbed in temperature. Her next spoonful produced brittle threads in the cold water and she quickly drew the pan from the heat. Her mother added the cinnamon extract, stirring rapidly.

"Now the best part." Lilly smiled as she spilled the syrup onto the greased cookie sheets.

"What's the best part?" Jacob asked.

She looked up to find Jacob watching with his dark hair slightly messed, easing himself into a chair.

Lilly's mother laughed. "A man knows when to come to the table."

"What are you making?"

Lilly drew a heavy ice-cream scoop from a drawer and poised its backside over the cookie sheet. She pounded lightly once and the now hardened candy shattered into a hundred pieces.

"Shatter Candy!" Jacob exclaimed. "I haven't had it since I was a kid."

"And you may only have one piece now. It's for the children for Valentine's Day." She scooped up a warm piece, dusted it with powdered sugar, and absently held it across the table to his mouth. He opened and she popped it in.

"Mmmm," he said as he nodded. "Wish I were ten again . . . in some ways. In truth, I could do with a primer lesson from my favorite teacher." Lilly heard the sensuous note in his voice and avoided looking at him while her *mamm* laughed.

Chapter 39

*J*acob walked into the nearly empty schoolhouse at 3:15 on the day before Valentine's and saw Lilly at her desk, Abel coloring busily at his own.

"*Ach*, Jacob . . . *danki* for coming. Did Seth mind you leaving work for a bit?"

"*Nee* . . . it's all fine." He was aware that the child had turned to look at him. He slipped off his hat and coat, laying them atop a desk. "*Hiya*, Abel. Did you see any animal tracks this morning in the snow?"

Jacob enjoyed the time he spent with Abel and had most recently been teaching him things about the woods.

"*Jah*, Mr. Wyse. I saw rabbit, deer, and chipmunk."

"*Gut* eye."

He held out his hand to the boy and Abel took it, following him up the aisle.

"Well, teacher, today we have a surprise for you." He exchanged a smile with Abel.

"What is it?"

Jacob half-laughed, knowing what her reaction was going to be to their plan.

"Today the teacher becomes the student. Right, Abel?"

The boy nodded.

"I've gotten special permission from Mrs. Beiler for Abel to come over to the horse farm."

Jacob watched Lilly swallow and couldn't help himself from studying the delicate line of her throat. "The horse farm?"

"Yep. Today you have your first riding lesson."

"Oh, but I have so much grading to cover. Maybe we should wait."

"You're scared," Abel said flatly.

Lilly looked at him and sighed. "Yes, I guess I am."

"Trust God," he replied, and Jacob watched her cheeks fill with delightful color. Then she nodded.

"You're quite right, Abel. I will have trust. All right, Jacob. Let's go."

He hadn't expected her to give in so easy, and he patted Abel on the shoulder for his help in the matter. Then they were off in the sled and soon to the Wyse farm.

Seth had Buttercup on a lead, and Lilly gazed in wonder as the horse walked with a bedsheet strapped to her saddle, billowing out on both sides.

"Best imitation of a woman's skirts that we could come up with . . . not that yours will do that. But I didn't want her to be spooked, so we've trained her to the sheet for the past week. You see, I'm taking every precaution." Jacob grabbed a helmet from the fence post and pushed it on her head, careless of her *kapp*. Then he strapped it securely beneath her chin and she had the sudden longing vision of him brushing his mouth across hers. But he tapped her on the helmet instead. "No worrying."

He turned and secured Abel's helmet, then motioned Seth over.

"Abel, you've met my little *bruder*, Seth."

The boy shook hands and glanced up at Seth's tall frame. "He's not little."

Jacob laughed. "You're right. He's not my little brother, but he's younger than me."

Abel nodded.

Seth glanced over to an adjoining paddock. "We've got a pony named Firecracker if you'd like to take a ride, Abel. Have you ridden before?"

The boy thought, then shook his head. "Once with my father, but then *Mamm* said not again. I think I got hurt or something."

Jacob met his brother's eyes and shrugged slightly.

"Well, no getting hurt today, young man. Come on now, let's leave your teacher to her lessons."

Seth started to walk away when he was stopped by Abel's uplifted hand. Jacob saw his brother study the child for a moment and then sigh. He finally took the boy's hand in his own and they started across the field.

"Does Seth like children?" Lilly asked as they watched them go.

Jacob smiled. "Oh, I think so. Maybe he just doesn't quite know it yet."

Lilly looked at him with curiosity but he waved a hand toward Buttercup.

"All right, Mrs. Wyse. On to your own tutoring."

He caught up the lead on Buttercup and brought the mare closer.

"So today, if you only learn one thing—"

"Only one? That's it?"

"Let me finish my sentence, *fraa*," he said in a teasing tone. "If you only learn one thing, I want you to learn that safety around horses has a lot to do with confidence and trust."

"That doesn't seem like a lesson to me."

"That's a lot." He slid the bedsheet from the saddle and laid it over a fence. "Horses are naturally herd animals. So they want someone to be in charge, to look out for their safety. If they can't find someone, they will take over. So, if you lack confidence, the horse knows it and becomes the herd leader, doing what he wants rather than listening to you."

"Kind of like Ruler being a tough horse to drive?"

"Yes. He knows you're not confident so he's nervous about you being in control."

"Well how can a scared person learn confidence?"

"By acting confident, being kind yet strong, teaching the horse to yield to you, and reminding her to stay out of your personal space. And doing it all in the language of a horse."

"Is that why you don't let them nuzzle you?"

"If I invite them into my space, I let them nuzzle. But no, they aren't allowed to choose to step close to me. It must be an invitation."

"Why not?"

"An eleven-hundred-pound animal is not something I'd like to have slamming its body into me at any time he chooses."

Lilly stepped back a bit, probably thinking about his last comment.

"Come here," he said. "Hold out your hand, palm down, fingers curled slightly. Let the horse sniff the back of your hand. That's your horse handshake, your introduction."

Jacob took Lilly's hand and gently pulled her forward a couple steps. He gestured for her to give her greetings. Lilly hesitantly held her hand out for Buttercup to smell.

"Once you've been introduced, you can scratch them on the withers—"

"The same way they scratch each other in the field?"

"Yes. They love that mutual grooming. It's a sign of friendliness and sends the message that you have no intention of hurting them."

Lilly scratched away, her body still stiff with fear.

"It's okay." He moved behind her, reaching over her shoulder to scratch Buttercup as well. Lilly's nearness distracted him until she spoke.

"I'm still scared."

"Lilly, one reason why I chose Buttercup for you is that she is very calm."

"But Granger beat her."

"We've worked a lot with her—every day—to teach her to trust us. I would not for a moment put you on a horse I thought might hurt you."

Jacob stepped back, took her hand, and moved her out of the way. He swung himself up into the saddle, flopping around a bit up there like he didn't know what he was doing, then dismounted. The worst thing Buttercup did was sigh and shift her weight. He pointed at her back leg which stood slightly cocked. "Horses only do that when they're relaxed. Now it's your turn."

She frowned at him and he smiled back.

"Well, all right . . ." She moved to mount on the left side, but then she discovered the problem of modesty.

"Jacob . . . I can't just gather up my skirts . . . why anyone will be able to see my legs!"

"Planning on donning pants and telling the bishop to jump in the crick?" he asked.

"No . . . but now that I've thought of it, Amish women do not ride astride . . . I don't even know if they ride when they're grown-up—" Her voice rose.

He smiled. "I think you need some motivation."

"Motivation? While I'm standing here feeling like a fool? No, I don't believe that I need anything."

"Here we go. You get on that horse and I'll practice reading with you for a straight hour. We could finish the primer . . ." His tone was faintly wicked, and he could tell she tried not to smile.

"I don't understand how that's supposed to be inspiring in this situation."

"Maybe that's the point. You don't need to understand every little thing right now. My *mamm* has always ridden astride and in her skirt too."

She glared at him. "*Ach*, all right. I'll try."

She gathered her dress and underskirt in a bunch, lifting them high enough to reveal her long legs encased in black kneesocks. Then she slipped her left foot into the stirrup and gave a little hop.

"Don't hold onto the saddle to get up . . . you can grab a handful of the mane but the saddle itself might slip."

"I don't think I'm getting up anywhere," she muttered, moving to do as he suggested and catching hold of the reddish mane. She apologized to Buttercup, who stood so patiently, and made another attempt. This time she got her leg up and tried to swing her right leg astride but her dress was in the way. She got back down and glared at him.

"Maybe I should just take the dress off."

"Now that's an interesting proposition. Of course, Abel and Seth might be a little surprised."

She turned from him, her small jaw set, and she caught an even better hold on the skirt of her dress. He admired her trim calves but quickly looked away, deciding it probably wasn't proper to ogle the student, even if she was his *fraa*.

She made another attempt, ruthlessly lifting the fabric that entrapped her and finally got her right leg over. She sat still and triumphant and slightly breathless.

"Very good," he praised, a warm lilt to his voice.

"Can I get down now?"

"No."

"Please?"

"No. You'll be fine. You might even like it."

"That's highly unlikely." Lilly gripped the saddle horn until her knuckles turned white. "How will I hold onto the reins?"

"No reins yet. Just a lead rope that I'll have control of."

Jacob put his hand on Buttercup's withers. "One of the first things to learn is to never squeeze with your knees! Squeezing tells Buttercup you want her to run."

Lilly's knees visibly relaxed.

"Then what do I do with my legs?"

"I'll show you. It's all about balance. Sit up straight like a good student."

Lilly started breathing hard.

"You can sit up better than that."

"I'm scared."

"It's okay, Lilly. I don't want you to get hurt. Trust me." He put the balls of her feet on the stirrups. "Okay, put your heels down. Like this." He placed one foot in proper position. "This gives you the balance you need to be safe in the saddle. Sitting up straight makes sure your heels are directly in line with your hips and your hips in line with your neck. Think about a stack of building blocks."

Lilly tried to get herself straightened up. When she did, her eyes lit up in surprise. "I don't feel like I'm going to fall off!"

"Right! That's the point. Okay, I want you to close your eyes. I'm going to walk Buttercup in the round pen."

Lilly's eyes flew open wide.

Jacob spoke to her as softly. "Trust me, Lilly. Close your eyes. Hold on. Breathe. I want you to just let yourself move with the horse. Think about not tensing and relaxing into the rhythm of the horse's walk and breathing."

He moved Buttercup toward the center of the pen, then

rounded her, leading her slowly. At first Lilly tensed and forgot to breathe. But at his encouragement, he could see her relax and begin to smile.

"Jacob," she said in a stage whisper. "This is amazing! I am on one of *Derr Herr's* creatures."

"Riding a horse is completely about mutual trust, Lilly," he said while continually leading the mare slowly about the pen. In a quiet voice he went on. "Horses are all about relationship and trust. Horses will only yield to you if they are forced or if they trust. They will only have a positive relationship with you if you spend time together, building that trust. I want that kind of marriage with you, Lilly. Where we spend time together, learn to trust each other."

He led Buttercup to the hitching post. "Okay, Lilly. You can dismount now. "

"What?"

"That's it—you're done. Lesson one is over."

He was delighted to see the look of disappointment on her face.

Lilly couldn't believe the feeling of wonder she felt when she finally relaxed into Buttercup's movements. She didn't dare tell Jacob she wanted another lesson right away. Well, as long as all she had to do was hold onto the saddle horn and let him lead her around. She wasn't certain she wanted to try any more than that.

Jacob began to lead Buttercup back to the barn, when the horse stumbled. "That's not right," he muttered. He lifted her foot and studied the hoof. "*Ach*, well . . ."

"What is it?"

"Buttercup needs a tire replaced. I didn't notice it when I picked her feet before you came. I was in a bit of a hurry. It just

goes to show that life is full of little things that can't be predicted."
He shot a glance at her. "And sometimes that's good."

Lilly nodded. "I agree."

"Okay, we'll have to go over to the smithy shed."

"Like a blacksmith shed? I thought people had to go into
Lockport to . . . er, change their tires."

"Nope . . . *Daed* taught us young and well how to do it our-
selves. Otherwise, we'd be going to town three times a week.
Come on, you might find it interesting to watch."

Lilly followed him and the horse, remembering to take off her
helmet, then grumbling as she felt her hair slip down a bit.

"Just ahead," he called as they crossed the paddock. "It's this
far building on the right."

He slid the door wide and led Buttercup inside while Lilly followed, blinking in the dim light until he turned up a lamp on a
workbench.

She glanced around the barn. It was reinforced with cement on
the floor and presented a neat and unusual arrangement of tools
hanging or attached to the walls or ceiling beams. And, of course,
horseshoes in all shapes and sizes resting in metal boxes. Buttercup
stood placidly where Jacob had tied her. Then there was an anvil
and hammer and a funny-looking post on a low tripod.

She looked over at Jacob, who'd taken off his coat and hat and
rolled up his white sleeves. He pulled a leather apron, obviously
heavy, from a peg on the wall and slipped it over his front. She
thought vaguely that it suited him, emphasizing the strength in his
arms and shoulders.

She moved to watch the proceedings from a better vantage
point when he gently lifted Buttercup's front leg and pulled it
between his legs. He had a hoof pick and was removing the dirt
accumulated in the hoof. "I picked it before, but now I need to get
the rest of the dirt.

"Do you see? The shoe is a little loose—it's pulling away from the hoof." He took out some kind of snippers and each little nail came out at his bidding.

Then he drew a tool from the workbench that looked like a cross between a tree trimmer and oversize pliers. With them he started to cut off about a good half inch of the hoof, going all the way around it.

"*Ach*, doesn't that hurt her a bit?" Lilly asked.

He had taken the funny tripod and had placed Buttercup's foot on the piece that came up through the middle of the tripod. He was busy now, filing and shaping the hoof with a large rasp, like he was giving the horse an *Englisch* manicure.

"It doesn't hurt her a bit. Her hooves are like our fingernails basically, only a bit harder, of course. Horseshoes keep the hooves from wearing down too fast on the road and from injuries due to stones. However, the hooves need to be shortened since they continue to grow—also like our fingernails. So, we need to reshoe every six to eight weeks, unless one works loose, like now."

She watched him take a new shoe from one of the bins. He held it up to Buttercup's foot, then began to hammer it out on the anvil.

"Now I just put the shoe back on again. It takes eight nails, and you drive them through the holes on the shoe until the point comes out at an angle through the side of the hoof." He bent and hammered while Buttercup stood unconcerned. "Then you hammer the points back into the hoof to anchor it and secure it a bit more with this little tool. All that's left is to rasp the hoof down even with the shoe. And there we go." He lifted his dark head, brushing his hair back out of his eyes, and looked at her.

"What do you think?"

"I think that life's little unpredictable happenings can sometimes take a lot of specialized knowledge to fix."

He laughed and laid the tools aside, then came close to where she stood. He lifted his hand to a stray tendril of brown hair that brushed her cheek, then bent his lips to the curl. She watched him, entranced.

"Do you enjoy the unexpected, Mrs. Wyse?" he asked, reaching his hand around to the nape of her neck and lowering his head.

The barn door slid open and he broke away with a rough noise.

"Hey . . . where'd you two go? Abel and I are done—" Seth grinned at them. "Are you?"

CHAPTER 40

*L*illy and Abel were already tucked snug and waiting in the sled when Seth motioned Jacob back inside the barn.

"Here," he said, "before you go. I've got your present."

"You didn't have to get me something."

"You always say that. Just open it."

Jacob tore the brown paper off the large rectangle, then stared in amazement at the running herd of wild horses that seemed to breathe across the canvas.

"Seth, it's remarkable. I've never seen anything like it. I feel like I can hear them running."

"That's what your *fraa* said when I showed her the painting. Remember? Upstairs? When I was a little too interested in my *schweschder*-in-law." His voice lowered with regret.

Jacob held the painting close to his chest, then reached out and gave his brother an honest hug.

"All right. Come on," Seth said, pushing him away. "*Hallich gebottsdaag* tomorrow."

"*Danki*. Oh, and how was Abel?"

Seth looked at the ground. "He's a great kid. Hidden, you know, like a pool in the woods. But great."

Jacob nodded. "You would see him that way—as a wonder to be discovered. You'll be a *gut* father one day, little *bruder*."

"I'll wait for you first."

Jacob laughed and felt something tingle in his belly when he thought of having children with Lilly. It was a primal, instinctive feeling that triggered a flash of heated longing to see a baby of their making and to discover what hazel eyes would look like washed with those as blue as the sea.

So, what are you going to give him?" Alice asked with interest as she poured them each a cup of cinnamon tea.

Lilly shrugged. "I don't know. I want it to be something memorable, but I'm not sure that I'm going to find that in a store. Seth gave him a beautiful painting of horses."

Alice stirred sugar into her cup. "Well, you can't top that."

"You are very helpful, Alice."

"I try to be."

Both of them stared at the table a few moments.

"Okay," Alice said. "I know this doesn't sound like much. But why not make him a card? I actually prefer a homemade card with someone's special note for me in it rather than a present."

Lilly frowned, remembering the valentine she'd tossed away in her youth.

"*Ach*, never mind," her friend said hastily, as if reading her mind. "Though you have to admit that it's odd that you tried to give him a valentine that long ago and now he is your husband."

"It is strange. It's clear I don't know him any better than I did as a *maedel*. He's—he's like something wild, you know? Like a storm coming over the mountain and you can feel that charge in the air." She lifted her cup to her lips and blew across the hot tea. "I guess I sound silly."

Alice patted her hand. "You sound like you're in love. So, he's wild, hmm? Maybe you could think of something along those lines."

*O*n the morning of Valentine's Day, Lilly was up at three o'clock, sitting in bed, waiting for her husband to stir from his nest on the floor. Her heart pounded with excitement as she considered what she planned to give him for his birthday—if he would accept.

Soon, the telltale rustle of the quilts and the sound of his sigh let her know that he was waking. She waited a minute more, then spoke softly in the still dark room.

"Jacob?"

"What? Yes? You scared me."

"Sorry. I wanted to wish you *Hallich gebottsdaag*."

"It couldn't wait?"

"I wanted to tell you what your present is going to be. Will you come here?"

She heard him fumble with the quilts a bit.

"Uh . . . sure."

She felt him feel his way along the side of the bed, then sit down next to her. The clean smell of his skin came to her in the dark, fresh like Christmas pines. She reached out and made contact with his shoulder, letting her fingers smooth up and down the muscle. "I thought I'd give you a gift that you might remember."

She felt him tense and she smiled at her devious ways.

"All right . . ."

"So, you agree to accept?" She slipped her hand to the base of his throat and then up around the back of his neck.

"I agree." His breathing changed.

"Then, for your birthday, I'd like to give you—twenty-six kisses."

"Twenty-six kisses?"

She wasn't sure if she heard relief or disappointment threaded through his voice.

"*Jah*. Twenty-five for your age, and one for the coming year."

"Do I . . . uh, get them all now?"

She laughed and let her hand caress his chest. "No, throughout the day. Anywhere, anytime that you ask or I choose."

She closed her eyes against the boldness of her own words. She couldn't quite believe she was talking this way.

"I think I'll start now." She felt for the spot on his body that she was envisioning in her mind. It was the underside of his upper arm, that silken play of tanned muscles just inches from where he'd been shot. She rubbed her fingers against the spot, and hearing his faint gasp, decided that *rumspringa* or not, no one had probably ever kissed him there before.

She flicked her hair over her shoulder and leaned forward, letting her mouth follow her hands until she drew her fingers away and then let her lips discover the spot in a long, heated breath. She felt him shake when she moved back and was more than a little shaken herself at the same time, but she kept her voice level and low.

"That was one. *Hallich gebottsdaag*."

"Uh . . . okay . . . thanks . . . I think I'll just get dressed . . . and go . . . somewhere . . . To, uh, work, I mean."

She felt him start to rise from the bed and slipped out from beneath the quilts. "Jacob?"

"Yes?"

"Would you like your second kiss? Because I can smell your hair—it's just like soft pine. And I can picture it shining in the sun, with the blond and chestnut highlights mixed together." She ran her fingers down the length of his hair and felt him shudder.

"Will you turn *sei so gut*, so that I can kiss you at the back of your neck?" He made a small sound, then she felt him shift on the bed. She stretched out her hands and the width of his bare back felt tense and drawn beneath her touch. She knelt behind him and lifted the back of his hair. She sensed when he bent his neck forward and then she was kissing him again . . . this time in two quick nips.

She sank backward. "That makes three I'm afraid. I guess I forgot myself."

"Me too," he mumbled. "Are you . . . done?"

"For now. Do you like your gift so far?"

He gave a hoarse laugh. "I love it. I'd say it's the best birthday present I've ever had."

"And your birthday's hardly begun." She trailed her fingertips down his arm and delighted in his shiver of response.

Jacob swung the axe with ruthless precision in the early morning light, setting wood chips flying. He felt restless and frustrated and upside down inside. He loved Lilly's surprising gift, and his scalp tingled at the thought of the remaining kisses. He found himself trying to figure out how she'd work them all in before the end of the day.

"Think that's enough wood, son." His father spoke from behind him, and he almost dropped the axe.

"*Daed*, don't come up behind me like that! I could've taken your ear off."

His father laughed. "Don't forget who taught you to cut wood. I'd say you've cut enough to last for the next three weeks."

Jacob glanced at the pile, amazed at how much he'd worked through.

"Put your coat back on, son. You'll catch a chill sweating like that in this cold."

Again, Jacob hadn't even noticed the cold; he'd been so occupied with his thoughts. Now he shivered in his light-blue, long-sleeved shirt and reached for the black coat he'd flung over a stump. He bent and gathered an armful of wood and turned with his *daed* to walk back toward the house.

"So, were you working off your first Valentine's as a married man or the fact that you've turned twenty-five?"

"No. I was just thinking. Uh, *Daed*—do you understand women?"

His father choked on a laugh. "*Nee*, that would be their Creator who best understands them."

Jacob tried to smile and his *daed* went on.

"Let's sit down for a minute, son."

Jacob sank down on the cold back porch step and moved to make room for his father. He stared at the wood in his arms. "Things are so much easier when you're working outside. I know what to do, how to behave—because you taught me all that, *Daed*."

"Then try and learn from what you know. Look, Jacob, nobody's born married. You have to work at it. Think about how long it took you to know everything that you do about horses. Pour that kind of interest into your wife. And remember, the family is the center, the place of true treasure."

Jacob was quiet.

"You think on it, son. Pray and see what comes to you." His *daed* patted his arm and rose to go inside while Jacob hugged the wood and bent his head to do as his father suggested.

*L*illy had difficulty concentrating at school, so she did what she'd never done before in all of her teaching. She took the liberty of calling an early dismissal on account of the holiday. The children stared at her at first as if she were *narrish* but soon gave way to clapping and whoops of joy. Even Abel smiled.

"So," she encouraged them, "go home . . . give your family their valentines, and remember Who it is who loves us all."

John Zook caught Abel's hand, and the rest of the group soon fled with them. She had no idea what the school board would say, but today she didn't care. She had twenty-two kisses left to give to her husband.

Jacob saw her buggy turn down the lane along the main fence and automatically started to head for the barn.

"Hey, where you going?" Seth called. "That's your *fraa.*"

"Yeah . . . uh, I know."

"Fighting on your first Valentine's Day? What's wrong with you?"

Jacob turned on his heel and strode back to the fence as Lilly pulled up, her beautiful smile lighting up her face as she peered from the buggy.

"Hello," she called. "I've given myself the afternoon off."

She slipped down and came over to the fence while he stared at her in wonder.

"You let the *kinner* go home early?"

"Yes. Hi, Seth."

"Hiya."

"Why did you do that?" Jacob asked, though there was something in her eyes that told him the answer.

"You know," she murmured.

He reached to cup her chin across the fence. She yielded to his hand, a smile playing about her lips.

"Two," he murmured, nuzzling closer to her.

"What?"

"Two kisses. Right now, if you would so please."

She leaned forward, careless of Seth, and let her hands slide up to his shoulders.

"All right, if you insist."

She kissed him twice, but he felt so enraptured that he couldn't tell where one kiss ended and the other began. Then she drew back and he gripped the fence hard.

"You did say two, right?"

He nodded weakly.

Seth cleared his throat. "I'm sorry for staring but odd behavior has always fascinated me. I mean, not that you look odd, but, well, I haven't seen kissing like that since . . . I don't think I've ever seen kissing like that." His voice took on a forlorn note.

"Go away, little *bruder*, and find your own *fraa*. Mine owes me some more of my birthday gift."

Seth grinned as he started past them. "I see, well, I bet that was a pretty present to open."

"I'm still unwrapping," Jacob confessed as he lowered his head to claim yet another of his sweet gifts.

Chapter 41

*T*wenty. Twenty. Twenty . . . Somehow, his innocent but clever wife had got him thinking about kissing in terms of delicious rationing, like drops of water to a thirsting man. But he found his thirst increased with each kiss so that their spontaneous walk in the woods near the Wyse farm became fraught with exquisite tension. He felt as *naerfich* as a colt and struggled to concentrate on the patches of snow and exposed tree roots along the trail he'd run as a young *buwe*.

"So, if you weren't getting kisses," she asked, shooting him a smiling sidelong glance, "what would you have liked to have had as a favorite supper for your birthday?"

You. He cleared his throat and shrugged. "Pork chops, scalloped potatoes, apple butter, and fresh bread."

"I'll have to remember."

"And what's your favorite food?" he asked.

"Funnel cakes," she answered without a pause.

"Funnel cakes? Really? Like at the fall fairs?"

"Mmm-hmmm. I love pinching off the warm dough and sliding it in the powdered sugar. I can eat a whole cake alone."

"There's a fun side to you that I don't know."

She slipped her hand into his. "Maybe there's a lot we don't know about each other."

"True. But I plan to spend a lifetime discovering your secrets, Lilly Wyse." He stopped, turned to her, raised her slender fingers to his lips. "I claim kiss number twenty." He carefully selected her left pointer finger and popped the tip into the warmth of his mouth. He heard her gasp as he drew upon her skin gently, letting his teeth edge against her. She tasted of summer and sky. He smiled at his pleasant fancies as he released her with reluctance.

"That . . . that wasn't a kiss," she declared.

He stared down at her, then tucked her arm into his, continuing the walk. "Now that presents an interesting topic for discussion, Mrs. Wyse. What exactly constitutes a kiss in your opinion?"

"Well, not that. I'm not a piece of candy."

He felt a delicious churning in his chest at her innocent words. "*Ach*, there are so many ways that I could answer that, but none are quite suitable for a lady, I'm afraid." He watched her delicately flush with delight.

"I didn't mean it like that." She sniffed, a cover for the smile he could see playing about the edges of her mouth.

"No worries. But back to the issue at hand. What exactly is a kiss?" He asked the question in a calm voice but the words did something warm to him as he tried to come up with his own definition.

"Well, I'm sure it's a question that's been asked through the ages—"

"No fair playing teacher," he chided.

"I'm not! Well, all right. I am." She laughed. "When I was younger I used to practice kissing my reflection in the bureau mirror."

"Really?"

"*Jah*, and I'm not going to ask how you practiced. I don't think I want to know."

"My wrist," he confessed, feeling himself flush.

"What?" She stopped stock-still.

He turned his free arm over, stroking the veins and underside of his wrist, and shrugged. "It's . . . it's kind of a sensitive spot. So, I'd practice."

"When?"

"You mean how old I was?"

"No. When would you practice?"

"*Ach*, when I was alone, of course." Then he laughed out loud, remembering something.

"What?" she demanded.

He shook his head. "Too strange."

"Now you've got me curious. What?"

"Well, I always practiced when I was certain to be alone—except once. I was supposed to be milking, and I was, but I had my other arm back against the cow, my mouth on my wrist, half asleep, when my *daed* walked in."

She giggled and he thrilled to the delightful sound. "What did he say?"

"He laughed and I woke up all the way and fell backward off the milking stool. Then he helped me up and warned me that I'd better not leave any marks on my wrists or my mother would know what I'd been up to."

"Marks?"

He lowered his gaze to her lips. "Yeah, you know."

She shook her head slightly and he felt a dizzying wave of desire. "Marks—from doing it too hard," he explained.

"Oh." Her gaze slid away to the safety of the ground and he cupped her chin, gently forcing her to look up at him.

"Do you know what I mean?"

She wet her lips. "Wouldn't—wouldn't that hurt?"

He smiled. "Wonderfully. Do you want me to show you?"

"Uh . . . I don't think—"

"Just watch," he whispered. He felt her shock when he pulled from her slightly and slid his black coat sleeve up from his wrist. He turned his arm over and lowered his mouth to his own skin, feeling a curious mix of excitement and exhilaration in the knowledge that she stared at him. He watched her from lowered lashes as he drew hard against the pulse point, feeling the throb of his own blood beneath his lips. He lifted his head after a few moments, then held his arm out for her inspection.

"See?" he asked hoarsely. They both stared at the reddened mark that stood out against the tan of his skin.

She reached delicate fingertips to rub against the spot, pressing slightly against the damp imprint. "It really doesn't hurt?"

He drew in a shaky breath and half-laughed. "*Nee.*"

He knew by instinct what she was going to do before she ever dipped her head, and the knowledge jolted through him so hard that he felt like his heart would stop. She kissed his wrist and he closed his eyes against the wet stinging movement of her novice mouth. She drew back after a few seconds and he forced himself to open his eyes. She stared up at him uncertainly and he smiled at her with dazed warmth.

"Was that . . . all right?"

"*Jah,*" he breathed. "More than all right. I'll never forget."

She smiled shyly. "Was that nineteen?"

"That might have to count for more than just one."

"So, that was a kiss, then?"

"If that's your definition of a kiss, Lilly, I'd say we couldn't agree more." He caught her hand and eased up her sleeve. "But what about your poor neglected wrist, my *fraa?*"

He watched her breathing increase as he encircled her delicate bones with his thumb and forefinger. "Have you ever heard of snow kissing?" he asked with husky interest and she shook her head.

"Noooo."

"Do you want to learn how?"

"To kiss the snow? Are you going to dump me in a snowbank?"

"Snow kissing has to be done just right before the snow melts." He stooped to scoop up a palmful of clean snow. "Let me see your wrist."

She offered her arm hesitantly, and he laid a finger full of cold snow across the delicate veins so clear beneath her pale skin. Then he bent his head, hovering near the wrist she'd reached to support with her other hand. "See," he murmured. "The cold of the snow against the heat of your skin . . . mmmm . . . makes it start to melt, but then I put my mouth over the snow . . ." He broke off to do as he'd explained and heard her startled gasp as he lapped the snow from her wrist then kissed the warm-cold spot with gentle pressure. He lifted his head to stare into her transfixed blue eyes, then placed a drop of snow against her parted lips. He meant to go slow, to entice as well as to teach, but one touch of the melting liquid cold giving way to the warmth of her lips and he lost all track of rational thought. He kissed her with such intensity that they both moved until her back was against a wide tree. His fingers dug into the bark of their own accord, heedless of the melting snow in his palm.

He broke away once to catch his breath. "Lilly . . . I think . . . do you want . . ." And then she stretched to encircle her arms about his neck and he was lost. One kiss followed another in mindless succession until he was sure he'd gone past the bounds of his birthday gift to something even more tantalizingly special.

But a sudden crashing through the undergrowth along the path followed by a strong whistling warned him that they were no longer alone, and he almost groaned aloud in frustration. He lifted his head and gently lowered her arms, pulling her to steadiness against his side.

Then Seth's tall form came around a bend in the trail.

*L*illy automatically ducked her head and clung to her husband's side and wanted to cover her cheeks with her cloak. She felt feverish and confused by her own intimate behavior and desire, and by the dazzling replay of images behind her eyes of Jacob's mouth against his own skin and then against her lips. Then she realized Seth was not alone. The presence of Abel walking along the path did much to help her regain her composure.

"Jacob. Lilly. I'm surprised to see you." Seth's voice was cheerful.

"And what are you doing here?" Jacob asked in a rough tone, reaching out to ruffle Abel's hair.

"Well, I saw Abel walking along the property alone, and I just thought he might need some company."

"Wait," Lilly exclaimed softly. "Abel, you were alone? Does your *mamm* know that you were going for a walk?"

The *buwe* shook his head thoughtfully. "You let us out early. She wasn't at home. So I just went for a walk."

Lilly glanced at her husband, trying to conceal her dismay. "Jacob, Seth, I'm sure Mrs. Beiler is bound to be concerned if she finds that Abel's not at school or at home. We'd better get him back quickly."

"No!" Abel said. "No. I'm getting my *mamm* presents for Valentine's Day." He opened a grubby palm and held three perfectly capped acorns up for their inspection. "I just need one more to have four."

"Well, three seems just as good," Seth remarked.

Abel shook his head, beginning to get upset. "I need four. It has to be even."

Lilly looked at the two brothers and shook her head slightly. She knew from classroom experience of Abel's need for the number of items to be even. "Abel likes things to be even when they can be—it comforts him somehow. Why don't I cut over to Mrs. Beiler's and let her know that Abel's all right, and you two help Abel find another acorn and bring him along when he's done."

"Here's an acorn—right as rain," Jacob exclaimed, scooping up an uncapped acorn from the snowy ground.

Abel turned his pug nose up in disgust and shook his head. "No cap."

"Oh." Jacob inspected it. "You're right." He tossed the offending acorn into the woods.

"They've all got to be the same," Lilly explained.

"Well, *gut* luck to us, then, finding a perfect acorn in the snow. The squirrels and chipmunks have probably gotten them all." Seth scuffed a foot at the ground, peering at it as though it might magically produce the right acorn.

"I found three," Abel pointed out.

"All right." Jacob gave Lilly a tight squeeze. "You go on to Mrs. Beiler's. We'll be back with you shortly."

"*Jah*," Lilly muttered, still warm from his kisses. She nodded to Seth and hurried up the path.

*T*wo hours later the sun began to sink in the afternoon sky, and the late winter day seemed damp and gloomy in the deep of the woods. They'd long left the trail in search of the perfect acorn. A fox skirted in front of them and darted into some dark evergreens. Jacob shook his head. "Abel, it's going to get dark soon. We've got to go back. Your *mamm* will be worried."

"No!" the boy yelled and darted off in the direction of the fox.

"Great, Jacob," Seth said. "Now we have to find an acorn *and* the kid."

"Come on. Quit whining. We have to move quickly. Not only can that boy outrun both of us, but I don't know this side of the mountain as well as I might."

They took off at a jog through the snow, calling the child's name as they went, looking for his footprints. In the places where the snowmelt left bigger patches of dirt than snow, and the footsteps disappeared, Seth stopped to catch his breath. "Wait. We'd better split up. The light's going to fade fast, and I don't need another reason for his mother not to like me by getting him home after dark."

Jacob raised a brow with a half smile. "*Another* reason?"

Seth shrugged. "All right. She's the most beautiful woman I've ever set eyes on, but I somehow have given her reason to hate me. Avoids me at all costs."

"You're imagining it." Jacob waved away his words. He started diagonally to the left. "Come on. We'd better move. I'll go this way."

"I wish we had a light," Seth complained, then began trotting off to the right.

"Abel!" Jacob's voice echoed hollowly through the trees.

I should go out and look myself." Grace Beiler stared out the kitchen window at the deepening dusk, and Lilly tried desperately to think of something else to distract the anxious mother.

She'd already run through every possible topic of conversation that she could come up with and truthfully had no explanation as to where the men and *buwe* could be. She, too, had expected them back by now. She stifled anxious thoughts of her own and glanced over the quilt top Grace was working on—one of many—that she sold to a distributor in Lancaster. It was laborious, tiring work, or so Lilly thought, and didn't seem to suit the delicacy of Grace Beiler's petite frame. Although she needed the work to support herself and her son, Lilly still considered that a woman like Grace should be cherished like fine porcelain by someone.

She dragged her wandering thoughts back to the moment. "Let's make something to eat for when they get here. Did I tell you it's Jacob's birthday?"

Grace gestured lamely to the pantry. "I have a bread pudding shaped like a heart I was going to surprise Abel with—he loves the raisins." Her voice caught for a moment. "Mrs. Wyse—Lilly. You needn't wait with me. I know your own *mamm* is at home. Won't she worry?"

"Anxious for me to be gone so that you can head out into the woods alone?"

The two women smiled at each other briefly.

"How did you know?" Grace asked.

"Teaching for a while. You get used to reading thoughts."

Grace nodded and sank down to take up anxious rocking in a bentwood chair.

They were both silent when the quiet was suddenly broken by the deep voices of men outside. Grace flew to the kitchen door and flung it open to let Jacob and Seth enter. Seth was carrying Abel in his arms.

"What's wrong? What happened to him?" Her voice was frantic as she tried to feel the child through the bulk of Seth's arms.

"Played out. That's all. Played us out too. He led us a merry chase up Keating Mountain. I thought we—"

"Put him down in here, in my bed, please." She cut Seth off and hurried to open a door off the kitchen.

"All right." There was a faint irony in Seth's voice that made

Lilly raise questioning eyes to Jacob's face, but he just shrugged. Seth soon joined them and then Mrs. Beiler gently closed the door behind her.

"I must thank you." Her voice was unsteady and she kept her eyes on Jacob's face. She opened her palm and held it out for them to see. "He roused long enough to give me my Valentine—four acorns."

"That's four—an even number, with caps," Seth noted lightly.

Grace skimmed a blank gaze over his face and then returned her look to Jacob and Lilly.

"Again. Thank you and thank you, Lilly. I couldn't have waited without you. If . . . if you all don't mind, I think I should go and sit by him in case he wakes or catches a chill."

"Not at all. Please have a *gut* night." Lilly smiled and embraced the woman, then caught up her cloak. Jacob reached to settle it about her shoulders.

Mrs. Beiler opened the back door. "*Gut* night." The door closed with a quiet click.

Lilly surveyed Seth's downturned mouth in the half light from the kitchen window.

"What did you do to her?" Jacob asked his brother, settling an arm around Lilly's shoulders in the evening cold.

"I told you. Nothing."

"I'm sure we're all just tired," Lilly said briskly, as if her point would explain Grace Beiler's undoubted coldness toward Seth.

Seth shrugged. "Yeah, right. Let's just go home."

Lilly snuggled beneath her husband's arm, flanked on her other side by Seth until they saw him off at the Wyse farm. She was sleepy but glad when the lights of home shown clear and bright across the fields.

CHAPTER 42

*S*now kissing. Yeah, I heard you. That's *gut*..." Seth's voice drifted off in the stillness of the barn and Jacob rolled his eyes.

"I'm trying to get some advice here, *bruder*."

"From your lecherous younger sibling? You're wasting your time. Remember, I tried to steal your bride."

"Why are you so down on yourself?" Jacob smoothed his hand across Thunder's side.

"You mean my tortured, longing self?" Seth sprawled across a bale of hay, his chin on his chest.

"*Jah*, that self. The one that's deciding to shut down because only one woman in a lifetime isn't swayed by your charm."

"I'd rather go back to snow kissing."

"Me too. I'm just not sure how to get there."

"Jacob," Seth groaned, lolling his head against a beam. "You are married! You know... marrriieeedd! Do what you want."

"You're no help. I think I went too fast and now I don't know how to reach her without seeming like I just want to—"

"You make me sick."

"*Danki*. Yet, I still have patience enough to tell you that you'd better get over yourself. You certainly aren't going to win her by wallowing."

"I don't want to win her—or anybody else for that matter."

"Okay. I'm going to go work with that colt now. I promised Tommy I'd give him some training time with me. Why don't you go paint?" Jacob slid the barn door open.

"I can't paint anymore. It doesn't work," Seth growled.

"Then you, my little *bruder*, are in deep trouble—heart trouble." He shut the door before he could make out Seth's furious response.

Lilly looked up from the projects she was grading at the kitchen table and wondered what time Jacob would get home. She sighed when she thought about how far he seemed to have drifted from her in the few days after their kisses on the trail. He seemed to be reserved and holding back for some reason, yet she knew he'd been intent in the woods. She wondered if she'd ever understand him and resisted the urge to bite her lip at the thought.

"Are you troubled about something?"

Lilly looked across the table into the sitting room where her *mamm* had been writing in her journal. It was still amazing to hear the warmth and tenderness that pervaded her mother's tone when she spoke.

Lilly shrugged. "I don't know. *Danki* for asking, *Mamm*."

Her mother patted the chair next to hers. "Come here, will you? Let's have a visit."

Lilly went, pleased at the diversion of her thoughts; she sat down and smiled.

"I've been thinking, Lilly. We've never had—well, a woman-to-woman talk about what to expect as a married woman."

Lilly raised a brow. "I think I understand the mechanics, *Mamm*."

Her mother gave a false frown. "Saucy-mouthed girl. That's not what I mean."

"All right. I'm sorry. I have to confess that I don't know what to expect from Jacob half the time."

Her mother patted her hand. "That's what I thought. I'd like you to read something from my journal, if you will."

"*Ach*, I'd love to." Lilly knew how important the journal was to her mother's recovery and felt honored to be asked to share a part of it.

Her mother riffled through the pages a bit, then found a certain spot. "Here. Read from here to the bottom of the next page."

Lilly took the notebook and thought how both familiar and foreign her mother's handwriting was to her; it seemed such an intimate thing. Something she remembered from childhood yet hadn't glimpsed in so long. She knew from teaching that handwriting revealed much about the personality of the writer. Her mother's strongly formed loops and word endings were a reassurance that her strength and will were present and focused. She began to read.

I think I married Hiram too young—or at least, I was too young in my mind. I didn't know half of what it meant to be a wife and mother when suddenly there was this sober, dark-haired baby girl staring up at me with all the trust in the world. I scarcely knew how to care for her. Oh, I understood the feeding and the diapering, but when she cried, it pierced my soul and scared me to death—especially when Hiram was out on a call. He always seemed to know how to comfort her better than I, and I found myself comforted just watching him hold her. But I also felt left behind. As though I were the one on the outside.

When we'd go to Meetings or frolics, I'd watch the other mothers with their babes and I'd wonder about the distance I felt from my daughter, though I held her close to my heart every chance I had. She didn't resist me, but I never felt that I was sure enough, gut enough, to parent her with confidence. I didn't know how to keep everything together—the running of the home, Hiram's involvement with his work, and the ever-watching beautiful blue eyes of my baby maedel.

Suppose I failed her? Suppose I let her get hurt? When she started to crawl and bumped her head or walked and skinned her knee, I was riddled with guilt. I should have watched more closely, not let her have gone so far away from me.

And then . . . somehow, she was grown up, and Hiram was gone. I was still too young to deal with everything. And then my baby married—became a wife, will surely someday become a mother, and still, I am unsure of how to help her. What to do for her—to keep her safe. Should I tell her the truth—that marriage is sometimes filled with expectations that are never met, that the heart gets bruised but must go on? Should I tell her of the moments of joy, the intense pleasure of holding the hand of the one you love and wishing that time would stand still? What about the differences that arise—the petty arguments and fault finding that you wish would all be gone, never having been said. What about when your heart's love takes ill and shrinks to some shadow of the person you knew. How do I tell her all of this and so much more? I love her . . . my Lilly. I told Hiram we must name her that, for I could think of no other flower so beautiful, and so delicate. She's grown to match her name. But she is her own woman too. A special, wunderbaar *woman. And for that, I am not too young to acknowledge and to be thankful to* Derr Herr.

Lilly looked up with tears in her eyes. *"Ach, Mamm."* She slipped from her chair to kneel at her mother's feet, laying her head in the warm lap and feeling the comfort of gentle hands brushing at the hair against the nape of her neck. "I never knew"—she sobbed—"that you thought all that."

"I should have told you," her mother whispered. "But I can

tell you now. And I can tell you that I know you've been struggling here and there with Jacob. I've prayed for you. I'll keep on praying. You will have a *gut* marriage, a *gut* life. And I . . . I love you so much."

"Oh, I love you too, *Mamm*." Lilly clung to her mother and felt a peace that touched the deepest shadows in her soul. She felt whole and renewed and ready to face life as Jacob's wife.

A sudden knock on the back kitchen door made her look up, startled, and she rose. She gave her mother a quick hug and quickly wiped away her tears. Then she went to open the door, wondering who might be calling so near to suppertime.

It was Alice, looking at her with suppressed excitement on her merry face. "Lilly, I have an idea. You have to come with me into Lockport right now."

CHAPTER 43

*L*illy's mother waved them off without question, with a promise to get Jacob his supper and the instruction to have a *gut* time.

Lilly stared at her friend as Alice urged the Planks' horse to pick up speed. "All right. What's this about?"

Alice glanced at her with an excited smile. "Okay, you know how you've been saying that Jacob has become distant and everything?"

"*Jah.*"

"Well, I've got a plan to get him *undistant.*"

"I don't think that's a real word."

Alice laughed. "You do not like surprises and you're not going to like my plan. But we're going to do it."

"What is it?" Lilly asked with both apprehension and interest, thinking of the birthday kissing gift they'd come up with together.

"We're going to Emily's Mystery."

"What?"

"Emily's Mystery. It's this store in Lockport that sells—"

"I know what it is." Lilly laughed, shocked. "But what could I possibly do there?"

"Buy something to entice your husband. It's my treat, by the way. Think of it as an extra wedding present."

"Alice Plank! You have got to be *narrish*. What would Jacob say if he knew?"

"Nothing." Alice smiled smugly. "He won't say anything, but he might do something."

Lilly studied her friend and shook her head. "You just want to see what it's like in there, don't you?"

Alice slapped the reins and shrugged. "Maybe. What's wrong with that?"

*O*nce Lilly got over the electric feeling that she was going to be struck by lightning the moment she crossed the store's threshold, she found herself in awe of the beauty of the undergarments and lingerie on display.

Lace and pastel trims were not what Amish women in their community usually wore—although, Lilly had to wonder, with a suppressed giggle, how was one to know that as a rule for certain anyway? She glanced at Alice, who boldly studied the mannequins with interest.

"I think I could sew some of these," her friend mused aloud, and Lilly wanted to shush her as the saleswoman came toward them.

"Ladies, good afternoon. Looking for something special?"

Lilly studied the woman covertly, admiring the carefree swing of her hair, but could find no words to offer in response. Alice, however, seemed to have no such problem.

"Yes. She's newly married and needs something to . . . make her husband happy."

Lilly wanted to crawl under one of the silk-covered tables.

"Hmmm . . . okay. I have to tell you that I'm surprised at the number of Amish who have come in here to shop lately," the sales-girl said as she studied Lilly, her head tilted to one side.

"Really?" Alice asked with interest.

"Mmmm-hmmm. Even a guy was in here not too long ago—with his mom or something." The woman smiled at the remembrance. "He was hot too, for an Amish man—tall, dark hair . . ."

Lilly and Alice exchanged glances and the woman went on. "So, what did you have in mind?"

Lilly shrugged lamely. "I . . . uh . . ."

"Is he a leg man?"

"A leg man?"

"Yeah. A man who especially likes women's legs. I've got some silk stockings in pale pink with the cutest little rosettes at the top. But I don't suppose you've got any heels to wear with them." She frowned down at Lilly's old-fashioned, sensible shoes.

"She needs a gown, maybe," Alice said, reaching to finger a blue lace confection with a plunging neckline and a satin waist tie.

The woman waved a dismissive hand. "She'd be lost in all that lace. I think something more simple with elegant lines."

Lilly almost choked on a laugh as she thought about her current nightgowns; the word *elegant* had absolutely no remote relation. *Serviceable* maybe.

"What about this?" The woman drew a simple white gown from a rack, but it was clearly cut to fall at thigh length with a tempting hem of rich embroidery around its base.

"What do you wear over it?" Lilly asked, rather in despera-tion at the thought of appearing before Jacob in such a garment. It would be like wearing nothing.

"Over it?" The saleswoman frowned, confused.

"She'll take it," Alice said decisively with a clap of her hands.

"I will not!" Lilly hissed, but the woman was already walking back to the counter with the wispy garment in tow. "Alice, I can't possibly wear that."

"Shhh . . . listen, do you want Jacob to be *undistant?* Well, this will do the trick; I guarantee it."

"How would you know?"

"Intuition." Alice smiled and winked.

Lilly frowned darkly. "He may well tell the bishop and think I've lost my mind."

"Somehow, I don't think so."

Somehow Lilly didn't think so either—not the man who'd revealed how he'd practiced kissing with such a blatant display. No, he'd probably be far from distant. She shivered in faint delight at the thought.

Alice was at the counter, paying the outrageous price for the gown, while Lilly watched in fascination as the woman wrapped it in pastel tissue paper and lifted an "Emily's Mystery" box from a shelf.

"Uh—" Lilly's voice made her pause. "You've wrapped it beautifully, but could you please put it in a—"

"A more Amish-appropriate wrapping? No problem." The woman smiled and slipped a simple brown bag from beneath the counter and gently tucked the wrapped item inside.

Alice passed the bag to Lilly, who took it with a murmured thanks.

"All right, ladies. Come again. Anytime. I'm beginning to think I should run an Amish discount now and then." She gave them a sunny smile and Lilly could not contain her mirth when Alice made a gay rejoinder.

"*Jah,* that would be a *gut* idea!"

Jacob entered his home as late as he dared without missing supper entirely. He'd been trying to hold off the last few days and treat his wife like the lady she was to him. He'd had no business making sensual and personal revelations to her innocent mind and kissing her senseless in the middle of the outdoors. She probably thought he was just interested in a hurried marriage consummation when he'd promised her a long courtship. It didn't matter what he desired or how irresistible he found his wife; he was determined to be a man of his word, no matter what torment it cost him.

So when he came into the kitchen to be greeted by his mother-in-law alone, he was both surprised and disappointed.

"To town? With Alice? At supper time?" His brow wrinkled in puzzlement.

"*Jah*, but a woman needs her time to do spontaneous things, Jacob. And she did want to make sure that you would eat."

He sat down to supper, not really sure what he ate. It was completely unlike Lilly to be impulsive—unless she was harboring a horse thief, or throwing away her reputation on someone like him. He frowned at the thought and concentrated on making pleasantries with his mother-in-law, trying not to notice the deepening dark outside. He was more than glad when Lilly burst breathless into the kitchen and rose to greet her.

"I'm sorry I'm late, Jacob."

Her beautiful face was flushed and her blue eyes sparkled with some suppressed excitement.

"That's all right. I was just worried a bit. That's all."

She brushed past him with a pat on his arm and a paper bag in her hand. "Nothing to worry about. Alice just wanted to give me uh . . . a late wedding present."

And with that he had to be content, he thought, as she put her parcel away and returned to calmly begin grading the papers waiting for her at the end of the table. He wondered what the present could be but couldn't think of a way to ask without appearing too interested in her doings. He had to remind himself that he was courting her, winning her, wooing her. So, half an hour later, he gave her a very chaste kiss on the brow and went to toss in frustration on the bedroom floor.

In the ensuing weeks, Lilly sought in vain for the courage and opportunity to try out the special gown, but nothing seemed to present itself. At first she tried it on, taking it off—immediately—her cheeks flushed, her heart pounding, and her entire self embarrassed. Once she rehearsed keeping it on and reminding herself that it was not vain to be beautiful to her husband, she was able to picture herself stepping out in front of him, wearing this airy gown.

Yet, even after a handful of more horse-riding lessons, where she thought she was progressing very well, he'd merely pat her back and give an encouraging word of praise. He simply continued to behave as if they were in a stage of early courting. Still, Lilly reminded herself with the stirring remembrance of his kisses on the trail, it was courting. And that had to lead to something else sometime.

CHAPTER 44

*O*ne evening in March, the small family was seated around the light of a kerosene lamp, talking pleasantly of the day's work while Lilly graded papers.

Jacob was pleased to see his mother-in-law looking so well and he'd come to enjoy her tart humor. But now she sighed with a dreamy look on her face.

"What, *Mamm?*" he asked with interest.

"*Ach*, nothing . . ."

"What is it?" Lilly looked up.

"I just had the thought that I wish I'd been well enough to host a wedding quilting for you, that's all."

Lilly smiled and rose to hug her mother. "I have you back, *Mamm*. A wedding quilting doesn't matter." But she spoke with such an unconscious wistfulness that it echoed in Jacob's heart.

*A*ll right, that's it!" Seth tossed a bridle at him, and Jacob caught it with ease.

"What?"

"You've been moping around here for the past two days. I took your advice and got over myself. Now I'll ask you what *your* problem is . . . besides the fact that you can't seem to bring yourself to . . . cherish your wife with husbandly affection."

Jacob hung the bridle up and looked at his brother with a growing light in his eyes. "Well, if you really want to know—you could help me."

Seth backed off, hands up. "Oh no, that's between you and your *fraa*."

"Seth," Jacob said, a bit disgusted, "don't let your artist's imagination run away with you. I need your help in a very different way."

"I wasn't offering help. I thought you were sad, not plotting. I don't want any part of this—"

Jacob linked his arm over his *bruder's* shoulders. "It'll only take a few minutes of your time."

Lilly kept her gaze discreet while sitting in the buggy in the cool evening air. By now, though, the group of Amish women who exited the church in Lockport where the depression support groups were held had become familiar to her, and her waiting presence to them. The group served a wide area of about fifteen miles or so and she didn't recognize anyone from her community. There were about twelve women in all, including her *mamm*, and they often bade each other good night or stood talking in pairs for a few moments when the meeting was done. For Lilly, it was exhilarating to see her *mamm* pause and speak to someone, sharing concerns and laughter before coming to the buggy.

"How was it tonight, *Mamm*?"

Lilly had discovered, to her surprise, that her mother liked to talk about the things she'd learned during the meetings. Lilly had grown to treasure the buggy rides home as a time to feel closer to her *mamm*.

"It was *gut*." Her voice was quiet.

Lilly glanced at her mother's profile. "What's wrong?"

"*Ach*, nothing. The discussion really was good, but one girl brought up the fact that she'd been told that if she only had more faith, then she wouldn't be depressed."

"Do you believe that?"

"No, not at all. But it's still difficult to hear such words."

"*Mamm*, Dr. Parker said that depression is a very real illness. Can faith help you as you recover? Surely. But to link faith or more faith with not having depression isn't fair—"

Her mother laughed and patted her arm. "It's all right, Lilly. I know all that. I felt bad for the woman who'd had someone say that to her; that's all. I don't want her to feel shame over false words."

"Oh."

"I'm feeling better, Lilly. Really. For the first time in months I feel like there's a break in the clouds. But I'm not fool enough to think it's over. I'll have to be careful and conscious of this illness for all my days."

Lilly nodded as her throat filled with happy tears. She was so pleased to hear her mother talking seriously, if not matter-of-factly, about her illness. She lifted her eyes to the star-strewn sky and thanked *Derr Herr* once more for using for good what had so recently seemed like such an irreparable time in her mother's life.

CHAPTER 45

*T*hree weeks after their secret plan was put into motion, Seth hustled Jacob upstairs after he'd dropped by his old home for a visit. Lilly had stayed home to do some extra school preparations.

"You'd better sit down."

Jacob dropped to his brother's bed and stretched.

"Now what's the matter?"

Seth tossed a stack of thick envelopes at him, then slid into a chair at the end of the bed, propping up his long legs.

"Letters from ladies for you, dear *bruder*. It seems that your brilliant idea for me to send out requests for quilt squares for your wife and a possible wedding quilting—hosted by us men—got circulated around. And, by the evidence, it has endeared you to the hearts of Amish women everywhere. All those letters have quilt squares and you're going to have to listen to each note because women will be able to tell whether or not you have read them."

Jacob picked up a handful of envelopes. "Women? How many?

How many requests did you write? Only a handful of people will fit around the frame, right?"

"Besides the fact that this is going to be the oddest quilting party in the area yet—being given by two men—I'd say we're going to have to have revolving seats for the quilters, because there are a lot of women who want to quilt." He stretched and scooped up a handful of the letters.

"*Ach,* here we go. One of my favorites—the lyrics to an *Englisch* quilting song, apparently from the late 1800s and dedicated to you by a Miss Lena Christner. I will not sing it, but I'll recite it later—much later." He rambled on. "Miss Lena also includes a patchwork square." Seth waved the fabric. "And, she wishes you the best in life and love and so on."

Jacob stretched out on the bed and yawned. "Keep going. I'm listening."

"You'd better be. Now we have a novel quilting technique from our local postmistress, a 'yo-yo' square."

"Like the toy?"

"Yeah, that will fit real comfortably into a bed quilt. No—circles of fabric are gathered into flat pouches and sewn together. See? It's like a bunch of little colorful circles; I like this one."

"Uh-huh."

"I've learned enough about quilting that I feel like I ought to wear a skirt."

"You'd look good in anything."

"I'll ignore that comment." Seth pulled another square out of an envelope. "I guess this one is called 'appliqué.' You see? This smaller piece of cloth is cut into a shape and sewn onto a larger piece."

Jacob stared at his *narrish bruder.*

"Then we have the French Knot—"

Jacob laid back on the bed, feeling his eyes drift closed. A moment later, the sudden weight of his brother centered on his chest.

"Get off," he gasped.

"Nope. Not until you listen."

"But it's boring, Seth."

"It was your idea. Now get up, gather your love letters and quilt squares, and go down and tell *Mamm* what you've done. She's the only one who can sew these all together in time to make the quilt top."

"The . . . quilt . . . top?" Jacob feigned ignorance to bait his brother.

"The quilt top! The thing that fastens to the frame that the ladies quilt on. I'm telling you this is the last time that I will ever—" It was probably Jacob's hiccup of swallowed laughter that clued Seth in. He gave a tremendous heave and landed his brother on the floor with a loud thump. A shower of envelopes followed.

"Boys!" *Mamm's* admonishing voice floated upstairs from the kitchen, just like when they'd been *kinner.* "What's all the racket?"

Jacob sat up and lifted a pretty pink rose square from the litter around him. "This is nice."

Seth narrowed his eyes. "You mock it now, but remember, this is important to your *fraa.* You can't make fun of things that are important to her." He shook his head. "Don't you know anything about marriage?"

"All right. I'll go talk to *Mamm.* But clean up the mess, Seth, and stop getting so involved in every little thing I ask you to do."

He was too fast for the long leg that shot out to trip him and laughed out loud on his way down the stairs.

CHAPTER 46

*T*he Saturday of his wife's wedding quilting dawned bright and clear. Jacob slipped out of the room at 4:00 as usual and rode Thunder as fast as he could to his old home. *Mamm* was already up cooking for the others sitting around the table—Seth, his *daed*, and a grinning Tommy.

The kitchen was filled with the smells of good things. Jacob hung up his coat and hat, then went to give his *mamm* a hug at the stove.

"*Danki* for doing all this . . . I had no idea how much work was involved."

His mother looked up from the huge tray of apple dumplings she was sugaring and raised an eyebrow. "I'm glad to do it, *sohn*, but to invite droves of women was a bit much."

Jacob turned to look at Seth, who was now fiddling at the quilt frame with their father and Tommy.

"*Droves*? How many are *droves*?"

"Who are these people?" *Daed* asked.

"Well-wishers, romance lovers, and quilters from as far away as two valleys over. I never put specific names on those letter requests, just handed them to whoever, and somehow or another they just got circulated around. And, I think most women want to come simply to see men try to quilt." Seth shrugged.

Jacob surveyed the huge frame that took up nearly all of the sitting room. He and Seth had hauled it from the Kings' largest barn when Sarah's mother remembered that the bigger frame had been stored there and hadn't been used in well over fifty years.

The long lengths of wood for holding the layers of the quilt taut so that they could be quilted together, without folds or puckers, had needed a few repairs. But now the full frame held the entire quilt, stretched out for the beginning of the quilting. Then the side rails would be rolled up within the quilt as sections were completed.

"Well, we ought to get it done fast, right? With all those ladies quilting?"

Seth rolled his eyes. "And talking, and eating, and visiting—and we're supposed to be the hosts! I can't believe I let you talk me into this."

"Boys!" Mary Wyse called. "This is for Lilly, for a lifetime of memories. And it's a *gut* symbol for the beginning of a marriage—you have to work to put things together, to make things work in your minds and hearts. And certainly everyone from here to Elk County will remember this quilting. Now come get the ham out and run down to the cellar for a half-dozen jars of white navy beans. Hurry. The guests start arriving in a few hours and I'm not near done cooking, even with all the dishes the neighbors are bringing."

Jacob hastened to obey and breathed a quick prayer that all would go smoothly on this special day for his wife.

It was a fresh Saturday morning, and Lilly sighed to herself that she was stuck in the classroom for an annual round of teacher training. The topics were really things she'd gone over before or already had teaching strategies for, and she thought she'd much rather be spending time with her husband. But, Jacob did say that he had a lot of things to catch up on. And, to make the day even more dull, Alice was surprisingly absent when she'd promised to come.

At 10:00 a.m. the mentoring teacher gave them a break. As Lilly stood and smoothed out the back of her dress, she had a sudden inspiration. She'd drive home and surprise Jacob with a half-day off, even though he was working. Perhaps she might arrive in time to have lunch with him.

She trotted Ruler, the buggy moving briskly, ignoring what stares she knew she was probably getting for leaving early, but choosing not to mind. She drove on and saw a lone Amish woman walking along the roadside. She would have passed by with a called greeting but when she drew abreast of the woman, she recognized Kate Zook.

She drew the buggy to a halt on some instinct and found herself asking if the girl needed a ride. Since the day of the cleanup at the classroom, she'd heard through the community grapevine that Kate had ceased to see Tommy Granger, even though the *buwe* was close at hand at the Wyse farm. Yet, she also knew that Kate was rather on the outside of the tight-knit community as she had yet to repent of her rebellion and express a desire to join the church.

Kate squinted up at her in the morning sunshine. "Why?" she asked. "Why would you want to give me a ride?" There was something flat and halting in the girl's tone. Lilly recognized the resignation of her expression and felt a surge of empathy.

"Because you might need one. Come on."

Kate clambered into the buggy and stared straight ahead.

"So, how are things going?" Lilly asked softly.

"Great." The girl's pretty mouth twisted in bitterness. "Just great."

Lilly though for a moment. "Kate, I know we've never gotten along. I was very jealous of you and your feelings for Jacob, but I'm over that now."

"And I'm supposed to say I'm sorry and that I'm happy for you, right?" The question wasn't antagonistic, just tired.

"No, I don't expect you to say anything. I just want you to know that I'd talk with you if you ever wanted. Believe it or not, I understand what it's like to feel trapped and unhappy."

Kate didn't respond and Lilly lifted the reins. "Where are you going?"

"I don't care. Anywhere."

"Fine." Lilly started Ruler back down the road and they soon came to the Wyse family farm. She would have passed when the sight of dozens of buggies gathered around the place made her catch her breath. Was someone ill? She could think of no other immediate reason but tragedy for so many to gather on a Saturday, and she hastened Ruler along and turned down the lane. "I'm sorry, Kate. I've got to stop. Something might be wrong."

"I don't think so," Kate muttered, but Lilly was already out of the buggy, barely noticing when Kate began to follow her but then turned and walked back up the lane. Lilly threw the reins over a post and flew up the steps and burst through the kitchen door.

The jumble of women, some unfamiliar, made her heart sink even lower and she frantically searched the group for *Mamm* Wyse.

Then she heard someone exclaim. "It's Lilly!"

The crowd stopped talking and slowly parted to reveal a giant quilt frame surrounded by women with their needles frozen mid-stitch. Then she saw Jacob and Seth and tried to assimilate the fact that they were, apparently, quilting!

Jacob stabbed his needle into the fabric and rose when her eyes met his. The contrast between his long, dark-clad legs and the bright colors of the unfamiliar quilt pattern was striking. He came around the edge of the frame and crossed the room to where she stood with his hands outstretched.

"Lilly! I thought that you'd be away for more of the day . . . I . . . I wanted us to get more done."

"I don't understand."

"It's your wedding quilt."

"My wedding quilt?" Her blue eyes flashed to his.

"This isn't how I planned for you to know," he whispered, pulling her close to him and shielding her with his broad back from the naturally inquisitive faces behind them. She saw him glance over her shoulder and heard a shifting as the women in the kitchen sounded like they'd turned away as a group.

"How did you plan it?" she whispered back, amazed and uncertain.

He smiled at her, his heart in his eyes. "With Seth. I just wanted to give you something to celebrate our marriage. I thought a wedding quilt made up of all kinds of squares, all kinds of love, might show you that . . . that . . ." He cleared his throat. "That our marriage is for real."

Tears began to flow down her cheeks.

"Even if it didn't start out in the traditional way . . ."

Jacob took her hand and turned to lead her to the frame where Seth sat grinning.

"Seth helped me write a request for some ladies to donate a quilt square and some of their time and skill. But *Derr Herr* had the word get around I guess, and all of these ladies wanted to celebrate in your happiness as a bride, even if it is a bit late."

"*Ach*, Jacob, do you even know what a gift this is? How much I've longed for this?" Her voice shook but she raised it so that everyone could hear her as she continued. "I have to tell you, even those whom I don't recognize, that this is something I never thought I'd have. Never really thought I deserved in some way."

She looked toward Lucy Stolis's sweet, young face. "But I think you're all here because *Derr Herr* brought you to add to this day."

She turned to Jacob and lowered her voice. "Thank you, Jacob. I can't imagine a greater gift of love." And she thrilled to the truth in the words. *Love. At last.*

A needle dropped, crystalline in sound, and went skittering across the wooden floor. The noise broke the silence and the ladies broke into an emotional response of laughter and tears.

Jacob drew her forward to walk her around the edges of the quilt.

"I've never seen such a large quilt!" she exclaimed.

"Well, all of the squares are *wunderbaar* but there are a few I think I should point out." He moved her to a corner to show her the square the children had made her for her wedding gift. He pointed to the next one, a marker-covered square showing a little boy, holding the hand of a woman outside a schoolhouse. "That's Abel's square . . . you and him together."

Lilly nodded, her tears falling unchecked.

"This is mine, sweet *schweschder*," Seth called, indicating a painted sunrise over the mountaintops with a well-held needle.

"*Ach*, Seth. It's beautiful. *Danki*."

Jacob pointed to another square nearer them. "I asked your mother . . . she said you wouldn't mind, right, *Mamm*?" He showed her the patch he'd cut from the Christmas tree covering that Lilly and her *daed* had sewn.

"Oh, Jacob, it's just too much."

"Well, there's one more." He took her by the hand to the square on the opposite corner of the quilt. "I made it—your gift to me and back again."

Lilly bent to look at the seemingly blank square that she'd given him for Christmas.

"There's nothing on that square you gave me," he said for

only her to hear. "Because I thought of a thousand ideas. And none seemed right. What finally came to me was that I wanted us to start quilting on it together. Just a few stitches now and maybe we could add to the design every year. Just like our lives together." His voice was hesitant.

She felt her heart swell with love. "It's like a patch of heaven, Jacob." She turned in his arms and kissed him full on the mouth to the delight of all the onlookers. Then she took her place at the frame, beside her husband, and began to stitch on her wedding quilt.

CHAPTER 47

*J*acob stood in the shadows of the storefront in the crisp
early spring air. He glanced now and then to the reassuring bulk of Thunder, properly hitched to the nearby post, and
wondered for the third time if he should wait in the buggy. Then
he told himself that he was on a fool's errand and almost backed
out entirely when the *Englisch* woman came down the street with
her keys jangling.

"It's you." She smiled at him and he swallowed, removing his hat.

"*Jah,* I mean—yes."

"Not bringing any ladies with you today?" she asked as she
opened the door.

He shook his head lamely and followed her inside.

She flicked on some lights, deposited her bag on a counter,
then turned to him with expectancy. "So, how are things going with
your bride?"

"Uh—good. Real good."

"She's a lucky girl."

"Thank you, but I think I'm the one who's lucky." He was

wringing his hat between his large hands, trying to study a nearby mannequin without appearing to do so.

The *Englisch* woman laughed. "All right. What can I do for you?" Her voice had lowered a bit at the question and he once again thought longingly of escape.

"Um. To the tell the truth, I wanted something for my wife, but I'm not sure. Maybe this isn't such a good idea."

"Every guy who comes in here thinks that," she said, shifting to business mode. "Tell me how she's shaped."

"Shaped? Uh, like a woman?"

"What size is she? Most of our items come in small, medium or large."

Jacob cleared his throat. "She's tall—but slender. Her waist has a gentle curve to it . . ."

"Bosom?"

"Yes," he choked.

"Yes, what?"

"It's . . . fine." He ran a finger around the inside of his collar and the woman seemed to take pity on him. "I want"—he gulped—"something beautiful." He felt the blush rising from his toes. "So she knows . . ." He cleared his throat. "She's, uh, never owned anything . . ." He couldn't finish his sentence.

The woman gazed at him speculatively, almost as if something funny had occurred to her, and she smiled. "Does your wife have dark hair? And fair skin?"

Jacob nodded in confusion. "Yes."

"I think I know the right thing. Follow me."

He tread across the velvety carpet in his work boots, further into the recesses of the store, like he was working himself deeper into a dark cave.

The saleswoman stopped and pulled something from a rack. Then she led him back out into better light.

"How about this?"

Jacob gazed at the simple lines of the cream and lace gown with its delicate inserts of light blue ribbon. His head whirled with the sudden vision of the thing shaped against his wife's pale skin; the ribbons matching the twin pools of her eyes, the lace pressing against the soft curve of her shoulder, leaving her neck bare . . .

"I'll take it."

Lilly made up the bed with deliberation in the late afternoon. A week had passed since the quilting and she had yet to lay her wedding quilt upon the bed because she'd just wanted some time to drink in the pleasure of remembering the quilting. And, she wasn't sure what Jacob would think if she used it. Would he believe it was some symbol that she wanted a marriage in truth? *She hoped so.* So now, she folded away Edith's quilt and glanced at the pile of Jacob's bedding on the chair near the dresser. She felt her heart begin to pound with expectancy as she considered the coming night. Her *mamm* was staying overnight in Lockport to help a new member from the support group who was having a hard time. This left her and Jacob in the house alone for the first time since they'd been married.

She smoothed the folds of the wedding quilt with a loving hand as she spread it over the bed, its generous size spilling over the sides and nearly brushing the floor. She fluffed the pillows a bit, then stood back to admire the bed.

The sudden rumble of thunder in the distance broke her reverie and she turned toward the window with a smile. Oh, how she loved a good storm.

Jacob arrived home in the middle of the rain, thunder, and lightning to an empty house. He knew *Mamm* Lapp was supposed to be gone, but he puzzled over Lilly's whereabouts late on a Saturday. The *gut* smells of food baking also had him worried. It wasn't like her to up and leave something she was cooking. He frowned and went to the kitchen window to peer outside. The rain made steady races of rivulets down the glass, but his sharp eye caught something white in the tree line beyond the barn. He laid the large box from Emily's on the counter and turned to hurry back outside. Careless of the rain, he sloshed through muddy puddles, then ran for the copse of trees.

Something came to him then and he almost stopped still. As he walked, he began to remember the dream he had on his wedding night. Clarity flooded his mind like the answer to a prayer. It hadn't been Sarah he'd been wanting. It was the dark-haired *mae-del* among the trees who drew his mind and heart—the vision of his beautiful wife.

He silently entered the leaf-strewn copse and turned to see the real Lilly with her *kapp* off and her long hair down, reaching to cup handfuls of the water that dripped from the canopy above into her mouth. Her back was half turned from him, and he thought he'd never seen anything so sensual in all his days.

He took a step forward, mesmerized, but not wanting to startle her, and she turned.

"*Ach*, Jacob. I . . . I love the rain in the springtime."

"I know." He stepped closer to her. "I saw you here before—once."

"Really? When?"

He caught her in his arms and he thrilled to the yielding of her damp, slender form against him. "The moment my heart turned to you."

Lilly smiled up at him, a secret, knowing smile, prompted by his words and the desires of her heart. She tipped his damp hat off so that it fell on the wet ground behind him and reached up to caress the soft lay of his dark beard and to brush his long hair away from his face.

"I've invented something," she told him, knowing her voice sounded warm and intimate, a competition for the fall of the rain.

"What is that?"

She could tell that he was having difficulty concentrating on the words as his gaze seemed to drink her in with his pupils dilated and his eyes gold with intensity.

She held out a cupped hand to catch some water then studied him deliberately. "Rain kissing," she confided. "Have you heard of it?"

He smiled and shook his head.

"Would you like to learn?" she asked, tilting her hand so that some of the water ran down her arm.

"*Jah*," he whispered breathlessly.

"Take off your coat then."

He obeyed with a haste that made her smile, shrugging out of the garment and carelessly letting it fall to the ground atop his wet hat.

He stood in his dark pants and long-sleeved white shirt, the press of his suspenders defining the strength of his shoulders already being revealed by the dampening rain.

"I think you can learn best by experience," she told him, dipping her finger into the pool of water in her palm, letting a drop of rain cling to her fingertip. She reached to rest the drop upon his lips. She stood on tiptoe to make her mouth even with the clinging droplet.

She closed her eyes and let her mind drift back to the day on the trail, wanting to kiss him with the same burning intensity he had brought her. She pressed her lips against the rain and tasted his lips, ignoring the low groan that reverberated from his chest as she lingered, making sure to drink deeply of the water and his scent before moving away.

"I think I get it," he rumbled, reaching out for her with intent. But she held him off with one hand against his chest and he reluctantly stilled.

"Just one more lesson, Jacob," she murmured. She took her cupped hand and pressed it full against the front of his arm where she knew the gunshot wound was laying its permanent scar—the mark of their love's beginning.

His shirt was already soaked but she knew it didn't matter when he shivered at her touch. She trailed her fingers down his arm, then back up again. "Beloved husband. Horse thief. Wild heart. Dream of my girlhood. Are you mine?"

"Yes," he choked as she moved to press her mouth against his wound. "*Ach*, Lilly, yes."

She kissed him through the fabric, the warmth of her mouth competing with the chill of the rain until she knew instinctively that he could stand no more. She drew back and he bent his head and kissed her once and hard. Then he scooped her up in his arms and carried her through the trees and back to the house.

*H*e crossed the room to the bed in two strides and sank beside her. "*Ach*, Lilly . . ." he breathed, reaching to touch her wet hair. "I love you. I love you. You were the perfect plan God always had for me, my love, my treasure." He trailed damp kisses along her shoulder, then yanked at his shirt in frustration of the barrier. She reached to help him with sure fingers and then he lost all thought as she whispered her love against his mouth . . .

A lazy smile tugged at his mouth. "Remind me that I've got a gift to give you later."

"All right. Want to know what I'm thinking?"

"Mmm-hmm?" He bent to nuzzle her neck and she laughed.

"Uncle Sebastian."

Jacob lifted his head and stared down at her. "What?"

"He told me a secret at Christmas—remember?"

"*Jah*, the thing you lacked."

"Well, I've found it."

"Have you?" He nestled her against his shoulder and caught a handful of her hair to spread across his chest.

"Yes," she whispered.

"What is it?"

She moved against him with a subtle pressure and he caught his breath.

"Joy."

THE END

ACKNOWLEDGMENTS

*J*would like to acknowledge the following special people who aided in the creation of this story:

For my husband and family, especially my mother-in-law, who constantly supports my writing efforts.

For my editor, Natalie Hannemann, who constantly encourages, strengthens, and helps me to grow in my work.

For the praying staff at Thomas Nelson.

For Lissa Halls Johnson, my line editor—a master at what she does.

For Brenda Lott, as always, my friend, brainstorming partner, and part of my heart.

For Natasha Kern and her encouragement of my reading *The Moral Premise*.

For Scott II and his words to keep me going.

For Donna Boudakian, who gave me precious laughter.

For Judy Murphy, who supported my efforts to write.

For the Prayer Room at JFBC.

And for the Amish people of the North Central Pennsylvania mountains.

READING GROUP GUIDE

1. How does Jacob's idea of focusing on the moment of "now" both help and hinder his life?
2. Jealousy often flares up in Lilly's life. What is a jealousy that you have struggled with personally? How can God help you handle jealousy when it happens?
3. Jacob prays about "choosing" to love his wife. What is the difference between the "feeling" of love and choosing to love?
4. Lilly's mother battles clinical depression. Have you or a loved one ever had to face this disease? How did you go through it? How did God help?
5. The bishop points out a difference between joy and happiness. What difference do you see in these two in your own life?
6. How does fear often keep Lilly from experiencing abundant life? What do you fear the most?
7. How did Abel's reaction to Kate's destruction at the schoolhouse change the moment in the story?
8. How does Seth and Jacob's relationship add to the development of the story?
9. Why is a quilting important to Lilly? What symbol is important in your own life?
10. How does the truth play a role throughout the story?

QUITE BY ACCIDENT, SARAH KING HAS
FALLEN IN LOVE. BUT THIS LOVE COULD COST
HER EVERYTHING SHE HOLDS DEAR.

"Kelly Long has hit it out
of the park, *Sarah's Garden*
is rich with Amish detail
and an endearing romance.
I highly recommend!"
—BETH WISEMAN
best-selling author of
Plain Paradise

Sarah's Garden
A PATCH OF HEAVEN NOVEL

KELLY LONG

ABOUT THE AUTHOR

 Kelly Long is the author of *Sarah's Garden*, the first novel in the Patch of Heaven series. She was born and raised in the mountains of Northern Pennsylvania. She's been married for nearly twenty-five years and has five children.